NICE DAY FOR A WHITE WEDDING

GEORGIA LE CARRE

Caryl Milton
Elizabeth Burns
Nichola Rhead
Kirstine Moran
Brittany Urbaniak
Tracy Gray
Cariad

Nice Day For A White Wedding

ISBN: 978-1-910575-95-6

CINDY

A light tap on my office door makes me look up from my computer screen. I check the time. It's only ten o'clock. Surely, we don't have trouble already! As the manager of The Macau, a small London casino, I have seen my fair share of trouble over the years; drunks, bad losers, cheaters, fights, drugs – you name it, I've dealt with it.

But at this time of night? No one has lost big yet and people are at the happy stages of drunk rather than the fighting stages.

The knock might not mean trouble, but something tells me it does.

"Come in," I call.

The door opens and Stewart, the casino's head of security, steps in. He grins at me as he comes over to my desk. So there isn't a fight then. He wouldn't be grinning like that if all hell had broken loose.

"What is it?" I ask.

"You might want to put the cameras on," he says. "We've got a live one."

That's Stewart's way of telling me we have someone winning big. Now don't get me wrong, we have big winners now and again, but this is someone who is having enough luck to raise Security's suspicions. Ninety-nine percent of the time it is someone who has found a way to cheat.

I open my top desk drawer, and pull out a remote control and fire up the bank of monitors on the wall to my right.

"There," Stewart says. "On the craps table."

He moves to the bank of monitors and points to a man. The man has his back to the camera, but even sitting down, I can tell he's big. He's both very tall and very well built. If he gets ugly, he might need all four of my security staff. He doesn't look rough though. He's wearing a black suit and I can see it's an expensive one, so that's something at least.

"You've checked the dice," I ask.

"Yup. And changed the staff."

I press another button on the remote control and the bank of monitors showing all of the public areas of the casino becomes one screen showing only the craps table from different angles. Whatever the man is up to, he's attracted quite a crowd of fans around him. It's often the case when someone is on a winning streak. Our clientele can't help enjoying seeing us taken to the cleaners. It's payback for all the times we take them there.

The man pushes a large stack of chips forward and nods to the croupier. Sasha looks into the camera before she pushes the dice with her stick towards Alex. I know she's wondering if we're watching from the office. Don't worry Sasha, we're watching.

Alex throws the dice.

They land and the crowd around the table raise their arms excitedly, high five and cheer. They stop short of slapping the big man on the back. By their reactions, it is clear he has won big. Again. A voluptuous woman in a long black dress moves in for her own slice of the action and slinks onto the seat next to him. He does not turn to look at her.

"How many is that?" I ask Stewart.

"I counted six in a row before I came up here," he says.

So that's at least seven wins. Probably eight or nine by the time Stewart got here and I got the monitor on. Sasha pushes a stack of chips towards the man and I have a quick tally of how many chips he has. There could be a little over two hundred thousand pounds in front of him. It's a lot of money, but it's far from a cause for panic. Some of our high rollers start with more than that. And of course, he could lose it all on the next roll, but somehow I doubt it.

I turn to look at Stewart. "But he has only won at most, two hundred K?"

"I know," he nods, "and I wouldn't even have come up here if not for the fact that one of the change guys was going off on his break and gave me the head's up to keep an eye on him. Apparently, he only started with a couple of thousand."

This makes me raise an eyebrow. The man's suit, his quiet confidence and the way he's throwing big money bets on the table tells me he's got plenty of money to lose. And guys in a casino with plenty of money don't start with two thousand pounds worth of chips. Guys like him start with five or ten thousand pounds.

Unless they know they can't lose.

I watch closely as the man lays on another bet. This time he pushes his full pile of chips forward and nods to Sasha. A few others follow his lead and push chips into the same box. I ignore those people. They're small fry, pushing on a few hundred. They're not involved in whatever scam the man is running. They're just taking advantage of what they now feel is a sure bet.

I curse as the man wins again. He isn't taking a huge amount of winnings and we can easily foot this kind of loss, but it annoys me because I can't for the life of me work out what he's doing. I can spot a card counter at a hundred paces. I've seen countless devices that cause havoc on the slot machines, but the craps table is the hardest one to cheat on.

I know of only two ways to rig the odds at a craps table. Either have the box person involved in your scam and have them use weighted dice, or attach magnets beneath the table that affect the dice. I know neither of those are happening here. Sasha has worked here almost as long as I have. She was one of my first hires and not only is she loyal, but she's also adept at spotting and reporting scams. And magnets would have sent an alarm signal to my office the second the man entered the casino, so even assuming he had managed to get them in place, I'd have known about them.

"What do you think?" Stewart asks me.

"I think our friend there has found a new way to rig the game, but I'm screwed if I can work out what the hell it is," I say, shaking my head. "Come on. I think it's time he met the manager."

I grab my keys off my desk and Stewart and I leave my office. I lock the door and we head down the corridor. I have no idea how I can prove the man is cheating, but maybe up close and personal I'll spot something. Even if I can't prove it, this situation still needs dealing with.

If a person is winning too much I tend to discreetly convince them to try another game, or move to a table with lower stakes. That way if they are genuinely on a lucky roll, there is a chance their luck will run out. Naturally if they are cheating they are shown the door and banned for life.

Stewart and I step out of the elevator and walk along the short corridor to the casino floor. I pause for a second before we go through the door. I run my hands through my straight blonde hair to make sure my hair is in place, then I smooth down my slim-fitted black skirt.

"You're going out there to ban a cheater, not go on a date, Cindy," Stewart mocks.

I laugh, knowing he'll never understand what I'm doing. Looking poised and in control is a part of my thing. I have to always look calm and unflappable, and messy hair and a creased skirt just don't give that impression.

I push my way through the doors and I am instantly assaulted by noise and activity. Although it is still early, The Macau is already busy. There are people everywhere and all the slot machines are taken up. Their whirling reels and bursts of music as they spin fill the air. Even the more obscure table games are full to capacity. Waiters and waitresses move around the floor with drinks trays. Stewart and I quickly make our way towards the craps table. A cheer comes from the direction we are heading. It sounds like mystery man has done it again.

Subtlety is going to be the key here.

I begin to make my way through the thick crowd gathered around the table.

"Excuse me. Excuse me," I hear myself saying over and over again.

Most people move aside easily at my request, but some, not realizing I work here and thinking I just want the best view-point for the game, give me dirty looks. I finally clear the throng and come out beside Sasha and opposite the mystery man which was my exact aim.

Mystery man has his head down, looking at his chips. I take a second to study him while he is unaware of my regard. He looks even bigger in person, and has a full head of shiny black hair. From what I can see of his forehead, I would guess he is in his early thirties. I was definitely right about him being from money. He has that casual confidence that only seems to come from having insane amounts of money.

Which begs the question of why anyone that loaded would risk getting caught cheating a casino out of what is essentially small change.

He must have felt my eyes on him because he looks up and straight at me.

Dangerous!

That is the first thought that flies into my head. The air of danger is all around him. From the unyielding jaw line, to the chiseled cheek bones, to the scar above his left eyebrow. There is a hint of a tattoo creeping out of the collar of his shirt and meeting the raven-black hair … and those stormy gray-blue eyes … they send shivers through my body.

I find myself staring into them, losing myself in them. There is a depth there that pulls me in, a sensual, sexual charm that sends fire racing through me and makes my clit throb. I subconsciously push my thighs together and it sends a little shockwave through my pussy. It takes everything I have not to gasp out loud at the sensation.

For the next few seconds I can't think straight. Neither can I break the spell of his mysterious eyes. I just stand there like a brainless goldfish gaping at his presence.

Dark and stormy. That's what he is. Dark and stormy and downright dangerous. He curls one corner of his sensuous lips up in a mocking smile.

Being mocked can tear you out of any sexual limbo. It does the job for me. I clear my throat, suddenly hyper aware of where I am, of the crowd around me. No more than two or three seconds have passed since dark and stormy looked up at me, but it feels like he's held my gaze for hours and I feel myself blushing slightly.

I force my eyes from his and his grin widens. Somehow, he knows exactly what he's doing to me. Hell, he probably has this effect on women everywhere.

"Good evening," he says to me.

His voice is low and gravelly, the perfect voice for his looks. The accent is Russian. For some weird, inexplicable reason, I imagine him close to me, whispering in my ear. I can almost feel his breath tickling my neck, his six o'clock stubble scratching my skin in a most delicious way.

For the love of God, get a grip, Cindy.

The casino is regularly frequented by members of the Russian Mafia, and this man certainly fits the bill to be one of them. I've never known them to cause trouble in the casino. They come here to have a good time and relax, but I am always on my guard around them. Dark and stormy is going to be no exception to that.

I flash him a totally professional smile as I get ready to give him my prepared spiel, but his next words stun me into silence.

"I was wondering when you were going to show up … Cindy."

ALEX

Her eyes widen with surprise when I say her name. I hold her momentarily unnerved gaze steadily. I want her to drink me in, to get a feel for who she's dealing with. The expressions that cross her face make her transparent. I can hear almost the wheels turning in her head as her brain tries to figure out how a man like me would know her name. I watch her lips curve into a cool business-like smile. Ah, she believes she's solved the problem; she's the manager of the casino. I've heard her name mentioned … somewhere.

She's wrong, of course.

In fact, I've gone to a lot of trouble to carefully engineer this situation to catch her attention. To get her down here. And now here she is. So beautifully predictable.

Look at her.

So confident. So smooth. So in control. Not a hair out of place, nude make-up, manly suit designed to hide even the smallest womanly curve, and uber-sensible shoes. She's almost a parody of a successful businesswoman.

I drop my gaze to her mouth.

Look at the professional smile plastered on it. I imagine myself getting up and going to stand in front of her. In my mind's eye, I reach out and shove my hand up her skirt. She struggles at first, but it's just a token gesture. She wants it as much as I do. I work her clit until she can't hold that condescending smile any longer. Her face changes, contorts with pleasure as I play sweet music on her clit. I hear her panting, hear her screaming my name as I push her over the edge. I imagine those full lips gasping my name incoherently after I make her come five times in a row. Her long blonde hair is all loose and hanging in sweaty straggles around her face. And I can almost feel her sticky juices on my fingers.

My cock stirs with interest.

She makes a small movement with her head and the strands of gold in her hair catch the light and sparkle, dazzling me. For a second she doesn't look like a mere woman, but an honest to goodness Goddess! My brain freezes and my gut tightens.

What the fuck was that?

It's my turn to be surprised. I try to keep my face expressionless, but I don't like the effect Cindy Forrester just had on me. She made me lose my mind for a moment there. This has to be business, nothing more. I need to get my head back into the game. She's no goddess. She's just a woman. A beautiful woman.

But it's not like I haven't been around beautiful women before. All my life stunningly fabulous creatures have swarmed around me. Money is a great aphrodisiac. It made them as relentless as the flies on those luckless beasts roaming the plains of Africa. No matter how hard they tried they've never distracted me before. Not once. I take them. I play with them. I give them expensive trinkets. Then I walk away from them.

She will be no different. I smile slowly at her.

Her cheeks become pink. She's blushing because she knows I've been undressing her. That I've already ripped away that ugly suit and starched shirt, seen the beauty underneath, and sucked on her large breasts.

She lives alone. Career women who live alone have dirty thoughts and mostly only their vibrators for company. Those poor nipples must be screaming for a real man's touch, a hard mouth that knows what to do.

Her hazel, almond shaped eyes flash as she catches herself staring back at me. She remembers where she is. She pulls herself back under control, at least outwardly, but she can't hide her pink cheeks, or the slightly glassy look of lust in her eyes as she looks at me. It's time to throw her a curveball and see how she really rocks under pressure.

I give her a half-smile, one that makes her clear her throat.

Holding her gaze, I push my stacks of chips forward. All of them. The game is on. She ignores the dice and keeps her eyes on mine. I never take my gaze away from hers, but I know I have won the bet when the crowd around me goes wild. They took a bet on me and won money.

The excitement around me is crazy and hands are trying to gain my attention, but for me the fun is over. Now it's time to talk business with Cindy, and we're not going to have this conversation over a craps table in the middle of a crowd.

I reach out and scoop up my chips, leaving give or take about a hundred thousand pounds worth behind. I stand and drop my chips into my pockets.

"Umm, Sir?" Sasha says, nodding at the leftover chips.

"It looks like it's a lucky night for both of us," I say with a wink. Then I walk away, leaving them all with open mouths.

I count my paces. I know if Cindy's any good at her job, she'll snap out of her goldfish moment and catch me within ten paces. She exceeds my expectations and catches me after just six paces.

I slow my pace, but I don't stop walking. "So have you figured out how I was cheating yet?"

I have to clench my jaw to keep from laughing at the look of shock on her face. She covers it quickly, her professional mask slipping back into place. Cindy stays at my side as I head towards the bar.

"I don't know what you're talking about," she says coldly.

I let myself laugh then and she frowns.

"Oh, come on," I say. "I know you were up in your office, watching me, and trying to work out what I was up to. So you can drop the act now."

To her credit, she doesn't try to deny what I'm saying is true, although she doesn't rush to agree with me either.

"I think we can both agree you've had a very profitable night," she says. "So how about you call it a night?"

I laugh.

Her jaw tightens. "What's so funny?"

"You are. Thinking you can tell me what to do. Let me tell you something, Miss Forrester. No one tells me when to call it a night."

She opens her mouth, but I don't let her get a word in.

"I'm not intoxicated. I'm not causing any trouble. And you and I both know you have no proof what happened back there was anything except a lucky streak. So tell me … do you make it a habit of trying to throw people out for winning here?"

"I'd hardly call what I was doing trying to throw you out."

I glance sideways at her. "What would you call it?"

"Discreetly suggesting you might want to think about moving on. Particularly when you've as good as admitted to cheating."

"I haven't admitted to anything."

We're almost at the bar when I stop and turn to Cindy. She stops too and I see her quickly assessing me, trying to work out if she's in danger. I am a very big guy, after all. She must have decided she's not because she's not calling for back up. Instead she faces me directly.

"Only twenty percent of communication is verbal. Everything else is body language."

I smile slowly. "Is that what my body has been telling you, Cindy?"

Under her creamy skin blood rushes up her throat and cheeks and I stare at her curiously. She looks exactly how I imagined she would look when my cock is inside her. I decide to change the subject. Obsessing about fucking her doesn't advance my agenda in anyway.

"I have to say that this is quite a clever set up they have here," I say.

I can see her wrestling with herself, not wanting to be drawn into conversation with me, but wanting desperately to know what I mean. Her curiosity wins out and she frowns.

"What do you mean?"

"Sending the blonde bombshell to deal with the situation instead of a bunch of goons."

Her cheeks flame brighter, and I watch her swallow hard. I decide to throw her a bone. I smile pleasantly, the smile I give when I want the other party to relax, to stop seeing me as the enemy. "It doesn't exactly make the place seem welcoming if it has teams of security dragging customers across the floor, does it?"

For the first time, the cool professional smile slips and I see the real smile beneath it. The one that reaches her eyes and makes them sparkle for a second. "I suppose not."

"And I guess there's a lot less bravado this way. Men who would fight another man to prove they're someone to be reckoned with are much less likely to react that way with … a beautiful woman."

She blinks. "Well, it seems like you have our system all worked out. So, let me ask you a little question. Are you going to be trouble?"

"Oh, I'm always trouble," I admit cheerfully. "But if you're asking if I'm going to start throwing punches at your under-paid, overworked security staff, I can assure you I'm not."

"And yet you are still here even after I've asked you nicely to leave," she points out.

"Ah, but you didn't ask me to leave. You told me to call it a night and I don't like being told what to do."

"Then perhaps I should reword it. I'm politely asking you to leave the premises and carry on with your night somewhere else," she says, flashing me her own version of my winning smile, this smile doesn't reach her eyes.

Her lines don't feel rehearsed although I'm sure she has had this conversation countless times.

"But the company here is so good. Why would I want to switch that out for somewhere less ... welcoming?" I counter with a smile that reaches all the way to my dick.

"Because I'm asking you nicely." She smiles, this one can freeze a whole elephant in a second.

I laugh. I can't help it. She has a way about her, a way that I imagine works on the average customer, but I am anything but the average customer.

"Will you answer me a question first?" I ask.

She nods, watching me warily like she's waiting for some-thing to happen. The air between us feels charged, and I find myself waiting for what might happen.

"When you use this tactic to get rid of undesirables from the casino, have you ever come across someone your charms don't work on?"

She laughs, a carefree, confident laugh that makes me want to reach out and pull her into my arms. She is more intoxicating than I had anticipated.

"No sir, I haven't," she says softly. "I always get what I want."

Jesus! Where did that come from? She's flirting with me. She is off book now for sure and bravo to her, she's completely thrown me off my game. Cindy Forrester is far, far more potent than I expected her to be. There is so much more to her than meets the eye … which actually makes her perfect for what I have in mind.

CINDY

Usually when I catch someone cheating in the casino I feel real anger, as if they have reached into my purse and stolen my own hard-earned money. It's not so much about the money, though. More about the fact that some jumped-up punk thinks he can get one over on me. That I won't see through his pathetic little scam and know exactly what he's up to.

This time, I feel angry with myself.

Dark and stormy has as good as admitted he cheated, and yet not only am I no closer to working out how he did it than I was in my office when I was watching him on the monitor, but he also seems to have the upper-hand in our power struggle. And I am in no doubt it is that.

I want to ask him, actually *demand* he tells me what he did, but I know it will do no good.

A) he won't tell me, and ...

B) I have a feeling letting a man like this know I want something from him would be a big mistake.

Another thing that unsettles me is the strong impression that he knows something I don't. That's something that has invisibly tipped the power between us so he is holding all the cards.

I don't buy his smooth exterior for a second. I've been around men long enough to sense when danger is bubbling beneath the surface. His is coming off him in waves, literally waiting to be unleashed. He has the air of someone from the criminal underworld, but I don't feel afraid of him. I probably should be, but I'm not.

He's undeniably flirting with me, but what the heck am I doing flirting back? Something even a fool can tell is a terrible idea. It's acceptable, expected even, to lightly flirt with customers. It oils the wheels and takes the sting out of the word no. But not in these circumstances. When the customer is clearly no ordinary con artist, and I feel as if I am the one standing on shaky ground.

The trouble is, I don't know what to make of him, or how to deal with him. He's told me he isn't about to let things get ugly, and I believe him, but he's also making no move to leave. I don't know how to make him go. Especially, as I get the impression he's used to getting his own way, and worse, he has some kind of ace card up his sleeve.

I've dealt with all kinds of men throughout my career. The billionaire who is used to bending people, particularly women, to his will. The gorgeous ones who think tipping me a wink will turn me into a giggling idiot. And the idiots who think pinching my ass as I pass by them is an irresistible compliment.

What I haven't dealt with is a guy like Dark and Stormy, who is confident to the point of arrogance, and yet doesn't make me want to barf on his handmade shoes. Who doesn't seem in the least bit perturbed to realize I am not about to become putty in his hands because he flashed me a sexy smile. And who is having such an effect on me I find myself flirting with him instead of dealing with the situation at hand.

He's not like anyone I've ever met before. I can usually read people pretty quickly, and knowing who they are behind their masks is the fastest way to knowing how far I can go with them. I have no idea who Dark and Stormy is or what he hopes to achieve here. One thing for sure he has an agenda.

I wait for his answer to my answer and he surprises me again now. Instead of a cocky comeback, he just nods, then he turns and walks away from me. Dammit. He really is good, because now, yet again, I am the one who has to go chasing after him.

From the first moment he looked up and saw me, he has managed to turn a situation that should have been a piece of cake for me to handle to one where he is holding all of the power. I am not used to not being in control, and I don't like the way he has so easily thrown me off my game.

By the time I catch up with him, he's sitting on a barstool and the bartender is fixing him a whisky on the rocks. I debate telling the bartender not to serve him, but something stops me. Although I did—well do, kind of—want him to leave, I

have to admit that I am now intrigued by him. He's danger-
ously attractive and I can't help but feel drawn to him.

What can I say? There's a part of me that wants him to stay. I
condone my crazy behavior by telling myself he's not
gambling anymore so it's not like he can cheat the casino out
of any more money. At least while he's spending at the bar,
we're getting some of it back. It's flimsy reasoning at best,
but I can't help myself.

Unfortunately, the more I tell myself I'm playing a dangerous
game, the more I seem to want to keep playing. The problem
with playing with someone like Dark and Stormy is I don't
think it will be a game I will win.

"Have a drink with me," Dark and Stormy says. It's not a
request, it's an order.

Immediately, I feel myself bristling beneath his gaze. I hate
being told what to do. I bite back my anger, reminding
myself to keep my composure. If he sees he's rattled me, then
all bets are off.

"I'm working. It's against the casino's rules to drink on duty,"
I tell him.

He ignores me and turns to Jerry, the bartender who has
placed his drink in front of him.

"Thank you." He smiles. "And a gin and tonic."

I frown. How does he know that's my drink? I shake my
head. It's a common enough drink. It means nothing.

"With a slice of orange rather than lemon," he adds.

That makes my jaw drop open. That's no coincidence. No
one would guess that. I don't know anyone else who has

orange rather than lemon in their gin and tonic. Who the hell is he? And how and why does he know so much about me?

He purposely avoids looking at me, keeping his gaze fixed firmly ahead of himself. Despite that, I feel as though he's watching me, as if he's waiting for my reaction. He's playing with me and I don't like it one bit, but I'm not about to give him the satisfaction of letting him know that he's touched a raw nerve.

Expressionlessly, Jerry puts my drink down in front of me, and Dark and Stormy pays for the drinks, leaving another hefty tip. Jerry's eyes widen. I don't know if the excessive tipping is meant to impress me, but if it is, he's wasting his time. Money is nothing when you have it, and watching a rich guy throwing it around means nothing to me.

My adversary swings his dark head back in my direction, and looks amused when he catches me watching him. I kick myself at being caught.

"Does the orange give the drink a certain sweetness that lemon just can't?" he asks mildly.

I nod, not trusting myself to form an answer with actual words. It's clear from his mocking expression that he knows I don't trust myself to speak right now. I stare down into the glass just so I have something to focus on other than him. What I wouldn't give right now to just be able to say screw the rules and neck that drink. I could do it. I'm the manager. No one is going to object. I don't though. He is having enough of an effect on me as it is without me bringing alcohol into the equation.

"You have to lift the glass and bring it to your lips," he taunts.

I feel anger start to swirl inside me. Who the hell does he think he is? I've already refused the drink, which he went ahead and bought anyway, and now he thinks he can sit there and order me around.

If I was in a bar and not at work, I would tell him exactly what I think of his chauvinist, piggish attitude, but here, I have to remain professional. I can't let him see he's getting under my skin.

"I've already told you it is against the casino's rules for me to drink while on duty," I say tightly.

I purposely avoid saying the phrase 'I'm not allowed to drink on duty' because I won't let him think I'm being pushed around by anyone.

"Rules are only fun when you break them." He smiles, that crazy-sexy smile. "Live a little."

"You have to break rules to have fun?"

"Ah," he lets the sound linger between us. "You don't dare."

"Oh, I dare. I just don't need to break perfectly legitimate rules to have fun."

"Said like a true follower of rules. I dare you, Cindy Forrester," he challenges with a mocking grin.

Dammit. Now he's done it. It seems he got the measure of me long before I've got the measure of him. He knows exactly which buttons to press on me. I never turn down a dare, especially not when it comes from someone who I want to like me. Fuck. I don't want him to like me. I don't care what he thinks of me. I just want him gone.

"If I drink it, will you leave?" I say.

He shrugs and watches me with a wry amusement. "Either you want to prove you're not a sheep blindly following orders or you don't."

So that's a no. I don't want him to think he's manipulated me into doing something I don't want to do, but the drink is starting to look mighty inviting now. Now I've asked him to leave, I can't just walk away from him until he has so maybe I should just see it through. With a sigh I reach out and pick the glass up.

"One drink and then you leave," I say foolishly.

He ignores my statement and clinks his glass against mine. "*Nostrovia.*"

He knocks his drink back, but his eyes never leave mine. Despite my instincts screaming at me that this isn't a good idea I bring my own glass to my mouth.

"*Nostrovia,*" I echo and take a long drink. Heck, G&T never tasted so good. I put my glass back down on the bar.

"You speak Russian?" he says, an eyebrow raised.

I debate lying but it would be the world's shortest lived lie if I pretend to speak a language I don't. And why would I, anyway? It's not like it matters one bit what he thinks.

I shake my head. "No. That's literally the one word I know. It means cheers, right?"

"It means 'to your health' and is typically used as a toast."

I remind myself I'm supposed to be angry with him, not chit-chatting about toasts. I straighten my back and keep my face impassive as I down the rest of my drink. Then I slam the glass back down on the bar.

"There! I kept my end of the deal, now it's your turn."

"That was your deal, Cindy. I didn't agree to it."

He turns back to the bar before I can reply, and asks the bartender for two more.

"Look, I really don't want another one. I'm working and I've still got a long night ahead of me. I don't intend to get sloppy."

"Something tells me sloppy isn't your style." There is a curiously intriguing look in his eyes. It feels as though he's looking deep inside of me, reading things about me in my eyes.

He pays for the drinks and pushes mine towards me again. I don't even glance at the drink. I give him a look that usually gets the message across that I am not playing around anymore. He looks back at me, his own gaze as steely and determined as mine is. I feel a shiver go through me at the sudden change in him. It is like looking at one of those transformer things. One moment it is a harmless toy car that you can play with, next minute is a red-eyed, machine of destruction. I can't help it. My eyes slide away.

He laughs softly and my eyes fly back to his face. He's laughing at me, teasing me, and I don't like it one little bit.

"Relax, Cindy. Drink as much as you like. While I admire your work ethic, I just gave you the rest of the night off," he says.

My eyes widen incredulously. Then I burst out laughing at the sheer audacity of him. He might be used to getting his own way, but it's a bit of a stretch for him to believe he has any control over my job, when I work or don't.

My laugh dies in my throat as he just sits there, cool as a cucumber, watching me patiently, as if he's waiting for me to catch up with the conversation. His expression tells me one thing. The reality of the situation hits me. What the fuck am I doing sitting here drinking with this guy? This guy who seems to know too much about me and is now behaving as if he has the right to tell me to take the night off.

I narrow my eyes, my suspicions well and truly up. He's still watching me, a predator waiting for his prey to slip up. What does he want with me? How has he managed to insert himself into my life like this? And why does he want to?

"Who the hell are you?" I ask, my voice a shocked whisper.

He looks down at his glass and then takes a slow sip of his drink. For a second I think he didn't hear my question, but he turns back to me and smiles oddly and I know he heard. He's playing with me again, keeping me on tenterhooks, making me wait until he's ready to talk.

"It's not so much a question of who I am Cindy. It's more a question of what I've done," he drawls.

I don't want to get lured down this path. This path where I can't seem to stop myself from playing into his hands and doing exactly what he expects of me, but I have to know. And his statement was a clear invite to ask.

"Ok," I say, my voice coming out a bit louder and sounding more like my own. "What have you done?"

"I've bought The Macau," he smiles. "It all became official yesterday. So … I'll say it again. Relax. Drink. You have the night off."

My first reaction is: he's lying.

There has been no mention of a sale, no mention that the business has changed hands. And surely as the manager, I would have been privy to that information, even if the rest of the staff weren't.

It would be such a stupid lie to tell, though. And one thing he is not is stupid. But what could he hope to achieve by making something like that up? And there's something disconcerting about the casual way he says it. He's not making it a big announcement.

That makes me think he's telling the truth.

ALEX

I gauge Cindy's reaction to my news out of the corner of my eye while I pretend to look at a man I'm vaguely acquainted with.

From what I've seen of Cindy so far, she seems to think she's hard to read, but her emotions play all over her face. She's easy to read if a person knows what they're looking for, and the first rule in my business is to learn to read people so they can never take you by surprise. Cindy has managed it once, but I won't let her catch me off guard like that again.

Her first reaction is, of course, disbelief. Then I see her mulling it over, wondering what I could achieve by such a lie.

I am quite impressed she's even giving it this much thought. I am a hard man to doubt. Nine times out of ten my inbred confidence makes people believe whatever I tell them. And the other time sheer confidence fails my poker face does the trick. If Cindy thinks I cleaned her out on the craps table, she should see me play poker. I've spent years perfecting the art of bluffing and reading people, and putting those two things together makes me almost unbeatable in business.

Actually, I am pretty sure I could walk into any business and announce I own it and within minutes, have all of the staff believing me. But Cindy is obviously different. She's one of those rare birds that doesn't believe easily. She wants to examine the idea, turn it over in her mind, and see if there's anything to suggest it isn't true.

In this case, there's no reason for her not to believe me. I'm not bluffing. I am the owner of this casino. Lord Alstree, the previous owner was happy to humor me and keep the deal on the down low. He didn't ask why. If I was up to something shady, he believed it was my affair not his. I like the English for that. They know how to mind their own business.

"I think I smell bullshit," Cindy says.

Her words doubt me, but her expression doesn't. She wants me to laugh, to tell her she's right, it was all a big wind up. But she doesn't really believe I'm going to. She knows.

"Then I think you might have some issues with your nose," I say.

She frowns at me. "So assuming you're telling the truth, then what was this all about tonight? Some sort of test to see if I was doing my job properly?"

"Not a test as such," I say. "I just wanted to make sure you are who I think you are. Someone responsible who takes their job seriously. And you didn't disappoint. Although you did take slightly longer than I thought you would to arrive at the table."

Like I knew she would, she bristles at the less than stellar evaluation I've made on her job performance.

I laugh. "But once you did arrive, you handled the … issue like a real pro."

She frowns again. "Nothing you've said proves you've bought this casino."

"Oh, Cindy, can we not get past this denial dance and get to the important details? We both know I'm telling the truth. It might interest you I looked up your HR file this morning. You started at twenty-one as an admin assistant and worked your way up. You were promoted to manager status four years ago. And if my math is correct, you are twenty-eight, almost twenty-nine. How am I doing so far?"

She pulls her drink towards her mouth and starts to drink it, really fast, but I don't comment on that. It's one more clue that she's shaken to the core. She wouldn't be sitting drinking with a customer she thought was cheating the casino under normal circumstances.

"Ok, so you know a few facts about me." Cindy shrugs. "They're hardly trade secrets. Maybe you've seen me here and asked around about me."

I laugh at her insinuation.

"What's so funny?" she demands.

"Your assumption that I have not only noticed you around, but also that I liked what I saw enough to go on an underhand fact-finding mission about you. You think very highly of yourself, Cindy."

She blushes and looks down at her glass. "I didn't mean it like that," she mumbles. Then she picks her glass up, drains it, and lifts her forefinger towards the bartender to indicate she wants another.

I take pity on her. I need her more than she needs me. If I push her too hard she could simply find a job elsewhere. "I know you didn't. It was just a last-ditch attempt for you to cling to the idea that I'm lying."

Her head swings back toward me. "You can't seriously expect to walk in here off the street, tell me you own the place, and have me just take your word for it. I'm the manager here. Why wasn't I told?"

My track record will show that is exactly what I do expect. As a matter of fact, I've never had to do any of the hand-holding I'm doing right now. I shrug casually.

"So what will convince you? Let me see," I say, pretending I'm thinking about it.

I know exactly how this will play out now. Play time is over and it's time to get down to business. I'm done toying with Cindy now. Either she says yes, or I start to look for my next target. I pull my phone out and scroll through my contacts. Once Lord Alstree's name is highlighted I hold the phone out to her.

"Would you like to call the previous owner and ask him about it?" I ask.

She doesn't take the phone, but she looks at the screen, and her face changes when she sees the name. Lord Alstree's a notably private man who doesn't give his contact information out to just anyone, and that should have told her something.

"How do you have Lord Alstree's phone number?"

I laugh softly. "Because I like to be able to contact a person when I'm doing business with them. It's kind of essential, don't you think? Now, do you want to call him or not?"

"No," she says quietly.

But she still looks skeptical. The truth hits me and I shake my head. "You don't want to call him because you've never spoken to him, have you? You would have no idea whether it was really him or not," I say.

She shrugs, but it confirms what I already knew.

"Maybe this will convince you." I reach into my inside pocket and pull out an envelope. "Inside the envelope are the deeds to the business that state I am the owner. Do you want to read them?"

She shakes her head slowly.

I eye her with disbelief. "You're telling me even if you see the legal documents, you still won't believe me?"

She smiles slightly and shakes her head.

"No. I'm saying I don't need to see the documents. I believe you."

I extend my hand to her and smile. "Allow me to introduce myself officially. My name is Alexander Obolensky, but you can call me Alex."

She shakes my hand. Her grip is firm, but her hand is warm and soft. I feel a burst of sparks run up my dick at her touch. Her sharp intake of breath betrays that she feels something too. She pulls her hand away, perhaps a little too quickly, but I understand why she did it.

The chemistry between us wasn't imagined, and it certainly wasn't a product of my charm. Charm is not one of my assets. It can even be said that I am a singularly charmless person. Raw chemistry could complicate my 'project', but I tell myself it won't. That this is business and I'll keep it that way. I won't let my attraction to her change my plans. I'm not a kid. I know how to ignore sexual attraction. I've done it before. Plenty of times. A little determination is all it takes.

I stand abruptly. It's a good thing for her to have some space. By the time I hit her with my proposal I need her to be back to her normal self.

"Meet me in Alstree's old office in twenty minutes," I say, all business now. "There is something I need to discuss with you."

I walk away without waiting for her to confirm her acceptance. I feel her eyes on my back as I make my way through the crowd.

I hate that it takes all of my effort not to look back.

CINDY

I watch Dark and Stormy, well, Alexander Obolensky, walk away. He walks like a predator. Confident and fearless. The whole jungle is his hunting ground.

My head feels like it is spinning. I shouldn't have drunk that last glass of G&T.

Even so … what the hell was all that about?

That was not … normal. Okay, I have to believe that cocksure bastard has bought the casino even though I find it almost impossible to get my head around the fact that the business has switched hands without me knowing anything about it.

But the way Alex made me find out about the sale was bizarre to say the least. It was almost as if he deliberately put me in a tricky position to see how I would react to him when I was outside my comfort zone. I frown when I remember our conversation. There was something disturbingly sexual about our entire exchange.

"Everything all right, Miss Forrester?"

I look up into Jerry's inquiring face and nod distractedly. "Yes, everything is fine."

"Can I get you anything else?"

"No, I'm fine."

He nods and walks away.

Because Lord Alstree is a notorious recluse who only came to the casino when it was closed and there was no one around, all casino business was conducted through Steven, his business manager. I could call Steven now and ask him about the sale, but something tells me he probably doesn't know much more than me.

So what now?

I've already wasted five minutes mulling this over. I have fifteen minutes left to decide whether to accept the change of ownership, or leave. Even the thought of leaving makes my stomach tighten. I love my job, I love the staff, I love everything about this casino. I've poured everything into this casino. When I first arrived it was a nondescript little place. The best that could be said about it was it had faded charm. I built it up to what it is today.

I don't want to leave it. Why should I? I haven't done anything wrong and Alex Obolensky doesn't look like a man who has time to waste on a small casino like this. Maybe he will run the same shop as Lord Alstree. As long as the casino is ticking over nicely there is no reason for him to chop and change anything.

I look at my watch.

Yes, I tell myself. I'll go and talk to Alex. In spite of the way he toyed with me he still seems like a reasonable man. If what he has to say sounds like something I can stomach, then I'll stay. If it doesn't, then I'll quit. It'll make me sad to leave this place and all the friends I've made here, but my mother always said, God never closed a door without opening a window. And in my life, I've learned to crawl out of the smallest little windows.

I'm not rich, but I have enough savings to see me over for at least a year. Hopefully it won't come to that. I think I have built up enough of a reputation to walk into any other casino in the city and get a job.

What I am worried about is how deeply attracted I am to Alex. If he's going to be a more hands on owner than Lord Alstree was I don't know if I can deal with seeing him every day while he has such a big effect on me.

I remember his smoldering eyes. The way they roamed all over my body. Even thinking about them now made goose bumps scatter my skin. He is a man you cannot ignore. He must have the same effect on most women. I'll just have to be professional about it, and ignore his magnetic eyes. I've worked with people I've been attracted to before, and nothing has ever happened between us. I didn't let it affect my day to day ability to do my job. And this will be just the same.

I'll make damn sure it is.

Alex might be able to swan in here and buy the place, but he can't make me act a certain way or do things I wouldn't usually do. Only I have that power over myself, and I intend to keep it that way.

It's not like I'm looking for a relationship anyway.

I check my watch and see ten minutes have passed. I stand up to head for Lord Alstree's old office. I make my way across the casino floor and along the hallway.

I reach his door and I pause for a moment, suddenly nervous. I tell myself I'm being ridiculous. What is there to be nervous about? I know this place like the back of my hand and I know all of the legalities of running a casino. If Alex is planning to test me, I know I'll be able to answer any of his questions, be they operational or logistical.

I pull a compact mirror from my jacket pocket and check my make-up. My mascara hasn't run and my teeth don't have lipstick on them. I snap my compact shut and slip it back into my pocket. It's as good as it's going to get. I knock smartly on the door.

"Come in," Alex calls.

I push the door open and step inside. Alex is seated behind a big ornate antique desk. Somehow this room is exactly how I pictured it might be. He nods towards one of the chairs on the opposite side and I sit down.

"You're punctual. I like that. Can I get you another drink?"

I stop myself from automatically saying no. That's not what a confident woman would do. I smile at him. "All right. I'll have whatever you're having. You did give me the night off. I might as well make the most of it."

"True," he agrees. "And I really meant it about giving you the night off. What I have to say won't take too long."

"Take your time," I say smoothly. "I expected to be at work tonight so it's not like I have any other plans."

"Then let's at least keep the drinks coming and make it somewhat sociable," he says, standing up and walking over to his bar. He fixes our drinks in silence and I resist the urge to fill the silence with babbling. To my surprise he puts a G&T with a slice of orange in front of me. He raises his glass of whisky. "To a mutually beneficial relationship."

I nod and take a sip. I watch him settle himself behind the desk again. I realize I feel better when he is not prowling about the room. I take another sip.

"So what was with all the theatrics, then?" I ask, the gin making me a lot bolder than I would usually be with a new boss. "You could have just come to my office and introduced yourself then run a performance appraisal on me to assess my suitability for the job."

He grins. Downright wolfish, that grin. "I could have. But where's the fun in that? Besides performance appraisals are useless. I needed a quick and dirty way to make sure you're the right person for the … job."

Did I imagine that slight pause he made before the word job? Besides my track record speaks for itself on that score, but I let it go. Maybe he was one of those bosses that was going to be weird. Maybe he wanted to catch us behaving badly while we did not know who he was.

"So how did you do it?" I ask. "Cheat the table?"

"You're the manager. You tell me," he says.

That twinkle is back in his eye, but I decide to be serious. I really could learn something here, something useful.

"I know of two ways to cheat at craps, and you were doing neither."

"Go on," he prompts me.

He leans forward, watching me with interest, and I try not to let his dark gaze distract me.

"One way is to have the box person use rigged dice. Sasha has been here far too long to be involved in something like that. The other way is magnets, but we have top of the range detectors at every entrance and I would have been alerted the second you stepped through the doors if you had magnets on you."

"There is a third way," Alex says with a grin.

CINDY

"You buy the casino and get your business manager to sneak in after the cleaning staff have left, and anyone else arrives. He attaches magnets to the table you will be sitting at. Then you count your losses to get the results you want."

I burst into laughter, shaking my head.

"Well, then it's fair to say that's not really a new threat I have to watch out for at least," I say. "You sure were committed to seeing how I handled a potential cheater."

"I think you handled me admirably," he smiles. "Most people get distracted by my brutish personality and forget themselves around me … but not you."

"Not me," I agree. "I've seen far too many psychopaths in here to let them disrupt the running of the casino."

"Fair enough," he says.

I think I detect a hint of disappointment on his face. Is he disappointed that I likened him to a psychopath? Did he want me to like him? No, I tell myself, quickly dismissing the idea. The gin has gone to my head and I'm starting to imagine things.

"Now, back to the job," he says, all business again. He leans back in his chair and studies me for a moment.

I take my chance to get in first. "Not to blow my own trumpet, but I think everything is run pretty efficiently here. Of course, today's take is going to be significantly lower than usual, but that's because of your little stunt so you can hardly complain about that."

He smiles and nods his head.

I go on quickly. "If there's anything you would like to change I'm open to a discussion about it."

He waves his hand dismissively. "You seem to know what you're doing here. I would never have bought the place if it was not a viable business option. But that's not the job I'm talking about. I have a proposition for you, Cindy. One I think will greatly benefit us both."

He pauses and I have to admit I'm intrigued. Does he have a network of casinos? Is he going to offer me some sort of area manager position? I'd definitely be open to that.

"I'll make you a fifty percent owner of The Macau, and after five years you can buy me out at the going market rate."

My eyes widen in shock. "What?"

"You didn't hear wrong," he says softly.

"Why?" I gasp out the word that is going round and round in my head like a dog chasing its own tail.

"In exchange for a few weeks of your time. During that time, you will act as my fiancée, and—"

I jump to my feet so quickly the fabulous velvet antique chair underneath me lands on the ground with a loud crashing sound. Ignoring it I glare bolts of fire at Alex. I'm so fucking angry I feel like I might burst into flames any moment.

"How dare you?" I yell furiously. "You waltz in here all mysterious and flirty and think you can buy *me*? I don't know what kind of people you usually employ, but let me tell you something. I am not that kind of woman and I never will be. And quite frankly, I'm disgusted you would even suggest such a thing."

Alex looks at me calmly as I shout at him. "Do you think it is possible, Cindy, that you could be holding the wrong end of the stick?"

I find that hard to believe. How else could he have meant it? I fold my arms across my chest and raising an eyebrow, wait for his explanation.

"If anything, I should be the one that's offended here. Think about it, do you really think I have to pay for sex?"

I have to admit it does seem extremely unlikely a man like him would have to pay for sex. He must have a string of women queuing up to get into his bed. And to pay that much for a few weeks of sex was sheer madness. And he didn't look mad. Quite the opposite. As a matter of fact, more and more he is looking like the sane one in our exchange ... but that doesn't change the fact he's just asked me to be his girlfriend for a few weeks in exchange for money.

"What exactly could your proposition mean except what I thought it meant?" I ask intrigued, but refusing to show it.

"If you'll just sit back down, I'll explain everything, I promise. And once I've explained, if you don't want to do it, then I'll understand. It won't in any way affect your job here," he says quietly.

"I won't be fired?" I ask, in disbelief.

"No, of course not," he says, looking slightly annoyed that I would even think such a thing. "This is a personal matter outside of the business. Even if you don't have the sense to see a good deal when one is offered to you, it doesn't mean you're bad at running the casino."

I ignore the dig at my business acumen and choose instead to focus on his deal. I have no intention of being a whore for any amount of money, but since he's claimed I got the wrong end of the stick, I'm now extremely curious to hear him out. Half of the casino I have given my lifeblood to for years is an unbelievable deal. It will change my life forever and I'd be crazy to not at least wait around to find out what I'd have to do to get it.

I turn around, pick up the chair I knocked over, and sit back down. "Ok, I'm listening."

"I have a great aunt back in Russia who is very important to me, but I haven't always done right by her. She's old now, and I don't know how long she has left," he explains, his face and voice utterly expressionless.

I know instinctively he's telling the truth. People who tell the truth don't have to varnish their words or create drama in order to be believed.

"Anyway," he adds, "she has this crazy notion in her head that I need a good wife to look after me. Clearly, I don't, but she's stuck on the idea, and I know she won't be happy until she thinks I've found someone. She's done a lot for me over the years, and I want her to die happy. I'd like to go visit her this weekend, and I want to take a fiancée with me."

"And that's where I would come in."

"Yes," Alex nods. "That's what I meant about being my girl-friend for a few weeks, broken down into perhaps three, but most probably only two trips. You wouldn't actually have to do anything with me. Your job is to be the best actress half a casino can buy. Babushka is a wily old fox and she will see through a wooden performance. I need you to be … and he began to tick the qualities off on his fingers.

"One, beautiful (easy – you already are),

Two, fiery (my aunt will expect the woman I chose to be a fireball),

Three, charming (I've seen you with difficult customers and I believe you have that in spades).

And finally, head over heels in love (that's the bit where you'll look deep into my eyes as if you can't believe your luck that you've caught such a man)."

Once more, Alex has taken me by surprise. I wouldn't have picked him as someone who would care so much about an elderly aunt's feelings to go to all this trouble. The proposal, at face value, sounds like a no brainer. Charm an elderly woman and make her happy for a relatively brief period. But I have a feeling there's more to it than that. It sounds too easy. Surely no one in their right mind will

43

dream of giving away half a casino for something so simple.

He must have taken my silence as hesitation, because he continues on.

"I assure you I will be perfectly respectful towards you at all times. We will have separate rooms and treat it like a business arrangement. So what do you think?"

"I think flying to a foreign country with a man I've just met, particularly one with enough resources to buy a casino on a whim is probably a bad idea. I don't know if I can trust you or not," I say honestly.

"That's a sensible reaction." He smiles as if what I have said is not a negative, but another step towards his goal. "I can't say I blame you for being wary. All I can do is assure you that no harm will come to you. I am a man of my word. You are welcome to check out my reputation before you agree. I just want to be able to make an old woman happy."

I'm inclined to believe him on that score, but something is niggling at me and I don't know what it is. It comes to me suddenly and I blurt it out.

"You're a ... er ... good-looking man," I start to say when he interrupts me.

"Are you afraid you won't be able to keep your hands to yourself? Don't worry, Cindy, I swear I'll somehow fight you off." His eyes gleam with amusement.

I roll my eyes. "That's not what I meant and you know it. What I meant was you can't be short of an admirer or two. So why me? Why not whisk some woman away for a couple of weeks with her dream man and save yourself a whole lot of money?"

"Let me start with the second part of your question. Do you think it would be fair of me to lead some woman on and let her think we have a real relationship when I would just be using her?"

"Hmmm." Wow, I really didn't expect a man like him to care about that side of the situation.

"There's another more important reason too. I want this to go smoothly. I don't want to get out there and end up spending the whole week bickering and breaking my aunt's heart because I only realize when I'm there that I don't get on with the person I take."

"How do you know we won't get there and realize we don't get on and end up bickering just as hard? You might have heard stories from Lord Alstree's business manager about my work ethic, but you don't know me as a person."

"Well it won't matter, will it?" he says with a shrug.

His blunt response takes me by surprise. I frown. Does he think that I am someone who will just swoon at his every word?

"It's a business deal, Cindy. You'll be getting paid handsomely to do a job. And that job is being nice to me and acting like you're my fiancée in public. It doesn't matter if you don't like me as long as you do what you're being paid to do."

"Ok, that makes sense," I concede. At least he's not arrogant enough to assume there's no chance of me not liking him. "But I still don't understand why you've chosen me. You must have female friends who could do this as a business arrangement."

"Would you believe me if I told you that you ... are exactly the kind of woman my great aunt would fall in love with?" Alex asks with a twinkle in his eye.

My eyes widen. "What kind of woman is that?"

He laughs. "If I tell you I will spoil it. Just be yourself and she will fall for you hook, line and sinker."

I scowl. "It sounds wrong when you say it like that."

"Wrong?" he queries, one eyebrow arched.

"Deceitful. We would be fooling an old lady."

"All of life is deceitful. When you wore your push-up bra this morning you made the decision to deceive every man that looked at you."

I blushed. He couldn't possibly know about my push-up bra. He had to be guessing.

He watched the color that flooded into my cheeks with interest. "My aunt wants me to be married. I don't want to be married. You want a casino and you don't have one, I think my proposal is an elegant solution that will keep everybody happy."

"Why did you offer me half the casino? I would have done it for less."

"Other than the fact that I find I get a startlingly better performance when I overpay my staff, I also didn't want to risk the deal because the bait I offered wasn't juicy enough."

"Actually, the job sounds too good to be true. Too easy."

"There's a little more to it."

My heart drops a little. I knew it was too good to be true.

"One of the reasons I chose you," he continues, "is because I've seen how you handle difficult customers and keep the peace. I've seen how you read people and instinctively know how to handle them. You're going to need those skills."

"You're not exactly making your great aunt sound like the sweet old dear I was imagining," I say with a frown.

"It's not my great aunt. She really is the sweet old dear you're imagining. The problem will be the rest of my relatives. Let's just say they won't exactly be welcoming."

"Why?"

"It's too complicated to go into, but it is also surplus information. Just manage them the way you would your most belligerent customers and you'll be fine."

I'm still not sure what to make of any of this and I don't quite know what to say. I guess I am intrigued enough by the offer that I don't want to just flat out turn it down, but I'm not quite ready to agree to it either.

On the one hand, my instincts are telling me to run away from this deal and never look back. But on the other hand, they're also telling me this might be the doorway through which a whole new world of adventure opens up.

Just imagine … I'll be able to buy him out in five years!

Oh my God!

I'll be the owner of my own casino!

The Macau will be mine! Mine! Mine!

Put like that I have no problem dealing with awkward people and I can talk myself into fooling a little old lady especially since it is all for her own good.

"Are you afraid of me, Cindy?" Alex asks suddenly, cutting through my thoughts.

His question is so far out of left field that I just answer it honestly without even thinking about it. "No. Should I be?"

"No." He smiles. "A lot of people are but let me tell you this, I'm the only person in my family with the sort of past and connections that could make people afraid of me. So if you're not afraid of me, the rest of my relatives will be a walk in the park."

I'm sure his words are meant to be reassuring, but I can't help but wonder if they're not a cleverly veiled threat. He's letting me know he has contacts, a past. Yet still I don't feel afraid of him. The more I think about it, the more I know why I'm stalling on giving him an answer to his proposition.

I am not afraid I'll get out there and he'll murder me and bury me in a shallow grave somewhere. I am afraid I'll get out there and fall for him and make a total fool of myself because that sexual attraction I felt when I first saw him has never gone away. It is in the background pulsing relentlessly.

Even when I was furious with him for thinking he could buy me like a prostitute and I flew out of my chair it was there, throbbing, throbbing, throbbing, like the heartbeat of a fetus, strong, sure, and undeniable. It wants to live. It has a will of its own. To abort it I will have to tear it away from my body and it will forever haunt me as a lump of flesh, blood and guts.

"While I don't want to pressure you, I really do need an answer," he murmurs.

"Can I take the rest of the night to think about it and let you know tomorrow?"

"Of course." He smiles that slow, sure smile.

I get to my feet and head for the door. He calls my name and I pause in front of the door and turn back to see him watching me thoughtfully.

"I told you there would be no hard feelings if you say no, and I meant it," he says.

I nod. "You'll have your answer this time tomorrow."

CINDY

I lie in bed and think of his strong hands touching the chips, almost caressing them, and I feel heat start pooling in my core. As if he was actually stroking my skin. Groaning at my needy response I turn to my side and press my legs together tightly. It doesn't help the least bit. My whole body feels like it is throbbing for him.

How long has it been since I last had sex?

A year?

Jesus, it hasn't been that long, surely. I frown. Actually, it may be even longer than that. I've been so invested in my career there was no time for fun and games. I roll on to my back and stare at the ceiling. It explains why I'm so hot and flustered for him. That and the fact that he is a very, very fuckable guy, after all. All that raw magnetism. Just thinking of those stormy eyes makes electricity race through my body. My skin tingles with anticipation.

Fuck it!

I slip my fingers into my panties and close my eyes. Suddenly, I'm back outside his office. This time I don't knock.

This time I walk in, and he doesn't talk. He looks up. Our eyes meet across the room, then he gets up and crosses the room in that wildly powerful panther-like stride of his. He grabs me by the upper-arms and slams me hard up against the door.

I open my mouth to protest, and he clamps his hand over my mouth and says, "You talk too much, Miss Forrester." Then he pulls my skirt up to my waist, rips my panties off my body and stuffs them in my mouth.

My whole body is shaking with excitement as he rips my blouse open. Buttons fly everywhere. He makes short work of my bra clasp and my breasts pop out. Immediately he bends his head, swirls his hot, velvety tongue around one nipple, then sucks it into his mouth. His mouth is heaven.

In the darkness of my bedroom I reach into the drawer by my bedside and let my hand close around my trusty old vibrator. I switch it on and push it into my wetness. A muffled moan escapes me ...

... as he sucks my nipple hard.

Holding me pressed tightly against the door, he kicks my legs so they spread wide open.

"Don't fucking move," he orders.

I don't even breathe when he knees between my legs, grabs my ass, and pulls me tightly towards his face. His five o'clock shadow rasps against my skin. And it feels delicious. He thrusts his tongue into my pussy, and tongue-fucks me like he can't get enough. The uncivilized, feral way he eats me makes me go crazy. My fingers

51

rake through his hair and I grind my pussy against his mouth. I feel my juices start to gush into his mouth. I am so close it feels as if I am going to cum in his mouth.

But he stands suddenly.

"Do you want everyone in the casino to know I fucked you?" he growls.

I shouldn't want that, but I find my head nodding.

He yanks my panties out of my mouth, and before I can even take a breath, he has grabbed my hips roughly and whirled me around to face the door. As my forearms hit the wood, he tilts my body so that my ass is jutting out. I scream in shock and pleasure when he rams his cock into me. Balls deep in one swift violent movement. He has entered me bare. Without protection. We are skin on skin. The way I have never been with any man in my life. Before I can even get used to the way his cock stretches me, he begins to fuck me like a madman. Like he damn well owns me. Completely and fully.

There is no way I will be able to walk out of the casino now without every single person knowing Alex Obolensky has fucked me in his office.

My hand thrusts the vibrator faster and faster into me, but I cannot match the speed of his cock inside me.

My body bows and locks and I come harder than I have ever come, on my own or with any man. For a long time, I lie staring at the ceiling, the vibrator still pulsating inside me. Shocked by the intensity of my orgasm.

Sleep becomes impossible.

I spend the rest of the night lying awake, Alex's proposal going around and around inside my head. I promised him I would think about it, and I meant it, but I didn't expect it to take up this much head space. I honestly thought that once I was alone, without his smoldering eyes on me, making the decision would be easy. I didn't expect those eyes to follow me home. Each time I tried to think rationally about the offer, all I could see were those beautifully stormy eyes boring into my soul.

Dawn creeps into the sky and I'm not even a little bit closer to making a decision.

Several times I decided I'm definitely not going to do it, but then a little voice speaks up in my head asking me if I'm actually mad? Half a casino for a few weeks of what is in essence an acting job!

Then I decide I definitely am going to do it because owning my own casino is my biggest dream, until another maddening little voice speaks up and asks me if that's a good idea. I have never reacted to any man the way I do with him. What if I fall in love with him? He has danger stamped all over him. What's the point of money if you're going to get your heart cut to ribbons in a metal shredder?

Basically, I waste eleven hours of my life trying to make a decision that should have been the simplest one I've made in a long time ... and I still haven't made a decision. But I told Alex I would let him know the next day and I plan to keep my word on that.

I considered just tossing a coin and going with whatever it tells me to do, but realistically, I can't make a potentially life changing decision on something so random. Finally, I decide to consult my two best friends who live in the city, Rosa and Star, to see what they think. Maybe they can look at the whole thing a little more objectively than I can and just tell me what the hell I'm supposed to do about it.

I text them and ask them to meet me for brunch and to bring along their thinking caps because I'm going to need them. Their replies are instantaneous and affirmative. Rosa because she is pregnant and her husband won't let her even boil an egg so she has all the time in the world, and Star because she married a billionaire and has dedicated herself to charity work and being a mother.

I step into the café where we always have our brunches and look around. The decor is light and airy and the smell of cooking food makes my stomach growl. I spot Rosa and Star at our usual table and make my way across to them.

CINDY

"You're late," Rosa accuses as she stands up to hug me. Her stomach gets in the way and we laugh. She kisses my cheek warmly.

"I know, I'm sorry. I lost track of time."

"What's with the dark circles under your eyes?" Star asks. And well she might. Even make-up wouldn't cover the blue shadows under my eyes.

"Couldn't sleep last night," I say moving to kiss her proffered cheeks. Star smells of expensive perfume and baby powder.

"Sit down and tell us all about it," Star invites. "We've already ordered you your usual by the way."

"Thanks," I slide into the seat.

Both girls lean forward eagerly.

"So here's the deal. I know it's going to sound crazy, but just hear me out. The Macau changed hands. Been bought out by a Russian."

"Wow! When?" Star interjects.

"Well, very recently. It was all so hush, hush, I didn't even know about it until last night when I met the owner in the most unusual way."

"Oh, my goodness. I didn't know it was going to be this good," Rosa says gleefully. She stops just short of rubbing her hands together.

"The new owner has offered me a deal. A business arrangement. I fly to Russia with him and spend a couple of weeks with him and his great aunt. Apparently, she desperately wants to see him married off … so I have to pretend to be his fiancée."

Star shakes her head. "What the …"

"You said deal. What do you get in return?" Rosa asks with narrowed eyes.

"I get ownership of half of The Macau with the option to buy him out after five years."

Both my friends' jaws drop open with shock. They stare at me for a few seconds, then they turn to look at each other.

"Well, it's a no brainer, isn't it?" Rosa says. "Do it. Get a flight booked quickly before he changes his mind. It sounds like the easiest job you'll ever do and it's a lot of money to turn down."

"Hang on. That's not right. Nobody gives half a casino for something like that," Star says worriedly. "There has to be more. To be honest I don't like the sound of it. My husband does business with Russian billionaires and most of them are out and out crooks. Think Kayser Soze from

The Usual Suspects and you've got the template for almost all of them."

"Er ... excuse me. Didn't you marry a Russian gangster, yourself?" Rosa asks, her eyes twinkling with mischief.

"That's different," Star says defensively.

Rosa doesn't let up. "How?"

"Nikolai is a good man," Star says primly.

"He wasn't when you met him. It was the love of a good woman who turned him into a good man. Maybe we should give Cindy's guy a chance too. He could turn out to be a good man too." She turns to me. "As much as I hate to rain on your parade, I have to agree with Star that half a casino does sound excessive for a pretend fiancée gig."

I shrug. "I know, but he says he did that because he wanted to make absolutely sure I didn't turn down his offer because the bait was not juicy enough, and also he likes to overpay to get the best out of his staff."

"Bait? I really don't like that word. It all sounds shady, Cindy. Who pays someone to pretend to be their girlfriend? Is it just a nice way of saying he wants a week of dirty sex with you?"

The thought of spending a week having dirty sex with Alex makes my body throb.

Rosa turns to Star. "You should know. Didn't Nikolai do exactly the same to get you?"

Star shakes her head decisively. "Mine was a unique situation. I got lucky. Since then I've learned a lot about Russian billionaires and most of it is not pleasant at all. Personally, I don't think it is a good idea. Anyway, if you're thinking about doing this, Cindy, just because you want to be the owner of a casino, why didn't you let me get you one when I wanted to? Why get it from a strange man?"

I sighed elaborately. "First of all, I'm not a charity case. I don't want you to buy me a casino. You already bought me a flat and honestly, I felt bad even taking that."

"And you feel better about having sex with your new boss to get it instead?"

"Hang on a minute. Who said anything about sex? It's not about sex. He doesn't want sex. He actually scoffed at the idea of him paying to get sex. And to be fair to him, he is what one would call a big catch. Girls must be queuing up to fuck this guy."

"Why can't he ask one of those women in the queue then?" Star retorts.

"He gave me the impression he doesn't want any emotional complications to follow him around once the deed is done. He wants to treat this whole scenario purely as a business transaction. Also, his family can be hard to deal with which is why he asked me as he's seen me keep my cool at work with difficult people. And the final cherry on the cake is I'm apparently exactly the kind of woman his great aunt would take a shine to."

"Well, that all makes perfect sense to me. You should go for it," Rosa encourages cheerfully.

Star gives Rosa an incredulous look. "Do you realize that you could be sending Cindy off to Russia with a psychopath?"

"Nonsense. This man has far more to lose than Cindy.

Besides, any man who is willing to throw that much money away to keep a great aunt happy is no psychopath."

Star turns back to me. "If everything is that clear and wonderful then what's holding you back? I know you're not worried about a few difficult relatives."

How do I even begin to explain this? "I don't know really. I just ... I kind of like him and I'm worried I'll get too attached to him I suppose."

"Well that's easy to fix. Just tell yourself it's business. You've never been one to mix business with pleasure. Don't let yourself get attached. Just keep it in your mind that it's all fake," Star says.

I look at her with surprise. "Now you sound like you're trying to talk me into it. A second ago, you sounded like you were trying to talk me out of it."

"I'm not trying to do either. It's your decision, Cindy. I'm just saying if that's all that is stopping you, then it's easy to protect yourself."

"Would you do it if you were me?" I ask her.

"I wouldn't do it. Not a chance in hell," Star cries passionately. "But I was never really a risk taker. I leave things like that to you and." She eyes Rosa. "And Braveheart here."

"What about you?" I ask Rosa.

"I'd do it in a heartbeat." She laughs. "A free holiday, half a casino, and a week spent with a guy you're clearly lusting after." She pauses. "But little Cindy, what aren't you telling us?"

"What do you mean?" I ask.

"There's something you're holding back. I know you said you're worried you'll fall for this guy, but there's more to it, isn't there?"

I sigh. I should have known they'd see right through me. They're my best friends and we've known each other since school. If anyone can tell when I'm holding something back from them it's these guys.

"I think he might be a part of the Russian Bratva, or something," I say.

"What makes you say that?"

"He kind of looks it. Besides, who do you know that has the money to walk into a casino and buy it on a whim unless their money is dirty?"

"What's the guy's name? I'll find out if he's legit."

I think about it for a second. Star's husband is well connected in the business world and if Alex is legitimate, his people will be able to trace him easily enough.

"Alexander Obolensky," I say.

Star takes her phone out and sends a quick message to her husband. "I've texted Nikolai the name. Let's just wait and see what he comes back with," Star says.

"Thanks," I say.

Our food arrives and I realize just how hungry I am. I tuck in immediately, enjoying the waffles with strawberries and chocolate sauce. I wonder if they have waffles in Russia.

We're about halfway through the meal when her phone pings. She picks it up and looks at the screen.

"It's Nikolai," she says. "Let's see what he has to say."

I can feel my heart racing as I wonder what Nikolai will say. I can barely taste my pancakes now, that's how nervous I suddenly am.

"Hey baby," she coos into the phone. He says something which makes her giggle, then she catches the expression on my face and quickly says. "So do you know that man?"

"You do? Great. What's he like? Can he be trusted?"

He must have asked why she wanted to know, because she mouths to me. "Can I tell him why you want to know?"

I shrug, then nod.

"Well," she tells her husband, "he bought The Macau, you know, where Cindy works and he's offered her half of the casino in exchange for her pretending to be his fiancée."

Both Rosa and I can hear the low whistle that comes out of the telephone speaker. For a while he talks and Star listens, then she coos her goodbyes, peppers them with coy kisses, and reluctantly ends the call.

"Well?" Rosa demands impatiently.

"Looks like he is okay," she says. "Nikolai knows him. Not personally, but he knows of him. He's from a fabulously wealthy old family, but for some years he did the rebellious thing and became the second man to a famous Russian crime boss, but he's gone straight since then and become a legit businessman. Nikolai says his word is good. If he says he's going to give half a casino then he's going to give it to you."

I feel a rush of relief wash over me, but Alex still seems like someone who's dangerous, and he must still have connections with dangerous people, but it's not like we're going to be smuggling drugs or something. Suddenly, my waffles taste pretty sweet again.

"Now that we've established he's legit, are you going to do him ... I mean, it?" Rosa presses me with a cheeky grin.

"I'm going to do *it*," I say with a grin.

"Good choice. Life is for living and taking risks. That's where all the fun lies," Rosa says.

Star stays quiet and I know she doesn't really approve of my choice, but like she said, she's not a risk taker. I am. Half of The Macau is just too good to turn down. Besides, I've never been to Russia. It might be interesting to see the sights.

But mostly, it's Alex who's made the final decision for me.

Those damned eyes. I'm too intrigued by him to say no. I think I like Rosa's take on things. Life is about experiences. Going out to Russia with a gorgeous billionaire must count as a great one. Also I'd like to get to know more about Alex. To be perfectly honest, I want to get to know everything about him.

"Oh my God, Cindy. You really are smitten with this guy, aren't you?" Star laughs.

I smile and shake my head. "Maybe," I admit.

"Well it can't hurt to spend some time with him then. But don't forget that it's just business. So don't lead yourself on and get attached to him. He sounds like a man who wouldn't know emotional commitment if it climbed into his bed and gave him a blowjob."

I grin. "Don't worry, I know the garden is not mine, but there's nothing wrong with admiring the flowers, right?"

"Nope," Rosa says. "As long as you only look and don't touch."

"Don't worry. I'll keep my legs crossed," I say with a grin. As intriguing and sexy as I find Alex, I have no intention of being unprofessional on this trip. And I'm certain he feels exactly the same way. I can put up walls and not let myself fall for him. I've done it before. Never with someone as hot as Alex, but I know I can do this. And who knows? Maybe after a few days with him, I'll see his bad habits and decide he's really not all that after all.

"So when are you supposed to be going?" Star asks me.

"He said this weekend," I reply. "Presumably Friday or Saturday. I'm not sure."

"You'd better get home and get packing then. You've only got two days."

I laugh along with them, then Star tells me what sort of clothes a person needs to go to Russia. I have no idea what to pack, but I'm sure I can work it out. Google will be my friend on this one.

"Isn't it like the Arctic out there?" Rosa asks.

"It is in winter," Star says. "But it's June, so it could be wonderful, but depends where you are. Even so I don't think it'll be that bad"

We finish our brunch and as we leave the restaurant, the girls make me promise to stay in touch while I'm gone and keep them updated on how things are going. I promise I will and I can't help but feel better just by knowing that they will know where I am.

That's the wrong attitude to go into this with, and I decide to let go of my fears. Nikolai has confirmed Alex's businesses are legit and Alex has promised me nothing bad will happen to me. I shouldn't trust a man I've only met once, but somehow I do. I knew instinctively he would keep his word even before Star confirmed it. The worst thing that can happen is a few snotty comments from his family. That I can live with.

I pull my phone out the second I get back home and I send a simple text to Alex.

I'm in.

H is reply is immediate. No messing about or playing games for him.

Good. My lawyers will Fedex your contract to you.

I text him back.

Great. When and where should I meet you?

My phone pings even faster than before. I read his message with a small smile.

Flying out Friday afternoon. My driver will pick you up from your house at 2pm.

I text him back.

See you then.

My phone pings again and I feel a rush of warmth inside of me. The business part is dealt with and Alex is still texting me.

You won't regret this. I promise.
And a GIF of a man repeatedly banging his head against a wall.

I laugh to myself. Whatever happens on the trip, I think Alex and I will get on ok. He has a sense of humor and I think we'll be just fine. I can't help but wonder what he's really like deep down, behind the dark and stormy exterior.

Just thinking about him, I feel a surge of excitement in my stomach which I swallow away quickly. I'm not meant to be excited about this. It's business, not a holiday. My fingers fly over my screen.

I'll hold you to that promise

ALEX

I stand on the steps of my plane and glance at my watch.
It's a little after 2.30. She should be here by now. I feel a
brief pang of worry, which I ignore. She'll come. Of course
she will.

My driver sent me a text when he picked her up.

I walk back into the cabin of the plane. The black leather
seats and the blue carpet are spotless as always. The bar is
well stocked with both drinks and snacks. Have they
prepared orange slices?

I tell myself to stop this.

What the fuck is wrong with me? *This is a fucking business
arrangement.* Nothing more, nothing less. I'm paying Cindy
handsomely for her troubles. If there are no oranges she will
just have to put up with lemons. They're fucking good
enough for everyone else.

Seriously irritated with myself I move back to the top of the
steps.

What the hell is it about that woman that has me so worked up? I decide not to even try to answer that question. The answer is dangerous and it sits in a place I don't want to go. I can't let myself think of Cindy as anything other than one of my staff. I promised her I would be respectful towards her on this trip and I meant it.

I finally spot my car coming along the road leading to the private airport and I relax. She's here. They must have hit traffic or something. I check my watch again. It's getting on for 2.45 and the pilot has a three o'clock take off booked. We have more than enough time.

The car pulls up alongside the plane and the back door opens at the same time as the driver's door. A smile twists my lips. How interesting. All the girls I've ever been with waited for the door to be open. Cindy clearly isn't used to being waited on.

I lose my train of thought when I see her emerging from the car. She stands looking up at the plane, shielding her eyes from the sun with one hand. She's wearing a canary yellow sundress that shows off her long, long legs and her stunning tan. Her hair is loose, blowing slightly in the breeze. My brain takes a mental picture of her standing there like that so I never forget this moment.

Cindy follows the driver around to the boot of the car and I have to laugh at his surprised expression. He speaks to her and she shrugs. Clearly, she thought she would fetch her own luggage. She doesn't, of course. Steven knows better than to allow her anywhere near the cargo area. She turns and starts walking towards me.

I remember the promise I've just made to myself.

No flirting.

Nothing even mildly inappropriate. Just cool and professional, nothing else. But the sight of her walking in the sunlight, gives my cock other ideas and I adjust my jeans slightly to make sure my hard-on isn't on show.

I shake my head at myself in surprise. I'm never ever like this around a woman. No woman has ever affected me the way she does. Best part is she's not even fucking trying. Hell, this is the behavior of a fucking horny teenager, and it has to stop. I dread to think what effect she could have on me if she actually wanted to seduce me. I'd be like a blabbering idiot, frothing at the mouth.

I force my eyes away from her legs. If I focus on them for too long, I know what will happen. This trip will become utter hell.

She comes up the steps and I smile as she reaches my side. I gesture for her to go ahead and enter the plane.

"Welcome aboard," the stewardess says as she steps into the cabin.

She turns back and looks at me over her shoulder, flashing me a quick smile and then she turns back to the stewardess.

"Thank you," she says quietly. Suddenly, she appears dignified, like a woman who has been flying in private planes all her life and I know for sure I have made the right decision. She will do a good job.

I walk past her and sit down.

She takes the seat opposite mine, adjusts her dress modestly, then spoils it by crossing her silky legs seductively. It takes all of my willpower to keep my eyes focused on her face rather than those long, long legs.

I picture her stretching out and kicking off one of her sandals. I see her lift her leg casually, then her toes are pushing inside my trouser leg, trailing over my skin, moving higher. I can almost feel her touch. Inside my heated head, she springs out of her seat, straddles me, and unleashing my cock, rides me.

Fuck!

"The captain will be doing his final checks now," I mutter, pleased that my voice doesn't give away the images my brain cooks up when I look at her bare legs. "We're due to take off in less than five minutes, and once we're up, the bar opens."

"Sounds good," she says, fastening her seat belt. "Can I ask you something? Something that's going to make me sound a bit naïve."

"Sure," I smile.

"What's the procedure to flying into Russia?" she asks.

"We'll touch down briefly in a normal airport and a customs officer will get on board, check our passports and the pilot's flight details. Once we're cleared, we'll go back up and land at the private airstrip on my aunt's land."

"I see. I guess the real benefit of flying private is not having to rub shoulders with all the rest of the cattle, isn't it?"

I arch an eyebrow. "You think I'm a terrible snob?"

"Oh, I do," she admits with tinkling laughter. "A snob and a queue jumper. The worst combination."

Her laugh is infectious and I can't help myself from breaking into a grin. It's good to hear her real laugh, see her real smile. This is a very different Cindy to the one I met the other night in the casino.

"Seriously though, I can see the appeal of not having to be at the airport for hours before taking off, and I can definitely see the appeal of skipping the lines at the other end."

"And it's always good to know your bags are definitely on board the right plane too," I add, trying not to stare at her. The sunlight is slanting in through the window, turning her hair gold and her eyes into twin blue fires.

"And we have blue skies," she says cheerfully, peering out of the window. She seems surprisingly laid back, and I feel as if I'm getting to know the real Cindy, the one behind the customer service face.

We're interrupted briefly when the air stewardess comes over to see that all is well. Then she closes the main cabin door. It gives a quiet hiss as the seal engages. She comes back over to us once the door is sealed and smiles at me.

"The captain is ready for take off. We're expecting a smooth and comfortable flight with around a three-hour flight time. I'll return once we're air bound to see if either of you need anything. Have a great flight."

"Don't worry about coming back, Gloria," I say. "Just chill out and enjoy the flight. We can grab our own drinks."

Gloria nods at me and moves away to the staff area of the plane.

"That was totally for my benefit, wasn't it?" Cindy asks with laughs.

"Totally."

The engines roar into life, the seat vibrates slightly beneath me, and we start moving.

ALEX

"So … what exactly is it that you do?" Cindy asks. Her tone is light and conversational but the question is not.

"You could say I'm a businessman although I don't really like the word. It always makes me think of a middle-aged, slightly obese man selling things nobody wants to buy. Not that there's anything wrong with that, but it's hardly me, is it?"

"No, because the middle-aged man wouldn't be so secretive about what he does," she says seriously.

"I'm not being secretive. Or at least not intentionally. I just don't want to bore you with the details. But you've asked for it now. I've acquired The Macau, obviously. I also have three others in Vegas, two in Madrid and one in France. I have hotels all across the world, and I have several clubs in London, New York and Moscow and I dabble in the property market quite a bit. Does that answer your question?"

"In a way." She gives me a teasing smile. "You're a jack of all trades."

I frown. "No, I wouldn't say that. I only know two things. How to recognize a good deal, and I know how to read people. It means I can negotiate deals most people wouldn't imagine possible. But once I sign on the dotted line, I rely on people like you who know how the business runs to keep it profitable."

"And The Macau is a good deal?"

"Yes. At a certain point other things become far more important than money. I can always earn more money, but this might be my last chance to make my great aunt happy."

Cindy mulls this over for a while. "Do you ever get lonely?"

I am a little surprised by her question and I frown.

"Sorry, was that too personal?"

"No. I never get lonely. Do you?" I ask curiously.

She shifts uncomfortably. "I have my job and my friends. So … no. I don't get lonely."

"Do you travel a lot on business?"

"Yeah, I guess I do."

"But London's your base."

"You could say that."

"So when your aunt asks, we live in London?" she asks.

"Yes, but not together. My great aunt's predictably old fashioned and she won't approve of the idea of us living together before marriage, anyway, so you can just tell her the truth about having your own place."

She smiles and looks relieved. She doesn't want to have to lie to my aunt any more than she has to. I don't much like the idea of lying to my aunt either.

"She sounds a lot like my grandmother." Cindy smiles. "She always wanted me to find a good husband and settle down and be happy. I don't think she ever accepted that I am happy as I am. She would have felt exactly the same about the idea of me living with a guy before marriage. Living in sin she used to call it. She was a great romantic, she believed love was worth waiting for."

"It sounds like my great aunt and your grandmother would have gotten along really well," I say.

"Yes, I imagine they would. I can imagine them now sitting side by side plotting our wedding," Cindy says with an uncomfortable laugh.

"Speaking of weddings … if my aunt asks, we haven't picked a date yet. We're taking things slowly." I lean to the side and dig into my pocket and then pull out a little box and I hand it to Cindy. "But you will need this though."

She takes the box from me and opens it. She gasps when she sees the gold ring with a large, sparkling emerald sitting in a bed of diamonds.

"It's beautiful," she says.

I smile. "I'm afraid you won't get to keep it. It's been in my family for years. Put it on and don't lose it."

She puts it on and holds her hand out in front of her, admiring it. She smiles a little sadly and then she drops her hand back into her lap and looks out of the window. The conversation seems to be over, and I am relieved when the light goes on in the cabin to tell us we can move around.

"I'll get us some drinks," I say.

"Just a diet coke for me please. I want to be levelheaded when I meet your family."

I decide that's not the worst idea and I pour her a diet coke and a large whisky for myself.

"Ice?" I ask.

Cindy nods. I add ice to both glasses, then I take the drinks back to my seat. I hand Cindy her Coke, and as she takes it, her fingers brush mine. Instantly, I feel that rush again. This is going to be a long week if I feel that every time we accidentally touch each other.

I take a gulp. "Shall we get our story straight?"

"Ah, yes, let's get our epic romance all synchronized, the moment we met, how long we've been together, the rainy day you got on one knee after a meal in a French restaurant and proposed ..."

I frown. I didn't expect her to get so detailed. I was actually hoping to wing it. No one needs details like that.

"If your aunt is so worried about your future, she will ask us questions about how we met. And if our stories don't match, she'll smell a rat," Cindy says, taking a sip of her drink.

She studies my face for a few seconds, then she laughs softly. "You don't have a story planned out, do you?"

I shake my head a little sheepishly. "No. I never considered going into that kind of detail. I was planning on keeping it simple. How about I'll grunt and pretend it's too private to discuss, and you can make up anything you feel will fly."

She pauses, her brow creased slightly as she thinks. "OK. Here goes. Let's say we met in a supermarket."

"Um … no. I don't shop for myself."

She grins. "Silly me, of course you don't. How about you ran out of milk and you popped into the supermarket for that?"

"Unlikely, but carry on," I said, intrigued.

"Well, I was trying to reach something off the top shelf and you got it down for me. And then, as we continued shopping … of course, you only came in for milk, but you were so entranced by me you couldn't help yourself."

I grinned.

Ignoring me, she went on with her story. "You made sure that we kept running into each other in each aisle. We ended up getting served at checkouts side by side, and when we got out of the store and went to the car park, our cars were parked next to each other." She paused. "Er … what kind of car do you drive?"

"Take your pick. A dark green Rolls, a yellow lambo, or a silver Aston."

She bites her bottom lip and my mouth waters.

"Let's go with the silver Aston Martin," she decides. "You told me it was fate and asked for my phone number. I was thinking the same thing; that fate had brought us together and since you were such a dish, I gave you my number."

I smiled at the cheeky look she gave. God help me, she was flirting with me.

"Anyway," she went on, "you texted me the same day. That was, shall we say, four months ago. For our first date, we went for the most delicious Italian food."

"Didn't you mention earlier it was a French restaurant?"

"I've changed my mind. Italian sounds more passionate," she says, lifting one shoulder.

"Right."

"We drank a whole bottle of champagne—"

"I never drink champagne," I interrupt.

She frowns at the way facts are ruining her pretty story. "Well, that night you did. Then you walked me home and we ended up on my porch for hours, just talking. There was so much about you I wanted to know and it was the same with you. We didn't even care that we were cold. You gave up your coat for me, and yet you barely even noticed the cold. Until dawn was in the sky and all around us was pink and rosy. At that moment, we both knew it. We were completely smitten with each other. Then to our surprise it began to rain. You bent your head and kissed me, and it was the most wonderful kiss in the whole world."

The muscles in my jaw twitch with the effort not to laugh. "Four months ago, would make it the tail end of winter. Wouldn't the rain be too cold to be hanging out in?"

"We were heated up with passion," she persists. "So with the cold rain splashing down on us, you just knew you had to propose. You went down on one knee. Obviously, I said yes, and the rest, as they say, is history." Cindy smiles.

"Did you just think that all up?" I ask with a raised eyebrow.

Sudden color races up her neck and she quickly turns toward the window. Wow! That's a turn up for the books. Has she been daydreaming about me? Concocting various scenarios in her head? I shake my head at the direction of my own thoughts. No, that's ridiculous. She's just being a professional and made the effort to come up with a story my aunt will buy.

Cindy turns her face toward me again and the blush from her cheeks is gone. "Well one of us had to think about it," she says. "And like I said, your aunt sounds a lot like my grand-mother, and I know those are the kinds of things she'd have asked me about."

"Were you close to your grandmother?" I ask.

"Yes, I was," she says. "When I was small, we spent a lot of time at her home. My grandfather died while I was little more than a baby and I think my mum was worried grand-mother was lonely. She never was though. I mean don't get me wrong, she missed my grandfather terribly, but she had lots of friends. She was part of a book club and she took cookery classes. She could never have been lonely. She had more of a social life than I've ever had. Bingo. Dances. Pie and pea nights down at her local pub. But I was always the apple of her eye. She doted on me. Even as a teenager I was always round her house. When she died … it was difficult." She trails off.

"I'm sorry," I say.

"Don't be," she says a twist to her lips. "My grandmother was a big part in making me who I am today and I would never change the time I had with her. That's why I'm so determined to make this work. I wish I had been given a similar chance to make my grandmother happy before she passed away. It'll be nice to make your great aunt happy."

"I know my great aunt is going to love you," I say with a smile. Right then, I knew without a doubt I'd made the right decision in picking her. Cindy is everything my aunt would love to have in my future wife. She's beautiful, smart, compassionate and kind. The only problem was how I was going to keep my hands off her. With every passing second that was getting harder and harder.

"I hope so," Cindy murmurs.

For a second our eyes lock and I can feel that thing between us again. It is so strong it's almost palpable. Then she jumps up suddenly. "I would kind of like to see the inside of a bathroom."

I point behind me. "Straight to the back of the cabin and it's the door on your left."

"Thanks." She turns to move into the aisle, cuts the corner a little too wide, and her leg brushes against my knee. I feel more than a spark this time. It's like she plugged me directly into a wall socket. An incredible jolt of tingling temptation slams through my knee and up my thigh. I feel goose bumps rising on my thigh and my cock jumps to life.

"Sorry," Cindy says as she steps into the aisle.

Her voice is low and breathy and I know she felt the burn of pure lust. That knowledge is going to make remaining professional over the trip a fucking nightmare. I don't turn to watch her go. I clench my jaw and get a control of myself. When was the last time a woman did that to me?

Never!

I take a couple of deep breaths and consider my options. Abandon the trip with some plausible excuse like a spineless coward, or bite the bullet and get the job done. Put like that my options narrowed down considerably. My control is back by the time Cindy returns from the bathroom.

I can hear her humming to herself as she walks back towards me. She gets to her seat, giving me a wide berth this time. She's fighting the attraction between us too. If she's as determined to ignore the raging desire inside her as I am, then I have a better chance of not behaving like a Neanderthal.

Cindy covers a yawn with her hand. "Seriously, there's just something about flying. I always end up so tired. I can sit in a car or on a bus or train for hours and be fine, but flying does it every time. I blame the air pressure."

"We still have hours before we land. Why don't you take a nap?" I suggest. "I have a whole briefcase of work. I'm sure I can entertain myself for a while."

"No, I don't want to fall asleep with my mouth open in front of you." Then she yawns again right after she makes her declaration and we both laugh.

"Tell you what. I'll move over to that corner and you can rest in peace. Hmmm?"

She shakes her head. "No, I don't want to trouble you."

"No trouble," I say, standing. It would be good to be away from her. She's too distracting.

"Thank you for being such a gentleman."

I nod and move away, but the term surprises me. No woman has ever called me a gentleman. Ever. Hard. Cold. Unfeeling. Bastard. Aloof. Heartless. Those are the words that are usually hurled at me.

I debate getting myself a whisky, but I would rather stay sober. I am thirsty though and I'm starting to get restless cooped up on the plane. I go to the bar and I pour myself a coke, add some ice and walk to the corner seat. For a second I stand looking down at the seat then I walk back toward Cindy. The word she used is still rattling around in my brain. Gentleman?

Cindy is already fast asleep. And her mouth is slightly parted.

I can't move. I stand over her and watch her with fascination. She looks so angelic, her long lashes lying on her smooth cheeks. Her skin looks so damn soft I want to touch it and let my fingers caress the curving contours.

What the fuck are you doing?

Waking up to find someone watching you sleeping is pretty fucking creepy, and the last thing I want is for Cindy to start thinking I'm a pervert. I turn away instantly and go back to the corner seat. I feel shaken. My lack of control is extraordinary. I'm never like this.

I open my laptop. Work. Work is always the answer. At least if I'm working, I know I have to focus on what I'm doing. I type in my password. I might as well get some emails out of the way since I'll be keeping work to a minimum while I'm at my aunt's house.

Cindy makes a little snuffling sound and shuffles in her seat and in spite of myself my head lifts and my whole body comes to attention and listens intently, the way a man in a jungle who has heard a twig break behind him might.

Resisting her is going to be hard. Much, much harder than I've imagined.

CINDY

Something wakes me up and my eyes flicker open. It takes a second for me to remember where I am. Ah yes, I'm on Alex's plane heading to Russia. I come awake fully when I think of Alex. Turning my head, I spy on him, sitting in his seat, a slight frown etched into his forehead as he types something into his laptop.

He must have felt my gaze on him because he raises his eyes and looks unsmiling at me. I have dragged him out of another world; there is no trace of the hunger/lust whatever you want to call it in his eyes. He is completely unapproachable and brutally distant.

"Just need to get this email sent before I shut down for landing," he says quietly.

"Of course," I croak and quickly turn my head back around. Frankly, it's a shock to see him like that, and I realize with a start that this is the face he shows the rest of the world.

I hear him typing furiously as I put my seat upright, then take my compact out of my purse. After I make sure I don't have drool running down my chin I snap my compact shut close. As I straighten my clothes, I hear him close his laptop.

He strolls over and slips into the seat opposite me. "Do you feel better for your nap?"

"Yes thanks," I say, searching his face. The hunger is back. Suddenly, I feel self-conscious. "Was I snoring?"

"Like a full-grown hog," he drawls in that deep, smooth voice of his.

My God, this man is calling me a full-grown hog and yet it sounds like he is making love to me. I feel heat rush up my throat and cheeks.

Alex laughs. "I'm joking," he says. "You slept like an angel."

I clear my throat. "How long before we land?"

He glances at his watch. "Less than half-an-hour."

"I've been sleeping for nearly three hours?" I ask surprised.

"Mmm ..."

"And you worked the whole time?"

"Three hours is not exactly a long time," he says quietly.

At that moment Gloria comes through to the cabin to check our seat belts are fastened correctly for landing. I fasten my seat belt quickly, then I peer out of the window. We're flying lower now, coming in to land over a vibrant city. I remember what Alex said about this part of our journey. We'll land at a normal airport and have our documents checked before we'll take off again to get to our final destination. Wherever that is.

Soon the plane lands, touching down smoothly on the tarmac. Within twenty minutes, the customs officer has been on board, checked our passports, and the captain's flight paperwork, then disembarked after finding everything in order. In no time we're taking off again. I go to take my seat belt off.

"Unless you're planning on moving around, I wouldn't bother," Alex smiles, nodding to my seat belt. "We'll be in the air less than fifteen minutes."

"How long would it have taken if we drove from the airport?" I ask, not heeding his advice and leaving my seat belt open.

Alex shrugs. "At least a couple of hours, especially with the early evening traffic."

I look out of the window as we leave the city behind. Through the wispy clouds, I can see we're moving across beautiful, rolling countryside. It seems like the summer fields are every shade of green imaginable.

Gloria comes flitting in again to tell us we'll be landing at our final destination within the next couple of minutes. She checks our seat belts again, then moves away.

I keep looking out of the window, watching as the ground seems to start moving up to meet us. This part of the country really is stunningly beautiful. I can't see a town or even a house anywhere and I imagine how beautiful this place will look in the winter, covered by a white blanket of snow.

I can't keep the smile off my face as excitement starts to grip me. As my mother would say, I am now officially on an adventure.

Alex seems completely unmoved by the beautiful scenery. He

doesn't even attempt to move closer to the window for a better view. I look at him curiously and he stares back questioningly.

"It's so beautiful," I enthuse. "Are you that blasé about it?"

"Yes, it is beautiful, but I've seen it all a thousand times. I grew up here."

"Ah, your parents lived here too?"

His face clouds over for a second and I realize he's never really mentioned his parents before. I hope I haven't forced him into revealing anything he doesn't want to.

"Yes. We all lived here together when I was growing up. My parents died when I was fourteen … a helicopter accident. My grandmother passed away soon after I was born so my great aunt was always *babushka* to me, that's Russian for grandmother. Once I became an orphan she raised me."

"I'm sorry," I whisper.

"It was a long time ago," he replies automatically, as if he had repeated that polite, overused, meaningless line a thousand times to a thousand people.

"What was it like growing up here?" I ask, trying to change the subject without making it too obvious.

"Perfect." He smiles. "All of this land you can see now belongs to my aunt, so as you can imagine, we were never short of outdoors space. We, my cousins and I, spent all our time out on the land, mostly riding."

"You had horses?" I ask eagerly. "Horses are my favorite animal. I've loved them ever since I saw Black Beauty, but ponies are for rich girls and my parents were strictly working class and proud of it. My father worked at building sites and read The Sun newspapers, and my mother cleaned houses and still smells faintly of bleach and disinfectant."

Alex nods. "Yes, beautiful Arabian horses. I'll take you down to the stables tomorrow if you'd like to see them."

"Oh, I'd love to," I cry eagerly.

He jerks his chin towards the window. "There's Winter House now."

CINDY

I turn my head and gasp as the house comes into view. Well, calling such place a house is like calling China a village. It's absolutely massive and mostly white, but with small areas painted with baby blue. The mansion stands out against the greenery around, seeming to almost shine with splendor, like something out of a fairytale. As much as it stands out, it doesn't look out of place. Somehow, it blends into the landscape as if it's as much a natural feature as the gorgeous tall trees that stand dotted around the grounds.

"Wow! Surely your aunt doesn't live here alone?"

"No," Alex says. "Petra and Anastasia, my cousins, live here with her. There's also Valeriya, her qualified nurse, assistant, and companion. Actually, she is almost part of the family. Most of the house isn't even in use anymore now, but my aunt has a whole team of house keepers who keep it in good repair. My aunt's daughter, Marina, and her husband, Viktor, live close by and they stay over if my cousins are out of town so my aunt always has some family with her. They'll be here tonight too to meet you. I guess you could say it's a bit of a family reunion."

"Oh wow. I'll never remember all these names," I say.

"You will." His lips twist sarcastically. "They're the sort of people who make an ... impression."

I feel a pit of dread in my stomach, which I quickly ignore. I know how to deal with difficult people. I've dealt with drunken men the size of Alex on my own and never felt afraid. I'm pretty sure his family aren't going to physically hurt me and I can definitely live with a few nasty words from a few rude, obnoxious people I'll never see again after this stint.

It'll be worth it for half The Macau.

We touch down on the runway and after we come to a stop, Gloria appears from the staff area of the plane to open the main cabin door. A set of steps are wheeled over to the plane by an ancient man in gray overalls. I squint out of the window once more before I release my seat belt and stand up.

Alex gallantly stands back and allows me to go first. As we walk down the aisle, Gloria wishes us a pleasant stay. I reach the doorway and stop for a second. The air is mind-blowingly fresh compared to London. I fill my lungs with it. I can see the mansion in the distance and any dread I had dissipates, replaced with a kind of nervous excitement.

Wait till I tell you all about this adventure, Mum.

I really hope Alex is right about his great aunt's preferences for a wife for him and she likes me. She is the only person he seems to care about keeping happy so I'll concentrate on being the perfect fiancée to Alex she could ever hope for.

As we walk down the steps the old man in the overalls ignores me and nods reverently at Alex. My feet touch the ground and a delicious cool breeze starts to roll in. I turn back toward Alex and watch it lift strands of his hair and drop them across his forehead. I feel my stomach do a little flip at the sight.

The temperature is similar to the evening air in London which reassures me that I have packed correctly. I gave up trying to work out what exactly the weather would be like, and I just brought a selection of my usual clothes. Thinking of my clothes draws my attention to collecting my suitcase, but when I look in that direction, I see the cargo compartment is already open and the ancient man in the overalls has already begun to unload our luggage.

In front of us there is a long black car waiting. The chauffeur who is actually wearing a peaked cap is waiting by the open passenger door. He nods politely at me.

I have a feeling I'm going to have to get used to being waited on for the duration of this trip. Alex is the sort of guy who has drivers back in London and maybe some other house-hold staff, and if I react like this is all new to me, then his aunt will know instantly that this is all a sham. Alex puts his hand on the small of my back to lead me to the waiting car.

He grins down at me. "Show time, baby."

The endearment is so foreign I have to laugh. But as soon as the laugh dies away it becomes impossible to concentrate on anything else except his hand on my back. I suddenly wish my dress wasn't forming a barrier between us. I want to feel his hand on my bare skin. I blink the thought away as we reach the car.

Alex allows me to get in through the car door closest to us and walks around to the other side. I smile my thanks at the chauffeur and slip into my seat. Alex slides in next to me as the driver closes my door. I can feel that dangerous heat from his body. I don't know whether he feels the pull I'm feeling, but he starts tapping his fingers impatiently on the leather seat, until the driver gets in and we're heading for the house.

I watch the house through the window and as we get closer, I see how grand and imposing it really is. It reminds me of Buckingham Palace. I am so far out of my depth here I realize with a sense of panic. It's all good and great saying it's an adventure, but how the hell can I convince a person who lives in a house like this that I'm good enough for her great-nephew? I've watched a program on TV about the complicated dinner table settings of polite society. How simply eating with the wrong cutlery can turn you into the uncivilized outsider. In fact, there are thousands of innocuous things that you can trip up on and out yourself.

"Hey," Alex says.

He brushes his fingers over mine and his touch does nothing to quell the rolling of my stomach. I blink and look at him.

"Relax, Cindy," he says. "It's just a house. Seriously."

I chew my lower lip. "I'm just a normal girl, Alex. Your great aunt is not just rich, she's practically royalty, isn't she?"

He shakes his head and laughs, a humor filled laugh that I don't quite understand.

"Once you get to know my aunt a bit, you'll see why I'm laughing. Honestly, she's the most down to earth woman you'll ever meet. She just happens to come from an old family with money, that's all."

I nod my head, not entirely reassured by his words. I remind myself I'm only here for a week or two. I can do anything for such a short amount of time, including pretending I fit in with people who are clearly only a step or two down from Russian royalty.

The drive is a short one and we pull up at the bottom of a set of white stone steps with huge fierce griffins standing on either side. Alex gets out of the car and even though my hand goes automatically to the handle, I resist the urge to open the door myself. Anyone could be watching out of the windows and it is time to get into character.

Alex nods approvingly as he opens my door and I climb out of the car. The boot of the car is already open and a man dressed in red trousers, a white shirt, and a matching red jacket starts unloading our luggage.

"Come on," Alex says with a panty-melting lop-sided smile as he offers me his arm.

CINDY

I slip my hand through it and square my shoulders. I've prepared myself for the sparks of electricity that fly between us, but that smile, though. My stomach rolls deliciously. One thing is for sure. I'm not going to have to work at faking the attraction between Alex and me. Even a blind person would be able to sense our chemistry.

He leads me up the stone steps and as I step on the final one, I get my first look at the family. Two young women stand side by side at the entrance of the tall blue door. One of them looks to be about the same age as Alex. She has blonde hair that is almost white and piercing blue eyes that look me up and down. The other girl looks a little bit younger. She has a short black bob, and while she couldn't look any more opposite to the other girl in her looks, her poise is the same. Haughty. She too is openly looking me up and down.

Instead of making me more nervous, I actually find that the girls' attitude helps me to relax. I've taken bigger people than these two down a peg or two, and I might even enjoy the task at hand.

The girls stand slightly apart from the other two women. One who looks to be in her early sixties and has the look of someone who has served faithfully and selflessly all her life. I take her to be Valeriya, and the other one has to be Alex's great aunt. She's small in stature but erect in bearing and confident of her place in the world. Although she uses a white and silver cane to support herself as she steps forward, she looks steady on her feet. She has the same stormy gray eyes as Alex, and when she looks at me, I see they are bright, alert and full of intelligence. She doesn't look me up and down, she just scans her eyes over me, taking me in quickly and efficiently. Then she turns to Alex and her expression changes to one of pure joy. It is clear he is the apple of her eye.

I hang back, a little unsure of what to do as Alex wraps his arms around the old woman and picks her right off the ground. Wow! I definitely did not expect that from him. She laughs a carefree laugh. Then she says something in Russian and immediately, Alex says. "English, please."

She turns her head in my direction, still beaming with happiness. "Ah yes, of course. Forgive me. I told my grandson to put me down immediately and not make a fool of me in front of you."

She has a heavier accent than Alex, but she speaks perfect English and I'm relieved there won't be any sort of language barrier between us.

"It's so good to see you, *babushka*," Alex says, and kisses her loudly on each cheek before gently setting her back on the ground.

She pats her iron-gray hair, her eyes are twinkling. "Not half as good as it is to see you, Alex. You always make the sun shine brighter when you come."

I can't help but notice the younger women have stiffened slightly during this exchange. They are both watching me now, the animosity in their eyes clear to see.

"Cindy," Alex says, smiling warmly at me. "This is my great aunt Babushka. *Babushka*, this is Cindy, my fiancée."

Alex's aunt steps towards me. For a second, she just looks at me with that same scanning expression, and then she beams at me too, and I feel like I've passed the first test.

"You have chosen well. She is beautiful," she says approvingly to Alex.

The cold, unknowable man I found cheating at the casino smiles slowly at her. Now I can see why he went to all that trouble to make her happy. He truly, truly loves her.

His great aunt turns toward me. "Welcome to Winter House my dear. As you're almost family now, you may as well just call me *Babushka* like everyone else."

She opens her thin arms towards me and I step up and let them close around me. She smells of dried flowers, a sophisticated, but old-fashioned smell that belongs in another world. I quell the unease in my stomach. I am deceiving this fine old lady. Her love for Alex is so sincere and so heartfelt. I promise myself that I will never do anything to hurt her. She releases me and I smile warmly at her.

"It's so nice to finally meet you. Alex has told me so much about you," I say.

"Oh, I assure you, it's all lies." she laughs.

I feel Alex's hand land gently on the small of my back. I look up at him unguarded and something sparks between us. It makes my heart skip a beat. He feels it too because I see a muscle twitch in his cheek, then he papers it over with a smile. "And this wonderful woman, my darling, is Valeriya,"

"Hello," I greet the unassuming woman softly.

She nods back. It's formal, but at the same time, her expression is warm and welcoming and I get the impression Alex wasn't making it up when he said Valeriya is almost part of the family.

"And these two young ladies are my cousins," he goes on. "Petra and Anastasia." He gestures to the ice sisters one at a time as he says their names. Petra, the blonde one, smiles, a smile so fake I almost laugh. Anastasia at least makes an effort and gives me something that could almost pass for a smile.

"Hi," I say, with a little wave.

I don't get a reply or a wave back, but before the moment can become awkward, Alex propels me away from them, and towards his *babushka*.

"Let's get you inside," she says with a smile. "Perhaps you'd like to freshen up before dinner. You must be hungry from all of the travelling."

"I'm starving," I admit.

Babushka laughs. "Good. Cook makes enough food to feed an army every time Alex comes."

We turn with her and go into the mansion. It is at least a few degrees colder inside. Must be all the stone and speckled-gray marble. I am instantly overwhelmed as I look around at the lofty ceilings decorated with intricate plasterwork and gold gilding. The house is a veritable palace with marble statues and the kind of massive old oil paintings that you'd find in a museum or art gallery. Our feet echo in the vast palace.

"You seem very surprised," Babushka comments.

"Oh, I'm sorry. It's just so beautiful …" I trail off as Alex's cousins giggle nastily.

Babushka throws them a look and the laughter stops instantly. She turns back to me and I can see the playful twinkle in her eye.

"Then you should have seen it all before the revolution," she says. "They carried away the best. It is the same with all revolutions. Fortunately, I like things bright and airy so they rather did me a favor here. Anyway, my rooms are over there. I don't like the stairs anymore. I look forward to seeing you at dinner." Turning away from me she says, "Val dear, would you show these two to their rooms please?"

"Of course," Valeriya replies.

"There's no need, Babushka," Alex laughs. "I think I can still remember how to find my way around."

Babushka smiles. "True enough, my heart, true enough. I've put you and Cindy in the South wing. It's warmer there this time of the year and you will have nice views of the rose garden. You're in the blue room and Cindy is next door."

"Thank you, Babushka," Alex says.

"Right." She smiles. "Dinner will be served at eight o'clock promptly. See you all then. Don't be late."

The two girls move away deeper into the house and Alex and I are left alone again.

CINDY

Alex takes my hand and leads me towards a sweeping marble staircase adorned on either side by the same fierce Griffins outside.

"Your ancestors liked griffins, huh?"

"They are part of our family's crest. They are supposed to represent courage and bravery."

I follow him up the staircase, glad to be away from prying eyes, and truth be told I'm enjoying the tingling feeling of my hand clasped inside Alex's big, powerful one. If only … I kill that thought right there. We reach the top of the staircase and Alex leads me along a hallway that perfectly matches the one downstairs, and stops in front of a door.

"This is your room," he says, letting go of my hand to open the door.

My suitcase is already inside, neatly hoisted onto a table. The room is grand and beautiful. I walk over to the window and the view is breathtaking. As far as the eye can see green grass and stately old trees. Right underneath the window is the rose garden Babushka talked about. It is in full bloom and quite a sight. I must take photos to show my mother.

"You have a private bathroom. It's the door on the left. The one on the right is a connecting door leading to my room. I trust that you won't be tempted to sneak into mine in the middle of the night."

He's laughing as he says it and I haughtily deny I'll be doing any such thing, but I think we both know I want him. The temptation is there. I certainly won't be acting on it though. That much is for sure.

"I'll let you get unpacked and freshen up, then," he says formally. "Meet me back here at half-past seven."

"Okay."

He turns to reach for the door knob.

"Alex?" I say.

He turns back to me.

"I don't think your cousins like me very much."

He grimaces. "I wouldn't worry about it. They don't like anyone very much. Not even each other. But don't worry about them. My aunt liked you, I could see it in her eyes. And she's the only person who matters to me."

I smile and nod, and he steps out of my room. The thoughts of Petra and Anastasia instantly vanish as I whirl around to take in my room without his distracting presence. It is huge, at least twice the size of my bedroom back home and I have a big bedroom. In the center of it stands a marvelous four poster bed. The bedding is all pristine white with gorgeously intricate antique lace. White netting cascades down from the posts. It's a bed fit for a fairy princess. As a child, this is exactly the kind of scenario I imagined Sleeping Beauty lying in when the Prince came to kiss her awake.

At either side of the bed are stunning blue bedside cabinets. Against one wall there is a large white double wardrobe and a matching chest of drawers with a large oval mirror on top of it. Both are elaborately and painstakingly carved. The walls are a cool white, almost with a tinge of blue, and the hardwood flooring is softened by what I imagine must be a Persian rug. It covers most of the room. Three doors lead off the room. The one to the right leads to Alex's room, and I resolutely give that one a wide berth, as though even getting too close to it will tempt me to head in there.

I open the first door on the left and find a massive bathroom. A free standing, claw footed bathtub takes center stage. In one corner is a large walk-in shower next to a wide sink. The toilet is tucked behind a small, waist high wall. That little quirky touch makes the bathroom seem at once foreign and prudish and I smile to myself as I step back out of the room and move to the other door.

Expecting some sort of walk-in wardrobe, I'm pleasantly surprised to see a gorgeous surprisingly modern lounge. A white leather sofa that looks soft and comfortable sits against the wall opposite a huge, wall mounted flat screen TV. The wall opposite the door is completely lined with shelves, half of which are taken up by books and the other half, by DVDs and CDs. I'm sure I could live in this room for a year and not get through all of these movies and books. There is a sturdy platform ladder with wheels tucked into one corner of the room, presumably to get at the books on the higher shelves.

I glance at my watch. The last thing I want is to be late for dinner. It's early still and I decide to unpack and take a shower. I want to save the bath for when I have time to really savor a good soak in it.

I unpack quickly and find the wardrobe packed out with coat hangers. In the chest of drawers, I find a hairdryer. Better and better. After a refreshing shower, I come back into the bedroom dressed in a fluffy bathrobe and dry my hair in front of the oval mirror. It is old and the silver behind the glass has tarnished over time. It reminds me of the one in my grandma's bedroom. Afterwards, I apply my make-up and then comes the hard part. What do I wear? Judging by the fact that the staff are in uniform, it should be safe to assume it won't be a normal family dinner where people rock up in jeans and a t-shirt.

So a formal affair then …

I don't want to get it wrong and be totally overdressed though. Eventually, I settle on a faithful friend. A black cocktail dress that isn't over the top, but isn't casual by any stretch of the imagination, either. I slip on a pair of black heels and look myself over in the full-length mirror inside of the wardrobe door. I turn around, twist my neck, and look at myself from the back. Hopefully, I've got it right. No doubt, if dinner is usually a super casual affair, Alex will tell me before we go downstairs and I can quickly change into something else.

I still have ten minutes before I have to meet Alex in the hallway and I decide to call Rosa. I pull my phone out and scroll through my contacts list until I find her. She answers quickly. She doesn't bother to say hello.

"You're still alive then?" she says instead.

"Just about," I laugh.

"Spill the beans? What's the aunt like?"

I vomit out everything. About the palace-like mansion, about the aunt who seems to like me so far, and about the cousins who Rosa instantly dubs the wicked stepsisters.

"The fact they're Alex's cousins and not his step sisters doesn't worry you in the least?" I ask with a laugh.

"Accuracy is more important than facts," she says airily.

"Actually, I've taken to thinking of them as the ice sisters."

"Take a photo of them when they're not looking and send it to me," she demands bossily.

I nearly jump out of my skin when I hear the knock on my door. "Shit, I have to go," I mutter. "I'll keep you posted. Can you tell Star and Raven the news so far?"

"Sure. Have fun and don't do anything I wouldn't," Rosa says with an evil laugh.

"That doesn't rule much out," I say as I end the call.

I know Star will text once Rosa speaks to her and the last thing I need is my text alert going off during dinner. Leaving my phone on my bed I go to open the door.

CINDY

Alex stands before me, in another wildly expensive suit. It's almost unfair how ridiculously good he looks in a dark suit. I feel my heart skip a beat just looking at him. In different circumstances I'd be quite happy to skip dinner and drag him into my lair. My stomach seems to disagree though because it chooses that moment to growl loudly.

Alex laughs. "Well that answers my question about whether or not you're ready for dinner," he drawls. His eyes linger on my chest for a moment and then they come back up to my face. "You look beautiful, Cindy."

"Why, thank you, Sir." I smile up at him coyly. Might as well get into character. "You don't scrub up bad yourself."

"Playing your best card already," Alex asks with a chuckle.

I arch an eyebrow. "Now why would you think that?"

"I don't know. How much further do you want to go?"

If he thinks I'm backing off, he has another think coming. "Well, you'll just have to wait and see, won't you?"

He smiles, a secret smile. "Yes, I'll just have to." Then he offers me his arm. "Shall we?"

I nod and take his arm and let him lead me down the grand staircase. We go along a hallway before Alex stops at a set of double doors where a man in uniform is waiting. Respectfully, he opens the door and steps back so we can step through. I find myself in a tall yellow reception room that one would find in any fine stately home. Beyond it, through another set of open doors I can see an extremely formal, deep-red dining room. Looks like the other guests are already there and they are dressed in evening dresses. I send up a silent thank you to God that I got the dress code right.

"Cindy, Alex," Babushka smiles, standing as the door closes silently behind us.

"No need to get up, Babushka," Alex says.

"Nonsense," Babushka retorts briskly coming towards us. "Anyone would think I was old or something."

This gets a laugh from the other guests, even Petra. Babushka is wearing a white lace top and a black velvet skirt. Around her throat is the most beautiful necklace made of pearls and a blue stone. She kisses me lightly on both cheeks.

"I love your necklace. It is so beautiful," I say impulsively.

Her white fingers finger the pearls as she studies me. "These belonged to my great grandmother and one day they will belong to you."

I feel Alex stiffen next to me. Forget Alex, the dismay in the air is actually palpable. It is clear no one in that room other than Babushka desires such an outcome. I am saved from answering by the arrival of a manservant with a tray bearing two drinks in crystal glasses. A whisky for Alex and tall orange liquid which I assume must be Gin and orange for me. Alex must have ordered it beforehand. I pick up my drink, the glass is cold under my fingertips.

"Come and join us," Babushka invites as Alex takes his drink.

Alex leads us towards an unoccupied sofa. It could have been the only quirky item in the room since the upholstery was printed with *Matryoshka* dolls.

Next to us is Anastasia and Petra and on the sofa opposite is a man and a woman I don't recognize.

"Cindy, this is my daughter, Marina, and her husband, Viktor," Babushka says, nodding at the couple.

I smile and say hello to them and they both return my smile, but say nothing. They certainly aren't as welcoming as Babushka, but at least they aren't as frosty as the ice sisters.

"This is Cindy, Alex's fiancée," Babushka announces joyfully, and I feel another pang of guilt at deceiving the proud old woman.

I remind myself we're only doing it to make her happy.

"Fiancée huh?" Viktor grins at Alex. "I never thought I'd see the day you'd settle down."

"Never met the right woman before," Alex says, turning to smile adoringly at me.

Jesus, that smile. I swallow hard and return what I hope is an equally adoring smile. I must have succeeded because something flashed in his eyes before he veiled and turned back to the rest of his family.

Petra says something in Russian and Anastasia laughs. I don't know what she said, but it's enough to make both her parents give her dirty looks.

"I've already told you we'll be speaking in English while we have our guest here," Babushka reprimands sternly. It is clear she didn't like the girl's remark either.

"Oh, of course. I'm so sorry, Babushka. I forgot that the English can only speak their own language because literally everyone else has to learn it," Petra says with an innocent smile that is anything but innocent.

"Petra," Babushka snaps.

"It's fine." I throw a reassuring smile at Babushka before I turn to Petra. "I know exactly what you mean. So many English people don't make the effort to learn other languages. It's very lazy of us as a nation, but our excuse is everyone speaks enough English to make communication possible. However, personally, I speak French, Spanish, Italian and just about enough German to get by. How many other languages do you speak? Since you seem to have an interest in them."

Then I give Petra a smile that is about as innocent as hers was.

"Just Russian and English," she mumbles, not meeting my eye.

"Oh," I murmur, feigning surprise. "Oh well, I'm sure that's enough to get by. As you said, everyone learns English, don't they?"

Petra's face sports an unattractive shade of red and she scowls at me.

When Babushka hides a smile I know I've just won a few more points with her ... and I've shown Alex I can handle his family. Petra mutters something else in Russian, too quiet for Babushka to hear her. I'm sure it's nothing complimentary.

"Please excuse our daughter," Marina says to me, as she glances uncomfortably at Babushka. "She's a little awkward around strangers."

I take a sip of my drink. "Oh, please don't worry on my account. I'm sure we'll be great friends by the end of the week," I lie smoothly. I can't quite get a measure of Marina. Is she apologizing for her mother's benefit, or is she's genuinely sorry for her daughter's appalling rudeness?

Another manservant comes in, bows, and says something in Russian. Babushka rises gracefully. "Dinner is served. Viktor, will you escort me in?"

Viktor quickly moves towards her and she slips her hand into the crook of his elbow. It is obvious that is the role usually played by Alex. I look up at Alex as I feel Alex's hand land lightly on the small of my back. He smiles down at me and a strange thought pops into my head.

How nice if this was all real?

As quickly as it came, I push it away. With his hand guiding me, we make our way towards the imposing dining room.

CINDY

The long grand table is set with fancy silverware. There seems to be an array of cutlery, but I have already decided that I will carefully follow whatever Alex does. I am seated between Viktor and Babushka and opposite Alex. The ice sisters are next to each other and Marina is next to Alex. Without Alex by my side I start to feel a tinge of nervousness, but when I catch his eyes he winks at me and suddenly I know I can do it. White wine is respectfully poured into my glass by a manservant. I smile my thanks and he nods gravely.

"Tonight, we'll be eating British food in honor of Cindy's presence," Babushka announces.

"Great. Fish and chips and soggy beef pies then," Petra sniggers.

Everyone ignores her as three more manservants troop into the room carrying silver serving platters with dome lids. When all the platters are on the table, the main headwaiter announces, "Potted crab with a hint of smoked paprika."

And all the lids are lifted at the same time with military precision. The effect is surreal. I can almost be persuaded I have gone back in time to a lost epoch where the very rich lived like Kings and Queens.

I look down at the tiny silver pot of potted crab with delicate fingers of sourdough bread on my plate. As the delicious smell fills my nostrils, the first of the barrage of questions arrives.

"How long have you two been together?" Viktor asks.

I spoon a bit of crab into my mouth quickly so Alex will have to answer. The crab is divine. It melts in my mouth. This is without doubt the best potted crab I have ever tasted.

"Four months." Alex smiles. "I know the engagement might seem a little quick, but when you know you know. And we're planning on taking things a little more slowly now with a long engagement."

"It doesn't seem that quick to me," Marina says. "Look at Petra. She met Anton in July of last year and they were married by Christmas."

I swallow the crab in my mouth and look at Petra in surprise. "You're married?"

"You don't have to look so surprised," she snaps.

"Actually, it's a compliment. You look too young to be married," I say evenly.

"My husband is away on business," she says haughtily. "Not everyone can take holidays whenever they like."

"Yes, I'm sure that is what all the truly poor people in Africa say," I shoot back, taunting her, almost daring her to say more. She sensibly keeps her mouth closed.

The servers bring us melon sorbet to refresh our palates.

"Where did the two of you meet, Cindy?" Marina asks me curiously.

I tell her the story about the supermarket. By the end of it, Babushka appears quite taken with it all, and Marina makes all the right noises, but the ice sisters roll their eyes to each other and mutter in Russian again.

The next course is served. "Roast wood pigeon with black pudding and baby beets," the main waiter announces as the domes are lifted. I have never eaten pigeon. I like pigeons. Sometimes I feed them in the early morning hours when I'm walking back from the casino. The meat looks dark pink. The black pudding is in little cubes and the beets are shaped into ovals. Some sort of red sauce is artistically dotted around the arrangement of food.

"The puree is made from dried and blended hibiscus flowers," Babushka explains.

I look up at Alex. He raises his eyebrows enquiringly? I glance at Babushka and she is looking at me with an expectant expression. She has gone to a lot of trouble to create this menu. I know I can't make a fuss. I cut off a piece of the dark pink meat and chew it. It's juicy with a deep flavor. If I didn't know it was pigeon I would have said it was perfectly cooked and seasoned.

Babushka watches me as I chew, and then she smiles. "At least it's not horse steak, huh?" she says.

Jesus Christ! I stop chewing. The tiny morsel of meat suddenly makes my mouth feel too full. I actually want to spit the mush in my mouth out. I catch myself and force myself to swallow the food in my mouth. No matter what I mustn't offend Babushka on my first night here. I nod my head, forcing myself to smile as I reach blindly for my glass of wine.

Babushka throws her head back and laughs.

"Your face," she cries merrily. "As if I'd condone eating horse when we have a stable full of faithful friends here. I just had to do it, I'm sorry."

I laugh, relieved that she's joking. I like the old woman. I like her wicked sense of humor.

"Babushka, behave yourself," Alex chides, but he's laughing too.

"Ah, come on now, Alex, I'm old now and I have to do something to amuse myself."

"You were doing this when you were not old," Alex says dryly.

"Yes, I suppose I was. Now, you said you're having a long engagement. How long is long? Because I'd rather like to see the wedding and maybe even a baby or two before I croak."

This time, Babushka doesn't follow up the comment with laughter. This time, she's deadly serious. My eyes find Alex's and for a split-second I catch that expression of dismay that crosses them. I feel my own face burning. I really hate that Babushka isn't going to get to see any of that. She seems like a genuinely sweet old lady and her affection for Alex is clear to see. We're lying to her and it's not right. And he knows it too.

"Typical bachelor reaction that, Alex," Viktor says cynically. He must have caught the quick expression too.

Alex gives him a pained smile and then turns to Babushka. "We've only been together four months Babushka. I know compared to Petra that's not a lot of time, but we want to do this right. We want to really get to know each other before we get married."

Babushka nods her head dutifully although she is clearly very disappointed. "I understand, Alex." She turns to me then, her eyes twinkling. "Just don't wait too long or Cindy might get bored of waiting and find someone who'll move a little faster."

I laugh, but I shake my head. "Oh, no chance of that. Alex is the one for me."

This gets another mumbling in Russian from one of the ice sisters. I don't know which one and quite frankly, I don't care. I'm already over their spoilt little asses. I do wish I spoke Russian now though. It would be good to know what they're saying, and then just drop in a casual comment in Russian later on and let them know I know everything they've been saying about me. The conversation turns to more casual topics. The general state of the world economy. I work my way through the wood pigeon, all the while telling myself it's not one of my pigeons. My pigeons are safe in England.

Then Babushka says, "I thought we'd give you a choice for dessert. You can either have Eton Mess or a traditional

Russian dessert call *chak chak*. It's fried dough coated in honey."

"The *chak chak* sounds delicious," I say decisively.

Babushka smiles at me. "You won't regret your decision. Our chef is particularly good at making it. We eat it at celebrations so it seemed fitting that we have it tonight to celebrate my boy finally finding a woman who can put up with his bad habits."

"Alex has bad habits? Pray tell me more."

This gets a laugh from Babushka and a quick shake of the head from Alex.

"Don't do it, Babushka," he warns with a laugh. "Not if you want the wedding to ever go ahead."

A plate set before me holding several small sticky balls and a scoop of delicate rose ice cream.

I slip a spoon of *chak chak* into my mouth and find it to be every bit as good as Babushka said it would be.

"How did Alex propose to you, Cindy?" Babushka asks.

I swallow and throw Alex a cheeky look. "I really should let Alex tell this story. It's a really good one."

Alex gives me an indulgent look, but underneath there was a subtle warning. "It was our three-month anniversary. I took Cindy to the same Italian place where we had our first date. Can you believe I was so nervous Cindy had to keep asking me what was wrong. I kept saying I was fine, but she must have known I wasn't because I was being so clumsy."

He lifts his glass of wine, takes a sip, and watches me from over the rim before continuing. I hope he doesn't overdo it because I can't imagine him being nervous around a woman.

"I knocked a glass of wine over and must have dropped my fork on the floor at least three times. Even so I managed to wait until after we'd finished our meal because I knew the manager would be playing our song. I took Cindy by the hand and asked her to dance with me. She was horrified."

He looks at me and smiles. "Do you remember how horrified you were?"

By now I am as enraptured by his story as Babushka, but I catch myself, and nod my head. "Yes, how could I forget?"

Where is he going with this story? I don't know but I am as eager to hear the end as everyone else. I think my delighted look will help convince Babushka we're in love, that I'm hanging on Alex's every word, and enjoying reliving the moment he asked me to marry him.

He turns back to Babushka. The whole table is listening, no doubt shocked that Alex would ever be so romantic and sentimental. Even the ice sisters are engrossed in the story.

"I told her it didn't matter if no one else was dancing. That maybe those people didn't have a reason to dance, but we did. I led Cindy out into the middle of the restaurant. She was wearing a beautiful silky pink dress, and she had never looked more beautiful to me than she did in that moment. I took her in my arms and we danced. And when the song ended, Cindy was laughing. She no longer looked embarrassed. I got down on one knee and asked her to marry me. She said yes, obviously."

Babushka looks delighted with the story. I can understand

why. My own heart is fluttering at the thought of being proposed to in that way. I can almost feel my supposed embarrassment and then my joy. It makes me see a new side to Alex. The side that maybe isn't quite so dark.

"Oh, look at her," Babushka says, clapping her hands. "She looks even more love struck than she did before, and she already looked like she was about to swoon."

I smile and look down at my now empty plate. Maybe I do look love struck, and if I really do, it's not because I'm acting. I'm not. Alex glances at me and smiles and I smile back at him, feeling my cheeks start to burn.

"You're embarrassing her," Marina says. "Leave her alone, mum."

Babushka laughs and shakes her head.

"She's not blushing. That's the flush of love," she says.

Now I'm definitely blushing. I look at Alex, wanting him to rescue me from this, to say something that will move the conversation on a bit. Instead, he just looks back at me with a smile. I don't know if he's smiling because my embarrassment is amusing him or because he is happy I'm giving such a convincing performance.

Petra says something in Russian and the attention finally shifts away from me and to her as Babushka reminds her to speak in English.

"Sorry," she says sweetly. "Force of habit."

Except, it wasn't. It was obviously intended to make me feel like an outsider.

"I was just asking if you're both planning to have a big wedding," she says in English.

"No," I say.

"Yes," Alex says at the same time.

Dammit. I laugh to cover up any awkwardness. "I guess we still have a lot to discuss in relation to the plans," I say.

"Yes, so it would seem," Petra says, her eyes shining with speculation and interest. She looks like someone who thinks she has found the code to a safe full of treasure.

God, what is her problem? It's almost like she's jealous, but what does she have to be jealous of? She's got her own husband, her own family. And Alex is her cousin. It's not like he's an old flame.

Alex swiftly moves the conversation on, asking Viktor a question about how his job is going. Viktor tells him about a new project he's working on and as I sip at the coffee that seemed to materialize in front of me out of nowhere, I relax a little. The heat is off me and Alex, and our imaginary romance, at least for a while. I marvel at how I didn't notice the coffee appearing before me. I wonder if I will ever get accustomed to be waited on in this extraordinary way.

Once everyone has finished their coffee, Babushka bestows both Alex and me with an indulgent, loving smile.

"Both of you must be tired after all of the travelling today. Why don't we call it a night? We've got plenty of time tomorrow to catch up and for me to get to know Cindy."

I nod, grateful at the excuse to slip away. I don't think I can handle any more questions right now.

"Alex, Petra, Anastasia," Babushka calls. "See your aunt and uncle out. I'm a bit tired. I think I'll retire for the night."

Babushka is clearly in charge here and it is kind of funny watching everyone take their orders from this tiny old lady. Viktor and Marina jump to their feet at her words. Alex stands up and even Petra and Anastasia get up with no argument.

"I'll escort you to your quarters," Alex offers.

"Ah, no. You stay with Cindy."

"No, no," I interrupt quickly. "I'll wait here for you, Alex."

Viktor and Marina bid me goodbye. I sit, enjoying the moment of silence as the others head out of the dining room. I still haven't decided whether or not Viktor and Marina like me. They aren't openly hostile, but there is an invisible wall around them. Maybe that's normal. Maybe they're just getting to know me in their own time. I can't say the same for Petra and Anastasia though. They clearly won't be joining my fan club anytime soon, but that's ok with me. As long as Babushka is happy, I'm doing my job.

After a couple of minutes, the door opens and Petra and Anastasia come back in.

"Alex is still with Babushka so we came to keep you company," Petra says. Her sweet smile would almost be enough to fool me if she hadn't been such a little bitch all night.

I don't bite. I just smile at her. "How lovely," I say, my sweetness as fake as hers.

"So you're staying in the room adjoining Alex's room?" she

says, as she takes a seat opposite me. Anastasia hangs back for a second, but then takes the seat next to her.

I wonder where this is going, but I nod my head.

"No one has stayed in that room for over fifty years," Petra says.

"Well at least not for more than an hour or two," Anastasia adds with a laugh.

It's clear they want me to ask why. I don't want to give them the satisfaction of playing into their hands, but I am curious as to what they're up to, and I decide to play along. "Why not? Is it haunted or something?"

Anastasia looks a little disappointed. It was clearly their intention to tell me the room is haunted and I've spoilt her fun. Petra, clearly the ringleader of the ice sisters, isn't put off from the game quite so easily.

"Yes," she says. "By Babushka's aunt. She went crazy in that room and hanged herself using the sheets. They locked her in there. They had to for the safety of the family."

"Sounds about right for the times," I agree, humoring her.

"People say she's still in there, howling and moaning, looking for a way out."

"Well the door isn't locked now, is it?" I ask with a wry smile.

"Well no, but her spirit is confined to the room with her dying in there," Petra says.

"Right," I agree slowly.

I hear footsteps echoing in the hallway and heading back for the dining room.

"Anyway, just be careful." Petra smiles. "We'd hate to see you leaving that room in a strait jacket."

I'm sure she would hate that. The door opens and Alex comes back.

"Are you ready for bed, Cindy or do you want to stay up for a while?"

The last thing I want is to spend more time with his cousins. I fake a yawn and stand up. "Bed for me. Good night ladies."

Petra and Anastasia wish me goodnight and Alex and I head for the stairs.

"What were those two saying while we were gone? They looked pretty sheepish when I came in," he says.

I decide against telling him what they were saying. They were just trying to get a rise out of me, and I think I made it pretty clear their stories weren't scaring me. I don't want to tell Alex and have him mention it to them. That would make it seem like I was partially buying the bullshit they were selling.

"Oh, nothing much," I say. "Just chit chat, really. They're very protective of you, aren't they?"

"That's one way of saying they're rude and standoffish," Alex says with a chuckle.

I laugh with him. He's seen straight through my attempt at being polite about them.

"They are protective though. Of Babushka," he says.

"Maybe you should tell them the truth," I say. "Then they'll know you're doing this to make her happy."

"Screw that," Alex says, stopping in his tracks and looking down at me with a frown. "They are extremely competitive and they'd do anything to make me look bad in my aunt's eyes. Promise me you won't let them manipulate you into telling them anything."

I quickly reassure him. "I won't say a thing, I swear. The less conversation I have to have with those two, the better."

CINDY

I wake up suddenly. The darkness around me is denser than I am used to. The city of London never sleeps and there is always light from the streetlamps or cars filtering into my room. For a second I am not even sure where I am. Then it comes back to me.

Alex.

Babushka.

I think I hear a tapping noise outside of my door. That must have been what woke me up. Is it Alex? But no. Surely Alex wouldn't come to my room in the middle of the night. He promised this trip wouldn't be like that, and I believe he meant it. Plus, there's an adjoining door. Why would he risk being spotted in the hallway when he could just come through there?

The noise stops. I strain to listen, but there is nothing. I must have imagined it, or it was the tail end of a dream ...

I close my eyes and let myself fall back to sleep, but just as I am starting to slip into the soft darkness, I hear it again. I jerk awake and stay unmoving, even holding my breath so there are no sounds coming from me, and listen more closely. It's not so much a tapping sound. It's more of a scraping sound, like ... wtf ... nails running over wood.

I sit bolt upright and listen again. Every sense in my body is wide awake and on high alert.

Now I can hear footsteps too. They cover the width of my room and then go back again as though someone is pacing restlessly outside of my door. Or something, I think with an icy chill running down my spine. My hand rushes out in the dark to switch on the bedside light.

Instantly, the sounds stop.

Breathing in quick shallow breaths, I stare at the door expectantly. But nothing happens. No movements. No sounds. Everything is still and silent. London is never this silent. The peace is broken when I start laughing with sheer relief. I realize what's happening here. It has to be one or both of the sisters out there, playing a trick on me, trying to scare me half to death.

I shake my head. What the hell is wrong with those two? They'd clearly decided to hate me before I even got here. They're like teenagers. So childish. I glance at the alarm clock. Well, well, it's just turned midnight. They have a sense of drama. I'll give them that.

Well girls, if you want to scare me off, it's going to take a little bit more than walking up and down scratching at the walls. I switch off the light and wait. The noises start again. I have to admit the nails against the wall is pure genius. Even knowing it is the two evil stepsisters doesn't stop the hairs on my arms from standing. I let them continue a few more seconds, before I push the light duvet back and get to my feet quietly. I tip toe across the room, hoping none of the floor-boards creak. They don't.

I reach the door without making a sound.

I almost give myself away by laughing when I imagine their faces when I throw the door open and turn the tables on them. I wonder what excuse they'll come up with to be prowling around in front of my room like two demented sisters in the middle of the night.

At the same time that I switch on the light, in one quick movement I grab the door handle and yank it open. I don't catch the girls in the act, or have the pleasure of shocking them out of their skins.

The hallway is empty.

I step out of my room and look up and down the hallway, but there isn't so much as a swaying curtain, or an open door anywhere to imply anyone was here. That's impossible: the noises were going on right to the moment I pulled the door open. I frown. There must be a reasonable explanation, and I'll get to the bottom of this.

I step back into my room, close the door, switch off the light, and walk to my bed. I am halfway across the room when I hear the footsteps again. But they are inside the room now. They seem to be so close behind me that I can't help feeling as if at any moment an icy cold hand will reach out to me and trail its fingers over my neck. I rush to the bedside lamp, switch it on, and look back around me, and of course, there's nothing there. No apparition reaching out to touch me. Everything is still. Except for the turmoil inside me. Every cell in my body is on high alert.

My heart is pounding in my chest. It's pounding so hard, Alex must be able to hear it through the walls. I look towards his door. There are no sounds coming from beyond it or light coming from under it. I tell myself I'm being ridiculous. I don't need him to tell me everything is okay. I'm ok. I'm tough. I'm just letting the ice sisters' stupid story get into my head and imagining stuff.

No, I didn't imagine it. I didn't imagine the footsteps or the nails running over the walls. I'm not crazy. Maybe they are just noises that old houses make. I've heard about it, but I've never lived in such an old house before. It could be the pipes, or the floorboards creaking as the house cools down, or something. It's what my grandmother used to call the sounds of an old house settling. She would know. She used to work as a maid in an old stately home when she was a young girl.

I get back into bed and pull the duvet back over myself. My body feels cold. I lay with my eyes wide open, waiting, listening. Finally, when nothing else happens, I turn off the light and close my eyes. There are no more noises. Perhaps I imagined them after all. I am three quarters of the way back into sleep when I hear a baby crying.

A baby crying? What the actual fuck?

Does Petra have a baby here? Maybe very rich people don't bring their babies to dinner, but surely someone would have mentioned it if she had. The crying comes again, a soft whimpering sound, and I realize with a start it's coming from the bathroom.

Now I know I'm letting my imagination run away with me.

There's no way there's a baby in there. And there's no way the ghost of a crazy old woman would be making the noise of a baby crying.

I switch on the light and jump out of bed. I rush into the bathroom and of course, there is nothing there. I look around me. It could be the wind. Sometimes the wind can sound like a howling wolf. To the best of my knowledge never like a crying child. I walk to the toilet and flush it. The sound is reassuringly normal. It's the pipes. Of course, it's the pipes.

I ignore the voice in my head. The one that tells me that this house truly is haunted.

CINDY

I fall back to sleep as dawn breaks over the horizon and some milky light starts to filter through the small gap in the drapes. By the time I wake up again the sun is already high in the sky even though it is only eight o'clock. I shiver as I think of last night; the scratching, the footsteps, the baby crying. In the sunny morning, it seems so ridiculous. I push the events of last night to the back of my mind. I know there must be a rational explanation and I will get to the bottom of it, but for now I'm not going to let it spoil my day.

Getting out of bed, I walk to the tall window, pull the drapes right back, and stand looking out over the beautiful gardens. The world is green for as far as I can see. It's the most profound thing. Just looking out into such endless, unspoilt beauty.

I've never considered myself to be a country girl. I've always been a city girl. Even our holidays when I was younger were always city breaks or beach holidays. But just standing here like this, I feel as if this is the way life should be. Not that empty rat race of the city. I don't feel isolated like I always thought I would in a house in the middle of nowhere. I feel wonderfully alive and enthusiastic to get out there and explore.

I don't know if we have anything planned for today, but Alex did mention showing me around the stables. I keep that in mind as I get ready. I don't own any jodhpurs or riding boots, but I choose a pair of black leggings and a long lemon colored top. I finish up with a pair of flat shoes. Sitting on the bed I French plait my hair. When I'm ready I take a look in the mirror. While I don't exactly look like a country girl, my outfit doesn't scream city girl.

I debate knocking on Alex's door, but I decide against it. I'd like to explore on my own for a bit. I head down the stairs, steeling myself to keep calm and unruffled if I meet the ice sisters. I peer into the dining room, but no one is around except for a man in uniform polishing the silver.

He puts down the silver piece and cloth, gives me a stiff bow, and says in a thick accent, "Good morning, Miss Forrester."

"Good morning," I say with a smile and a nod.

He doesn't smile back, but beckons to me with his hands. "Come, please. I will show you."

Without waiting to see if I will follow him, he leaves the dining room by a different door than the one I had come into. Clearly, he has been instructed to take me to the others. He leads me through what must be a music room since there is a gleaming grand piano in it and then down another short hallway. When he reaches the end, he throws the door open with a flourish, gesturing for me to enter.

"Thank you," I say with a smile.

I step through the tall open door and smile with delight as I come out into a huge, sunny conservatory filled with padded delicate metal chairs and matching tables. Alex stands from one of the chairs as I enter. He says something to the manservant in Russian, and the man nods politely, then closes the double doors and leaves Alex and I alone.

"Good morning," I say brightly.

"Did you sleep well?"

"Sort of," I reply, sliding into the chair opposite him.

"Was the bed not to your satisfaction?"

I make an offhand gesture with my hand. "I'm not used to the sound of pipes in old houses."

Alex lowers himself back into his chair. "Pipes? The pipes were troubling you?"

"That and the child crying."

One eyebrow arches. "What?"

"Isn't there a child somewhere in the house?"

He looks at me strangely. "Not to my knowledge."

"Well, that's strange, because I could have sworn I heard a baby crying last night."

He rubs his chin. "I've never really heard anything, but some people do say that old houses freak them out with all the sounds of floorboards creaking as they cool, and old pipes moaning and crying. I guess that must have been what you heard."

I wanted him to tell me about a baby somewhere in the

house and how sound echoes and carries through old houses, but I suppose it's more believable that the pipes make noises like that than the idea that there's a ghostly baby in my bathroom. Apart from anything, the ice sisters wouldn't have been able to resist mentioning the ghost of a baby as well as the ghost of a crazy aunt.

"Oh. Uh … where is everyone?" I ask, to change the subject.

"Babushka doesn't come down for breakfast anymore. In fact, she doesn't usually leave her quarters before midday. I have no idea where my cousins are, but I'm getting the impression you'd actually prefer me not to run into them," he says with a crooked smile.

I nod vigorously.

Alex gestures to the side table which is laid out with a breakfast spread fit for a king. There are croissants, grapefruit, yoghurt, cereal, toast, jam, honey, and just about every berry imaginable. In the hot plates are bacon, sausages, and fluffy scrambled eggs.

"All this and I can have the cook make you something else if you'd prefer," he offers.

"This is more than fine," I assure him. "But coffee first, I think."

"Let me," he says and gets up before I can.

I watch him walk across the room to a trolley I hadn't noticed. On the trolley is a jug of fresh coffee, a jug of what I assume is tea and a range of different milks, sugars and syrups.

"It's like being in a hotel," I laugh as Alex pours me a coffee.

"I know. Babushka prides herself on being a good host. She insists that every option is available to make her guests feel at home. Cream and sugar?"

"Please," I say.

He finishes making my coffee, then pours himself one, which he leaves black. Dark and stormy. Just like him. Except being here, I'm starting to see a very different side to him. A caring, almost gentle side comes out in him when he is around his great aunt. I smile to myself as I remember the way he lifted her in the air when we first arrived yesterday.

"What?" he asks, as he brings my cup over to me.

I shake my head. "I'm just thinking how different you are here."

"Different?" he asks with a raised eyebrow.

"Sweeter," I say teasingly.

He laughs shortly. "I don't think you'll find too many people to agree with you."

"Babushka would."

He smiles slowly. "No, she wouldn't. She knows exactly what I am, but she loves me anyway."

I take a sip of my coffee, savoring the rich taste and the caffeine hit I so desperately need first thing on a morning. I look up and find Alex watching me in amusement.

The hunger is back in his eyes. He masks it almost immediately though. "You like your coffee, don't you?"

"Oh, God yes," I agree with an awkward laugh. "It's pretty much an essential if you want me to string together a sentence of more than three words." Avoiding his eyes, I quickly stab my grapefruit half with my spoon and slip the segment into my mouth. The grapefruit squirts its tart juice onto my tongue.

"Juice?" Alex asks, his voice courteous. Like he is a stranger, which I suppose he is.

I nod and he pours me a glass from an elaborately cut crystal jug. I smile my thanks at him and sip the juice. It's icy cold and so refreshing.

"So what's the plan for today?"

"I thought I'd make good on my promise and take you out to the stables. If you still want to see them," Alex says.

"I'd *love* that," I gush enthusiastically.

"Good. We might even go for a ride up to the lake," he says. He laughs when he sees the horror on my face. "What's wrong? Do you not know how to ride?"

"I rode a few times when I was very young. I had a rich friend who owned a pony, but that was a long time ago. I'm not sure I'd be brave enough to try it now," I admit.

Alex throws his head back and laughs. "You? Scared of riding? Cindy Forrester, either you are just being coy, or you don't know yourself."

I mean when he puts it like that, how can I really refuse? And to be honest, I'm not afraid of riding. I'm exhilarated by the thought of getting up on a horse again after all these years. "The thing is I might need a few lessons to get started …"

"You never forget how to ride. Once you get back in the

saddle, it'll all come back to you. And you can take Nikita. She's very gentle."

"Ok," I agree with a laugh. "But no galloping off and leaving me behind."

"Ah, you spoil all the fun," Alex mocks.

Something about the way he says that makes a completely unrelated thought flash into my head. One where we are both naked and having fun. Avoiding his eyes, I put the grapefruit aside and stroll over to the long table. I drop four slices of bread into the toaster. Then I pick up a couple of sausages, some slices of the bacon and put them on my plate. As the toast pops I add them to my pile of food and make my way back to the table. There I start to assemble myself a breakfast sandwich.

At first Alex watches me with amusement as I make the sandwich, then he shrugs and, using my left-over sausages and bacon copies me with a grin.

"Good?" I ask, my cheeks full of food.

"Very good," he agrees, his eyes full of surprise and the sunlight slanting in through the half-open blinds on the glass walls.

CINDY

When we've finished eating our sandwiches, Alex stands up. "Are you ready?" he asks me.

"Yes," I say confidently, even though I have visions of me lying in a ditch somewhere with my neck broken.

Alex opens the door for me and waits for me to step outside. As I do he puts his hand on my arm and stops me for a second. "Really, there's nothing to be afraid of."

I don't think that's entirely true though. I think there's plenty to be afraid of. Like the way my whole arm is tingling where his hand is. And like the way he's holding my gaze with his eyes, which are all dark and deliberately unreadable. And the way I know if we stand like this for much longer, I'm not going to be able to stop myself from reaching up, touching his aristocratic face, and pulling it down to meet mine.

He takes his hand away from me and the spell is broken. I clear my throat, and lurch past him into the sunshine. My clit is throbbing. Oh God, why couldn't he be unattractive?

Alex comes to walk by my side, and I hope he puts my flushed cheeks down to the fresh air and nerves. That would be a lot better than him knowing it's because I'm such a little slut. A barn filled with sweet smelling hay. Alex and I naked. Me riding him.

God Cindy, stop it. Now!

I push the image away, although doing it is harder than I expect it to be, and I turn to Alex determined to stop being so silly, as he starts to talk.

"Can you see the treehouse?" he asks, pointing up into a large tree in the distance.

I squint against the sun, spot it, and nod.

"That was mine growing up. I was a terrible tyrant. No one was allowed in there. Petra was only allowed once because she had broken her arm and she begged Babushka so I allowed her that one time."

"Goodness what did you keep in there? Porn?" I ask with a laugh.

"Of course not," he says scornfully. "I stored the shrunken heads of my enemies."

I laugh again. I like this version of Alex. The sun beats down on our faces, making me feel carefree and relaxed. "Didn't Anastasia want to go up?"

"She was too young to climb up so high. By the time she was old enough to even be allowed up there, I'd outgrown it."

"How come? Did you discover girls or something?"

He throws me a sideways glance. "I found the *bratva*."

135

My eyes widen. In my mind's eye, I see a young Alex not yet tattooed, but already lean and tough. "So you really were in the Russian Mafia?"

"I was."

"Why would you do something like that after all this?" I sweep my hand in an arc that encompassed the stunning landscape and the palace like house."

He shrugs. "I craved something more. Something real. I felt as if I had been eating the frosting on a cake all my life. I wanted blood and guts. I was looking for meaning."

"Did you find it?"

His eyes are on a distant point on the horizon. "Yes."

I shade my eyes with my hand and stare at his hard profile. "But you gave it up?"

He swings his head to look at me. "Yes."

"Why?" I ask curiously.

"I wanted frosting again," he says, just as we reach the end of the house and turn around it. There is a long path leading to a large courtyard lined on three sides by stables.

"Wow," I say. "There must be room for fifty horses here."

"Fifty-seven to be precise, but not a bad guess," Alex says quietly. "When she was a lot younger, my aunt used to fill the stables with her horses. There were so many beautiful horses from all over the world. Now she only has a few here. There's Nikita who you'll be riding, Milan who I'll be riding, and a couple of others. I think she has six all told, unless she's acquired any new additions since my last visit."

A fair-headed lad appears out of one of the stables with a brush in his hand. He waves at Alex and shouts what I assume is a greeting. Alex replies in Russian, then turns to me. "I need a quick word with him, but he doesn't speak English so please bear with him."

"Sure, that's fine," I say, meaning it. It's not like he's Petra and Anastasia, using another language so he can berate me without me knowing about it. Alex talks for a bit longer, then the stable boy nods and disappears into one of the buildings.

"Boris knows these horses better than anyone, except maybe Babushka, and he agrees that Nikita will be perfect for you. She's gentle and calm."

I nod. Now I'm here, I can feel my nerves giving way to pure excitement. I actually can't wait to get on a horse again. I want to remember what it felt like to be so high up. I want what I never got when I was a child. To actually ride and feel the wind in my hair as I flew over open ground.

While we wait for Boris to get the horses ready, Alex leads me up to one of the stables.

"Come meet Polnoch," he says.

Inside, is a midnight black horse that stands at least twice my height. The horse is so majestic and so incredibly sleek and beautiful that I gasp when I see him.

"He's my aunt's prize stallion."

"I can see why," I say.

I step forward and Polnoch comes to meet me. I reach up and

stroke his neck and he nuzzles his head against my shoulder with a little snort. I laugh with delight.

"You're a beautiful, beautiful boy," I tell him.

Alex stands back a little, watching as I continue to stroke Polnoch.

"See. You're a natural," he says. "Polnoch doesn't easily accept a stranger's touch, let alone nuzzle one. He likes you."

"The feeling is mutual. He is absolutely gorgeous."

Boris comes in and says something to Alex and Alex turns around to tell me our horses are ready. I give Polnoch's neck one last rub and whisper goodbye to him before I follow Alex and Boris back out into the sun.

A large, chestnut-colored stallion stands beside a smaller gray mare. Alex takes my hand in his, and I feel a rush go through my body as he leads me towards the horses.

"This is Nikita," he says.

I reach up to pet Nikita and she accepts my touch with calm acceptance. Alex gives me a moment to get comfortable with her before he nods to the stirrups. I swallow hard. It's been so long since I've been on a horse, and I was never worried about making a fool of myself. Now I am. I try not to show it as I walk around to Nikita's side. I put one foot in the stirrup, and before I can talk myself out of it, I push myself off the ground and launch myself strongly onto Nikita's back. Some part of me didn't expect me to succeed at my first attempt, and I laugh with joy. I'm sure it wasn't the most graceful moment of my life, but I don't care. I'm on a horse. I settle into the saddle before looking down at Alex.

"Very good," he says approvingly.

I feel myself blush at the compliment. I quickly bend my head and stroke Nikita's mane to cover my embarrassment.

"A gentle tap with your feet will get her moving when you're ready," Alex says. "Use the reins to guide her. And when you want to stop, just pull back on the reins."

I nod. Now I'm up here, I feel confident and ready to go. Alex was right. You don't forget. I wait for him to mount Milan; his mount is by far more elegant and accomplished than mine was. He speaks to Boris for a moment before he turns to me and asks if I'm ready. When I nod, I see him gently touch his feet to Milan's side. I do the same and Nikita begins to walk. I sway a little in the saddle, but I soon adapt to her rhythm, moving with her rather than against her. I start to relax, enjoying the freedom I feel riding on Nikita. Alex was right about Nikita too. She is very calm and gentle. As if she senses my initial nerves she keeps her movements slow and steady. I pat her neck, wanting her to know I appreciate her.

"You're doing really well," Alex throws over his shoulder.

I beam happily at him.

We move away from the stables, and once we're out in the open fields, Alex slows Milan down a little, and the two horses walk side by side. I turn my face up to the sun and let it warm my skin. It is the best feeling in the world. The Macau feels like another life.

We've been riding for about half an hour when Alex points to the left. "The lake is that way."

I nod and pull on the left of Nikita's reins. She turns immediately and I pat her neck again. I am feeling braver now, and I tap her with my feet again, moving her into a slow canter to keep pace with Alex's horse.

Soon I spot the lake coming up in front of us. The sun shines on its surface, making it look like a sea of sparkling sapphires. It's so quiet and peaceful out here. We ride to the edge of the lake and I pull Nikita to a stop. We climb down from the horses and Alex takes the reins from me. He leads both horses to the lake and lets them drink their fill. When they're done, he leads them into the shade and secures them to a tree. When he returns, I'm sitting on the grass looking out across the surface of the lake watching a lone swan bob for seaweed. In the sun it seems to glow with grace and flawless beauty. Alex lowers himself down beside me and lays back on the grass.

"It's so peaceful out here," I say in a hushed voice.

"Mmm. It's a great place for thinking," he replies.

I look down at him. His eyes are closed. The desire to reach out and touch his face is so strong I have to stop myself.

"Relax," he murmurs.

I let myself lay down beside him and look up at the sky. It's mostly clear and I focus on the one fluffy white cloud that meanders lazily over our heads. I feel different. More centered. More like myself. As if this is the real me. I'm not entirely sure if it's the country setting making me feel that way, or whether it's Alex, but whatever it is, I like it.

"I never imagined myself being so comfortable in this kind of setting," I say after a few minutes. "I always thought I was a city girl through and through. But there's something so damn good about watching clouds float by that aren't just smog. And the lack of dirt. It's amazing."

"The city has a certain appeal, but it has too many people."

"You don't like people much, do you?"

"Not much."

I turn my head to look at him. "Why? Is it because of what you saw when you were in the *bratva*?"

His lips twist, he turns towards me. It is a shock to look into his eyes this close with only blades of grass between us. "What do you want to know, Cindy?" His voice is quiet, magnetic. I can't look away from them.

"Did you ever kill anyone?" I whisper.

"Dead people sometimes feature in my nightmares," he admits quietly.

I feel my stomach lurch. I know so little about him. How could a man who lived in this paradise give it up for the life of a criminal? "Was it worth it, Alex? The excitement?"

He looks away from me and stares up at the blue sky for so long I start to think he's not going to answer me. Finally, he turns his head towards me again and looks deep into my eyes. "No. It wasn't worth it. If I had to do it all again I would do it in a totally different way. I was seduced by the idea of power and violence because I was furious with the world for taking my parents away. It was a terrible mistake, but the past cannot be changed, and regrets are useless."

We stare into each other's eyes. The air changes, becomes more viscous. I can smell the grass, but I can also smell his cologne. It makes my head swim. The rest of the world falls

141

away. The lake, the lone swan, the blue sky above, the springy grass underneath … there is only me and Alex. My hand lifts on its own accord and gently touches his cheek. His skin feels like raw silk. I see him swallow hard.

"What are you doing, Cindy?" he asks hoarsely.

"I don't know," I whisper.

"Are you sure? Every woman I've been with I've let down."

"I don't care, I want you." My voice sounds different, thick and guttural, and throbbing with strange need.

His head lifts, moves towards me, then suddenly, jerks away. He sits up. "We should go," he mutters as he springs up.

He goes for the horses, taking them for another drink and then leading them over to me. I'm on my feet by the time he reaches me and I climb onto Nikita's back wordlessly. I can't even look at him. I feel as if I've been slapped with a cold fish. He mounts Milan and we start back towards the stables.

"Babushka asked last night if I would ask you to have lunch with her today."

"I'd love to have lunch with her," I say automatically.

He says nothing and for a while we ride without speaking, until I can bear it no more and blurt out, "Have I offended you?"

"No, of course not," he frowns. "Why would you think that?"

"Just the way you reacted."

He stops his horse and I follow suit. He looks at me and his eyes are hard and hostile. The eyes of a stranger. "I didn't bring you here to fuck you. You're here to do a job. Don't let what happened just now change anything. Babushka has the intuition of an animal with many predators. She will detect even the smallest change in you."

"Don't worry I won't be any different around her," I say tightly.

"Good. Never forget that nothing is more important than the role you have been hired to play. Is that clear?"

"Crystal," I reply tightly.

CINDY

"Oh no, I couldn't eat another thing," I protest, rubbing my stomach and smiling at Babushka as she tries to tempt me with another rich cake.

"Come, come now. Just one bite of this. I promise you won't regret it."

"Honestly, Babushka, I've already eaten far more than I ever normally would eat at lunch time, and I really think my stomach is on the point of bursting. Especially since I was still full from breakfast.

"All right," Babushka concedes with a laugh. "I can't help myself. I'm a feeder. Just ask Alex. Seconds, thirds. He had them at every meal. I have to wonder how he didn't turn out to be about thirty stone."

I laugh with her, although I can't picture Alex as anything other than toned and muscular.

"The old saying is true dear. The way to a man's heart is

through his stomach. But you already have Alex's heart, I can see that much, so I guess you don't need to resort to such mundane tactics."

I feel a strange pang of pain at the thought that I can't go after Alex's heart. Not now, not ever. It's just a professional relationship. Nothing more.

"Alex is very good looking," she continues. "He always was. But it takes someone special to love him."

I raise an eyebrow, wondering if she's going to reveal some deep family secret.

She laughs uproariously. "You should see your face. Don't look so worried dear. He's not a closet axe murderer or anything like that. I just mean it takes someone special, someone he really clicks with and trusts for him to let his walls down. For you to have got to the man beneath the hard exterior, you must be special."

Have I ever seen the man beneath the hard exterior? I think I have. Once, when we were at the lake, I saw something more, but he shut down faster than I could blink.

"Then you must be too," I say with smile. "Because he talks about you a lot, and it's obvious how much he loves you."

"Ah, he's a sweet boy." Babushka smiles, clearly pleased to hear that Alex talks about her a lot. "He has a heart of gold, even if he does try his best to keep it hidden. Enough of my ramblings. Tell me about you, Cindy. Where did you grow up?"

She seems interested in what I have to say and she asks a lot of insightful questions and I am enjoying talking to her now we're on a safer subject than Alex and I. So I begin to tell Babushka what amounts to pretty much my life story.

When I finish telling her all about me, I ask about her life and I am instantly enthralled by her stories of growing up here in Russia, about what life was like when she was a child and then a teenager. She is full of amusing, fascinating anecdotes and I realize I really do like the woman a lot, and I can see why Alex dotes on her so much.

We both lose track of the time, and Babushka seems as surprised as I am when Valeriya comes in and asks if she's ready to get changed for dinner.

"It's that time already?" Babushka exclaims. "Well I never. I'm going to eat dinner in my room tonight though, so no need for a fuss."

"Are you alright?" I ask her, concerned that she wants to hide away in her room.

"I'm fine," she smiles, waving away my concern. "I just want you and Alex to spend an evening together without me in the way."

"You're not in the way. We have all the time in the world to be alone when we get back to London," I say immediately.

Babushka shakes her head decisively. "No, no, you are on holiday and there must be a million things you want to do together. I'll eat in my room where I can watch an old James Bond movie. I like the ones with Sean Connery best. Doesn't he remind you of Alex?" she asks with a twinkle in her eyes.

I smile at Babushka. "I never thought about it, but you are right. There is something about him that is similar."

We exchange goodbyes as Valeriya leads her from the room. I guess I'll be spending tonight in my room watching movies too, and tomorrow, Alex and I can come up with a story about what we're supposed to have done together.

CINDY

I was wrong about what would happen.

Visions of sitting in my room making a start on the DVD collection weren't to be. Just as I got into my room, Alex knocked on the connecting door. He surprised me by telling me he'd made reservations at his favorite restaurant in the nearest city, and that we would be leaving the house at seven thirty.

As I zip myself into a slim fitting white dress I wonder if after what happened this morning Alex thinks it will be easier to keep our ruse up if we go out and not join the others for dinner. Whatever his reasoning, I know for sure it's not because he really wants to spend alone time with me. His complete and utter rejection earlier still stings. The only good thing about it is I now know exactly where I stand. There are no more illusions about what he wants from me.

There is a soft knock on the door and I take a deep breath and go to open it.

Alex is dressed in a white dinner jacket, black shirt and black pants and I realize Babushka is right. He is very, very James Bondish with a sexy, devil-may-care look around him. I can see the lower half of several Celtic design tattoos poking out from beneath the sleeves. He looks so hot I am finding it hard to tear my eyes away from him for even a second.

"Are you ready?" he asks quietly.

I nod. I'm not sure how to play this anymore. We walk down the empty corridor silently and when we reach the staircase we meet a servant who politely steps back to allow us to pass.

Downstairs the driver is waiting next to the open passenger door of a long black Rolls Royce. I thank him and slip in. The door closes, a heavy reassuring thunk. Classical music fills the faintly perfumed air as Alex slides in next to me. Instantly, I feel my heart start pounding in my chest. Even though he rejected me, my body still responds to him.

"Are you familiar with Russian food?" he asks quietly.

I turn to look at him. Gosh, he is so damn handsome. "My first introduction was last night when I tried the *chak chak*."

"Good. You'll like this restaurant."

After that he keeps the conversation light and casual. The restaurant is in a grand old building. The staff are ancient and dour to say the least, but shockingly efficient.

"Since I know nothing about Russian food, why don't you choose for me?" I say.

As I sip my champagne, very delicious by the way, he orders some fish appetizers for which the English translation is 'herring under a coat', and for the main course, meat stew, but no doubt a fancy version. I look around the grand, beautifully preserved surroundings curiously. There is something unreal, almost fairytale about the best of Russian architecture and this interior exemplifies that idea. One can imagine splendidly robed Tsars and Tsarinas in these lofty, gilded spaces. The Macau and my unrelentingly hectic life in London seem a million miles away.

"Like it?" Alex asks, cutting into my thoughts.

I look across the table at him. He looks so at home here. So regal. This is his birthright. I tried to imagine him as a thug and couldn't. Not even with his huge, thickly muscled body or the tattoo poking out of his shirt collar. I smile at him. "What's not to like? The architecture is stunningly beautiful. Almost as beautiful as Babushka's palace."

He glances around as if seeing the interior for the first time through fresh eyes, through my eyes, then looks again at me with a strange expression. "Yes, it's very beautiful. I'm afraid I took … I take all this privilege and splendor for granted."

"I can't imagine taking something this marvelous for granted."

He leans back. "What was your childhood like?"

It is flattering how interested he seems in what I have to say so I tell him about the small apartment we lived in, the neighbors next door who fought night and day, the school I went to, and my three best friends. I'm sure I would have carried on if the first course had not arrived. It is a colorful dish that looked like a layer cake. On the top was mayonnaise, then the fish, followed by the onions, carrots, apples and a bottom layer of boiled potatoes. Even though it looks beautiful I can't imagine I would like cold fish, but it is surprisingly good.

I put the fork down and find Alex watching me.

"Well?" he asks.

"It's actually excellent," I say honestly.

He smiles slowly and I have to remind myself this is not a date. The conversation flows easily and I find myself revealing even more unnecessary stuff about myself.

Next, an old Russian favorite, the *Zharkoye,* beef stew arrives. It is what the phrase 'something to write home about' was invented for. The meat is full of intense flavors that melt on my tongue. I close my eyes to shut out every other sensation but the taste explosion going on in my mouth.

Alex laughs softly. "If this is your reaction, I wish you could have tasted Babushka's version of it."

I look at him in surprise. I can't imagine Babushka cooking. She has staff for everything. Alex seems to read my expression and he laughs.

"Babushka has always had plenty of staff. And I'm sure you can see why."

I nod, thinking of the sheer size of the place.

"But her real love is cooking and horses. She had a real talent too. She would cook up the most amazing meals and up until five years ago, she even tended to and rode her horses. No matter how wet it was, or how much snow there was, she'd be out there with them every morning."

"She sounds like a hell of a woman," I say.

"Oh, she is," he agrees. "What you see now, is just a ghost of what she used to be."

"I don't know, Alex. She seems very spritely to me and in good spirits. I think she is a very lucky woman to have you and Valeriya. Especially since Valeriya seems to have a genuine affection for her."

"Babushka is more her family than her own," Alex says. "And I suppose compared to her actual family, we are. Her mother, who used to work as a maid for Babushka, died when she was ten. Her father immediately began to beat her. Because of the loss of income, he tried to send her out to work the streets."

My jaw dropped. "Oh my God. Why didn't she go to the police?"

Alex shakes his head. "It was a different time then, Cindy. The police would have done nothing to stop it. If anything, they would have taken her father's side. Women's rights were barely even a thing then, and Valeriya was only allowed to stay with us because Babushka stepped in and paid him enough money for him to go away. She didn't tell Valeriya for a long time, because she wanted Valeriya to stay because she wanted to, not because she felt like she had been bought."

"It sounds like something from a Victorian novel. It's hard to believe this happened in the eighties."

"Russia in the eighties was like the Victorian times in many ways," he admits.

At that moment a woman passing by our table suddenly stops and gives a little shriek. She says something excitably in Russian. The only word I catch is Alex. Alex stands and, resting her fingertips on his arm, she reaches up on tiptoes and kisses him lightly on his cheek. I'm sure she whispers something in his ear before moving back and flicking her hair seductively.

"Well, hello to you too," I mutter.

I didn't mean to say it out loud, and I feel my cheeks blushing when both Alex and her turn towards me.

"Natalia, this is Cindy, my fiancée. She's English," Alex says. "Cindy, this is Natalia, an … old friend of mine."

"Less of the old, you," she scolds, fluttering her fake eyelashes coyly at him, before glancing at me, her eyes are suddenly cold and appraising.

"Hello," she says.

Even before I can return the greeting she has already turned her attention back to Alex. Well, at least she's switched to English so she's slightly above the ice sisters in terms of friendliness. Natalia is clearly more than an old friend of Alex's, or at least she wishes she was judging by the way she can't take her eyes off him even for a second.

"How's Babushka?" she coos.

Great. She's close enough to know the family.

"She's good," Alex replies.

"Still keeping you firmly in line?" she asks with a giddy giggle.

I want to jump up and throttle her. Her giggly laugh is freaking annoying. She's starting to say something else, but Alex speaks over her, cutting her off.

"It was nice to see you, Natalia, but you've got to get on. And I'd like to get back to my fiancée."

He's looking at me when he says it, and I hate the fact that I feel a moment's triumph when I look at Natalia's dismayed expression. She glares at me, then says her goodbyes to Alex, back in Russian I notice. Then she flits away.

"An old friend, huh?" I say as casually as I can when Natalia has walked away. I can feel the spikes of jealousy inside of me and I'm so angry at myself for feeling this way. After what happened this morning when I was told in no uncertain terms that I'm on the job. None of this is real. Except to me. The more I try to hold back the more it's starting to feel real. I have to find a way to stop myself from falling for Alex. Maybe it's too late for that, but then I have to get a hold of myself, stop the rot.

"Yes," he says.

"And why not? She's gorgeous." I can't keep the petulance out of my voice, but I'm not sure I succeed. Especially because I'm telling the truth. Natalia is gorgeous. She has long red hair and curves in all the right places.

He looks at me seriously. "You have nothing to be jealous of, Cindy."

"I'm not jealous." I try to laugh but the laugh won't come and I look down at my plate so I don't have to meet Alex's eyes.

He does laugh though. "You've almost turned green."

The truth hurts and I look up at him with a cold smile and lie through my teeth. "It's an act, Alex. How do you think I would react as your fiancée if some ex was hanging all over you? I wouldn't be too happy about it, would I? And if this story gets back to Babushka, I want my appropriate reaction to the situation to get back to her as well."

"Whatever you say, Cindy," Alex says with a small smile. It's clear he doesn't believe a word of what I said.

I double down. "I'm serious. Why would I be jealous?" I demand.

"I have no idea, but you're protesting way too much." He grins, his eyes twinkling with mischief.

He's right. I am protesting way too much. If it had been an act and he had questioned me, I would have rolled my eyes, said whatever, and moved onto a different topic of conversation. It's too late for that now though. Alex sees straight through me. He's so exasperating.

"For what it's worth, I would have reacted exactly the same way if I was you," Alex concedes.

That brings me up short. What does he mean? That he would be jealous if my ex came up to me. He doesn't give me a chance to respond to that. Instead, he signals to our waiter that we're ready for dessert. I decide to let it go. I have to. If I bring it up again, then I'll only make it worse. And to be fair, Alex didn't show the least bit of interest in her.

By the time we finish our desserts, the tension between us is gone and I'm relaxed again. Alex is even making me laugh with his dry humor.

As I scoop up the last bit of my ice cream Alex gets our waiter's attention again and says something to him in Russian. The waiter moves away and comes back quickly with two small glasses of clear liquid. Alex thanks him as he places one down in front of each of us, and I hear myself echoing his thanks, even though I have no idea what this is. I certainly didn't ask for it.

"Vodka." Alex smiles at me. "I know it's a cliché that every Russian drinks vodka, and generally I'm a whisky man, but you can't come to Russia and not try the real stuff at least once. It's so much better than the commercial stuff you get in England. Or pretty much anywhere else in the world."

He picks his glass up and smiles at me, challenging me with his eyes. I pick my glass up and clink it against his. The challenge is well and truly accepted.

"*Nostrovia*," I grin.

I hear him echoing me as I bring the glass to my mouth. I throw my head back and swallow the huge measure. It burns my throat and my insides all the way down to my stomach, but I hide it well, smiling at Alex who has taken only a sip of his.

"We're Russian, not Mexican." Alex grins. "We sip it here, savoring the flavor."

"What can I say," I smile. "You can take the girl out of London, but you can't take London out of the girl. We're more of a go big or go home crowd."

Alex looks me straight in the eye, and I feel my breath catch in my throat. He doesn't take his eyes off mine as he downs the rest of the drink.

"I guess we're going big then," he says softly.

His eyes darken and I feel a pulsing energy running all through my body. I swallow hard and force myself to smile at him. Then I pretend that something in the room has caught my eye and quickly look away. The spell he held me under breaks, although my clit doesn't get the memo, and it continues to pulse with desire. Ruthlessly crushing down the desperate urge to reach across the table and touch Alex's hand, I shift uncomfortably in my seat to try and find a position that doesn't tease my clit. I fail. The shuffling around only intensifies the feeling.

Alex looks at me with wry amusement and I feel as if no part of me is private from him and he's reading my internal thoughts. I hate the feeling and I stand up rather abruptly.

"I need to use the bathroom."

He frowns. "To throw up?"

The moment of feeling like he can see inside of my soul passes and I laugh, a normal laugh. He thought the vodka had hit my stomach and made me feel sick. He didn't know what was really going on inside my crazy, lust-filled head.

"No chance," I say. "I wouldn't be much of a Brit if one shot affected me that much."

Alex chuckles as I walk away. Inside the bathroom I look in the mirror. My cheeks are flushed. I blame the vodka for that, although I secretly think it's more about my close proximity to Alex and what that does to me. I fluff my hair, reapply my lipstick, and wash my hands, to pass a few minutes so it seems I've had time to use the toilet. When I feel a little more composed, I go back to the table. Two more glasses of vodka have materialized there.

"This time, we're going to savor it," Alex says as I take my seat.

I'm not sure it's a good idea, but I pick my glass up and take a sip.

"It's not exactly something I could savor," I say with a wince as the liquid fire runs down to my stomach.

"I think you'd feel differently if you came out here in January when the temperatures reach around minus twenty and the nights are dark from around three o'clock. There's nothing better than sitting in front of an open fire sipping a glass of vodka."

"Or whisky in your case."

"Actually, I was a bit more of a vodka drinker before I moved to London."

We finish the vodka and I have to say I'm kind of glad when it's gone. I'm definitely a gin girl through and through.

"Would you like to go through to the bar for drinks, or do you want to head back to the house?"

"It depends on the drinks," I say. The vodka is loosening my tongue. I can hear the flirty tone to my voice. I'm pretty certain drinking anything else would not be a good idea, no matter what it is, but what the hell. The worst part is Alex doesn't look like he's even a tiny bit tipsy.

"You can have whatever you want," he says suavely. "The vodka thing is a rite of passage, like drinking a pint of Guinness in Dublin, even though the stuff is vile. You don't have to have any more."

"A drink it is then," I decide with a lopsided smile. The truth is I can't bear for the night to be over.

CINDY

Alex nods and we stand up, then I follow him through to the bar area. It is smaller than the restaurant and the lights are subtly dimmed. He tells me to find a seat while he goes to the bar. I bristle at his commanding tone, but a small part of me likes the way he takes control of a situation … of me. It makes me ponder what he'd be like in bed. Dominant I imagine. Dominant and extremely skilled.

I take an empty table in the back corner. A small candle flickers in the center of the low table. I swallow hard. Anything could happen with Alex and I in a place like this. A place where no one will be able to see what we're doing.

I shake my head slightly to clear it. Whoa! That vodka must be hitting my brain cells.

I'm *not* going to throw myself at Alex, with or without vodka. After what happened this morning it would be too pathetic. Besides he's my boss. This is business. I have to treat this like a business meeting, not a damned date. I've already embarrassed myself tonight by acting jealous of his stupid ex. I'm not going to embarrass myself further.

Alex comes to the table and confirms everything I already know by taking the seat opposite me instead of sitting down beside me on the plush sofa. It annoys me even more when I feel a pang of disappointment. My body wanted to be able to feel his leg pressed against mine, the heat coming off his body.

He pushes my drink towards me and I smile when I see the slice of orange in it. He remembered. I pick my glass up and take a sip. The gin and tonic is heaven after the neat vodka.

I put my glass down and lean back. "Have you never wanted to get married?"

"That's a bit out of the blue," he murmurs, studying me above the rim of his glass.

"I don't really know what made me ask it. The question came into my mind, and it popped out of my mouth before I had chance to think about it. I blame the vodka. And the wine."

"I've never met anyone I could imagine spending forever with. What about you?"

"I always seem to hook up with Mr. Wrong," I say. "It got so bad I swore off dating forever."

"And yet here we are." Alex drawls. "It's a good job this is fake. I would hate to compromise your principals."

Must be the vodka, or the lack of lighting, but the look on his face as he says it tells me, actually, he would very much like to compromise my principals. I take a very, very large gulp of my drink. It goes down the wrong way and makes me cough.

"It's a good job then that we're both on the same page and nothing will be compromised," I gasp.

He frowns suddenly and I know whatever moment of weakness in him is gone. He finishes his drink and asks me if I'm ready to leave. Since he still seems mostly sober, it makes sense that he's the one to take control and put an end to the madness. I nod and stand. As we make our way out to the waiting car, he keeps a safe distance between us. We sit at opposite ends of the back seat, not touching.

I look out of the window, peering through the darkness at the passing houses and then at the countryside. Alex looks out of his window too, but like me, I have a feeling he's not seeing anything.

I'm filled with regret at what might have been, but can't be. I'm missing something I never even had. I tell myself it doesn't matter. That it's only the alcohol making me feel this way, and tomorrow, when I'm sober again and no doubt hung over, I'll be back to normal again. Just a girl with a crush and nothing more.

But right now ... God, I wish he felt the same clawing need for me that I do for him.

We barely speak on the ride back home, and then we go into the house and I follow Alex up the stairs, still in total silence. It's awkward to say the least, and I can't wait to get to my room. I almost wish one of the ice sisters would appear so we would have to act like everything is normal between us so they don't think we've had a fight or something. In fact, I think a fight would be easier to get past than this burning cold.

We reach the door to my room and Alex stops. I turn to look at him. His face is set, unreadable.

"Goodnight," he says curtly.

"Goodnight," I reply. My voice is slightly breathless. I step towards the door and reach for the doorknob, but I don't want to leave things like this between us. "Thank you for dinner. I really enjoyed it, especially the food."

It's not much, but it's the best I can come up with and it seems to thaw Alex a little.

He gives me a half smile. "It was my pleasure."

I step into my room then. As I close the door on the raw animal magnetism that he exudes, I tell myself I should be glad to be away from him. Away from the relentless attraction, and the awkwardness of not being able to do anything about it. But, it's simply not true. I'm horribly, horribly disappointed that he didn't try to kiss me, or make some lame excuse to come into my room. I couldn't have made my availability clearer. It tells me everything I need to know.

To Alex I am, and always will be, just business. I can only hope that in the morning, without the tipsiness, I will feel exactly the same. Or at least I'll convince myself I do.

Kicking my shoes off, I strip off, and leave my dress where it falls, then I pad into the bathroom and use the toilet. I don't even take my make-up off. I'll sort it out in the morning. Right now, I'm so tired all of a sudden and I just want to go to bed.

$\approx$

I wake up in the dead of night to the sound of footsteps in the hallway again. I close my eyes and try to ignore them, but they're so loud, I can't ignore them. I roll over and realize how cold I am. I'm shivering and my teeth are chattering. I can see the plume of white in front of my face as I breathe out. So much for spring not being cold.

I sit up quickly, ignoring the frigid air that wraps itself around my bare skin as I hear footsteps in my room. They run from the bed towards the bathroom. I reach out and snap the light on, but the room is empty. I hear a noise like a door slamming and I tell myself it's the pipes. Nothing but the pipes. I have to know for sure though, and I push the duvet back and stand up. I move slowly and cautiously towards the bathroom door.

"Hello?" I say.

I feel foolish talking out loud to what is almost certainly just the pipes, and I get annoyed with myself suddenly for letting fear consume me to the point that I'm whispering at doors like this. I reach out and throw the bathroom door open, almost daring there to be a crazed ghost in there. The bathroom is empty, as I knew it would be. Its emptiness seems to mock me, laughing at the dumb foreign girl who doesn't understand the ways of the house.

I feel a shiver run down my spine at my strange thoughts and then I force myself to laugh. It comes out a little shaky, but it makes me feel better. As if the house is mocking me. I shake my head and turn to go back to bed. I grab my robe from the chair in the corner first and slip it on. It's short and silky, extremely thin, and it's almost useless against the cold.

It's only as I get back into bed that I realize the bathroom wasn't cold. I felt the wave of warmth coming out of it as I opened the door. I wonder if I've accidentally knocked the heater off in my bedroom and I get back up and go towards it. The dial is still where it should be, and I reach out hesitantly to touch the actual radiator. I half expect it to be warm, to prove to me that this room is indeed haunted and the ghost of the crazy old aunt is making the temperature plummet. Of course, that's not the case. The radiator is stone cold. I shake my head at my own imagination and head back to my bed again, making a mental note to tell Alex about the heater in the morning so someone can come and take a look at it.

I sit back down on the bed and reach for the duvet. My hands have just grasped it when I hear a woman's voice from the bathroom. The voice says my name as clear as day.

"Cindyyyy," I hear again, the Y sound on the end being dragged out until it's barely a whisper, and fades altogether.

I freeze, my eyes wide open and staring straight ahead in terror. I feel the hairs stand up on the back of my neck. That sound is most definitely not the pipes, and nothing will convince me otherwise.

"Cindyyyyy."

I jump to my feet, no longer frozen to the spot. I run across the room like I have all the hounds of Hell on my tail, and slam open the door that connects my room to Alex's, and step into his room, instantly noting the warmth in here compared to my room.

I expected Alex to be asleep in bed, and my plan was to sneak through to his lounge area and sleep on the couch in there. I was wrong though. He's wide awake and sitting at a small table with a pile of papers in front of him.

He looks up, a frown on his face, obviously pissed off at the intrusion. His face changes when he sees me, and I know my terror must be written all over my face. He jumps to his feet and crosses the room. He takes my hands in his.

"Cindy? What's wrong? What happened?" he asks urgently.

I don't have the words to explain and I just shake my head mutely, aware that the only warm spots on my body are the places his hands are touching.

ALEX

Choosing Cindy was a stupid mistake.

I knew it the moment our eyes met that night, but I couldn't damn well help myself. And now I've dug myself into a hole I can't seem to dig myself out of. I find it almost impossible to stop myself from flirting with her and touching her. I know I'm giving her mixed signals and it's a low despicable thing to do, but I'm losing control over my own actions. For the first time in my life I'm doing things almost against my will.

It's clear she is feeling the rush too. The way she reacted to Natalia is the way I would have if one of her exes came up and tried to flirt with her. No, it's not the way I would have reacted: I would have punched a hole in his damn head.

I want her more than I've ever wanted any other woman, but I'm not going to jeopardize the fantasy I have created for Babushka. It is going so nicely. Everything is as perfect as I thought it might be. Babushka loves her. I'm not going to spoil it.

As I shrug off my jacket and shirt, the image of her lying on the grass, the sun in her hair comes into my mind. God, I could have taken her then. How easy it would have been to move my head closer and just kiss that soft, pink mouth.

I knew I had to shut the moment down, but once I did, the tension that wasn't there between us became something impossible to disregard. Before it was in the background, humming gently. Now it's like a relentless gnawing in my gut. It won't be ignored. It won't even let me sleep. I take off my pants and go to the bathroom in my boxer shorts. When I come back I toss my laptop onto the bed and settle down next to it. Work. Work might be able to consume my attention.

It always has in the past.

It takes ages to get back into working mode, my thoughts keep straying to her sleeping next door. Does she sleep naked? Fuck. I pull my thoughts away from the image furiously. I hate how weak and vulnerable I have become. If the men I ran with could see me now. How they would laugh. I think of my best friend, Yuri. How annoyed I was when he fell in love. For the first time I understand how he must have felt as he found himself being helplessly twisted around the little finger of a woman.

I force my attention back to the figures in front of me. This time I succeed. The deal sucks me in and I work steadily. I'm so involved I jump when the connecting door to Cindy's room crashes open.

My head jerks up and the sight of her cuts the words off in my throat. Her hair is tousled and loose all around her shoulders, and she has hastily thrown on a short red silk robe that is barely long enough to conceal her pussy. She is clutching the robe tightly in her hands, but I can still see a deep triangle of the skin all the way down to her waist. It's more than enough to tell me she's probably naked beneath the wisp of covering. Her long, long smooth legs are a potent invitation all on their own.

None of that is what makes me freeze, though. It's the expression on her white face.

Her eyes are wide and staring and her mouth is pressed tightly closed in a grimace. She is so terrified her hands are shaking. I jump to my feet and rush to her side. I take her hands in mine, ignoring the heat that flows through me when I touch her skin. Heat is just how she makes my body react. From day one. Her hands aren't warm. They're so cold, it's as though she's been outside in the dead of winter dressed in the flimsy robe.

"What's wrong?

She just shakes her head and I give her a moment to get her words in order. I want to pull her against me and stop her from shaking, but I stop myself. I don't trust myself. She's nearly naked. I try to think what could have happened to scare her this badly. Has she had a phone call with bad news from home or something? That must be it. She's only been in her room. What else could it be? I'm already making silent calculations in my head for when we can fly home. This might be for the best, because I don't think I can take much more of being around her all day long and pretending I'm not burning up inside to fuck her.

"There was someone in my bathroom. I heard footsteps and

then someone saying my name," she blurts out. Her voice is husky with fear.

I frown. There's no one in her room. I know that for a fact. Even to get on this land someone would have to negotiate an electric fence, then the up-to-date security system I installed five years ago. It must be those damned pipes again. I'll have to talk to Babushka and try to convince her to allow me to update those ancient things.

"It's just the pipes, Cindy," I say, releasing her hands. Now that I know there is no emergency, I feel a burst of desire rip through my body.

She shakes her head. "When I thought I heard crying, I could buy the pipes theory, but I swear, you have to believe me, something in there called my name, Alex. As clear as day. And it's icy cold in there too."

The first thing that comes into my mind is: Petra or Anastasia are playing a cruel joke, hiding out in Cindy's room to scare her.

"Wait here," I say and stalk through to her room. If I find one of those little bitches in there, or any sign they've been there, I swear I'll kill them. They used to be spoilt brats, but now, they've turned into grasping witches.

The light is still on in Cindy's room and the duvet is pushed back. Nothing else is out of place, but I do notice the unusual chill in the air almost immediately. I go through to the bathroom and switch the light on, but the room is empty, and there's nothing to suggest anyone has been in there.

It's warmer in the bathroom than the main bedroom though and a quick touch on the radiator tells me the heating is working fine, but when I go back through to the bedroom and touch the heater in there, it's stone cold. Even though the temperature during the day is nice, the nights can get surprisingly cold in this big old house. At least now I know what's happened. I go back to my room.

"The heater in the bedroom is broken," I say. "That's why the pipes are being so loud. They're trying to heat something that isn't working."

"But the voice ..." she insists miserably and trails off.

I don't want to make her feel stupid. "Maybe you were dreaming."

She seems to have gotten a grip of herself while I was gone. She no longer looks so afraid, but she's still making no move to go back to her own room. In fairness, I can't really expect her to go back and sleep in there while it's so cold.

"Do you want to sleep in here tonight? I'll have one of the staff look at the heater first thing tomorrow," I say.

"Thank you," she says.

She heads for the door that leads to my lounge.

"Take the bed," I say.

She stops mid-stride and turns around. "No, it's fine. I'll be alright on the couch."

"Take the damned bed," I growl, a little annoyed that she always argues with me about ... everything.

As if I'm going to let her take the couch. I snatch my laptop off the bed and take a few steps away.

"Thank you," she whispers and moves towards the bed. There

is something wooden about her movements. She climbs onto the bed, but instead of getting into it, she just lays down and closes her eyes. Must be the shock of thinking she'd been visited by a ghost.

"Shall I switch off the light?"

Her eyes snap open. "No, don't do that. I like sleeping with the lights on."

I hide my smile at her antics and move towards the lounge.

"Um … if you're not going to bed straightaway, maybe you can work here."

Concentrating with Cindy so close to me and her legs on show like that is going to be damned hard, and I know for sure now I won't be getting any work done. I'll be far too busy thinking about what I want to do with those legs, but I sit at the writing table by the window and try to lose myself in my work again. It is impossible. Cindy is quiet and after a while I assume she's fallen asleep and I begin to think about going to the lounge. I glance back at the bed and she looks to be fast asleep. Her chest is rising and falling evenly. Even that one glance has me all heated and I quickly turn away. I close my laptop and as quietly as I can I start to push my chair back.

I jump when Cindy speaks suddenly into the silence. "What are you doing?"

"Going to bed," I mutter.

I don't want to be rude and ignore her completely, but I don't want to get drawn into a conversation either. Her being near naked on my bed is a recipe for disaster. I hope my tone gives Cindy the hint that I don't want to talk, but it doesn't.

"I guess it's too late to continue working," she says.

"Uh huh," I grunt, as I push back my chair and stand.

"Were you working on The Macau?" she asks quickly.

God, it's like she thinks we're teenagers at a sleepover or something. I glance at her. She is up on her elbows and staring at me. "No," I say.

"Oh."

"It's late. I should get some sleep."

"Yes, it's late. You should get some sleep, but can we just talk for a bit." Her voice sounds chatty and wide awake.

"What's so important that it can't wait until the morning?"

"Oh nothing. I just thought we could talk a bit, you know? We could talk about The Macau, if you like."

The last thing on my mind was to stay here and talk to her about The Macau.

"I'd love to talk to you about The Macau, but probably not at this time of the morning. Perhaps we'll go over it over breakfast."

I look at her as I say it, expecting her to look a little sheepish. Instead, she looks like she hasn't heard a word I've said. Her eyes are all over my body, taking in my abs, my legs. I have to stop this, because if she keeps looking at me like this, I know exactly what will happen.

"Goodnight," I say.

She looks up at my face and now she looks a little sheepish, but also a little sly. That look that women get when they know what they want. She gives me a half-smile and I hurriedly move towards the lounge. The longer I stay here with her, the more dangerous the situation gets. I step through to the next room, and go to pull the door closed.

"Leave it open," she says softly.

I turn back to her, but this time, she isn't messing about. That scared look is back on her face.

"Please," she adds.

"Fine," I agree with a sigh.

ALEX

I leave the door open and for good measure, I leave the lamp on. As much as I want Cindy to go to sleep and stop fucking tempting me the way she is, I don't want her to be afraid. I go to the couch and lay down. It's anything but comfortable. My knees sit on the arm and my feet dangle off the end, and I know they'll be dead in the morning. But I can hardly turf her out of the bed now.

Even in the dark I can feel her eyes on me. I close my own eyes, hoping she will take the hint and do the same. She speaks again after a few minutes, dispelling my notion that she might make this easy. Doesn't she know what she's doing to me here? Clearly not if her words are anything to go by.

"You're too big for that couch," she says. "The bed is big enough for both of us." Her tone isn't flirty; she's just stating a fact.

I make a grunting sound and hope she'll leave it at that, but of course, she doesn't.

"Why don't you just come and get into the bed and then I

won't have to feel guilty about turfing you out of your own bed."

"Because if I do that, I guarantee you neither of us will get any sleep," I growl.

This finally shuts her up.

"Oh!" She snaps her mouth closed and falls silent.

I let some time pass before I open my eyes, but only to tiny slits. If Cindy is still awake, I don't want her to see that and start with the questions again. I can't resist looking at her.

The lamp provides light for me to see her. Her eyes are closed, but I don't think she's sleeping. She isn't underneath the covers, and she keeps moving her legs. Inch by inch, her robe is moving upwards, revealing the creamy white skin of her thighs.

She moves again and I know if her robe moves even an inch more, she's going to be flashing her pussy at me. It makes me feel like a pervert to think that she is unaware of how much of herself she is revealing to me. The thought doesn't make me feel bad. Instead I get even more turned on at the thought of her forbidden flesh.

She moves again and the silk robe shifts again. There can only be one inch left between the edge of her robe and heaven. It drives me crazy. I can't just lay here and not do anything about this.

I get up from the couch and stalk towards Cindy. Her eyes open as I am halfway to her and I know she wasn't sleeping at all. And she knew exactly what she was doing too. I keep my eyes firmly on hers. I'm kind of pissed off now. She's fucking teasing me, knowing I can't let anything happen between us.

I reach the side of the bed and look down at her laid out seductively. I want to reach out and pull that robe apart.

"Changed your mind about getting in with me?" Her smile full of fake innocence.

"No," I bark.

God, I want to rip that robe away from her curves. Instead, I reach down and pull her robe together. Then I tug at the duvet so I can pull it free of her. I pull it up over her and tuck it in tightly.

"There," I say, finally allowing myself to look at her properly. "Now stay beneath the covers."

It takes every ounce of self-control I have to turn away from her. Before I have even taken a step, she's talking again, teasing me. Her teasing is a mistake, because I only have so much self-control, and she's a hair-breaths away from pushing me past my endurance.

"Why do I have to stay beneath the covers?" she asks in a teasing voice.

I don't turn around to look at her. "Because if you push that sheet away, I'll take it as an invitation to fuck you. And once that happens, there is no going back."

I start to walk away again, knowing that now she under-stands the stakes, she'll stop messing with me. I don't have to look to know she is wearing a shocked expression. She won't be asking any more questions of me tonight. In fact, I think she'll actually just go to fucking sleep and leave me alone now.

But I underestimate Cindy. I hear a rustling noise from behind me and then she speaks again.

"I was starting to think you would never get the hint," she says breathily from behind me.

I can't help myself. I stop and turn back to her. She's pushed the sheet away again. I make a low growling sound in my throat and I cover the distance between me and the bed in two long strides.

"You shouldn't have done that, Cindy," I say from between clenched teeth, as I climb on top of her. Her body is supple and her skin is baby-soft.

"I know. It was a mistake, but I ..." she agrees as she lifts her head to meet my kiss.

She doesn't get a chance to say anything else as I crush my lips against hers. Fire floods my veins, moving through my whole body as Cindy's tongue snakes into my mouth. I can feel her writhing beneath me, her hands all over my body.

A voice in the back of my mind whispers to me, telling me this is wrong. This could ruin everything. Too much is at stake. This isn't about my pleasure. It's about Babushka. Don't think with your dick, the voice scolds.

I ignore the voice.

Too late for that now.

I move my mouth from Cindy's and let my tongue trail up her jawbone. Her skin is like warm silk. I nibble on her earlobe. I push myself up onto my knees and reaching down

I do what I've been craving to do since she ran in here all wild-eyed with fright. I pull her flimsy robe open. As I figured, she's buck-naked underneath it. The sight of her body sends a pulse of pleasure slamming through my cock.

There's truly no going back now.

I grab her ankles, pull apart those gorgeous long legs I'd been lusting after, and look down at her open pussy. I gaze at the small blonde locks shaved into a neat triangle, the pretty whorls of pink flesh, the engorged clit with its inner white bud showing, and the tiny, little hole that is dripping with her arousal. If this doesn't look like heaven, I don't know what does.

I run my fingers down Cindy's throat all the way to her stomach. Goose bumps rise on her flawless skin as my fingers dip lower still. I insert my thick finger into that warm throbbing hole. She jerks, clenches, and arches her body. I look down at my dark finger buried inside her white body, and a thought flashes into my head:

Mine. All mine. Only mine.

The thought is not tentative or newly born. It is fully grown and utterly fierce. Like a lion guarding its hunting ground, its mate, its life. I lean forward and flick my tongue over her clit. Cindy gasps as her hands comb through my hair. Her smell and taste flood my senses. I swear this girl was created to drive men mad. I pull my finger out of her and slip my tongue in, and she moans helplessly.

Her body jerks with surprise when I suck her whole pussy into my mouth, but the pleasure is so forbidden, so unexpected, so keenly anticipated, she comes in a gush of cum. Her sweet juices fill my mouth and run down my throat. I keep her inside my mouth while I wait for her body to stop convulsing. It seems as if her orgasm goes on and on. When it finally ebbs away she lifts her head and looks down at me with wide eyes.

"Wow, that was so freaking amazing."

"I'm not finished yet," I tell her.

"Not so fast. It's your turn now," she says in a sultry voice, as she pushes my boxers down. My cock snaps out, tight and heavy, and her eyes become saucers. She doesn't take her gaze off my erection as she speaks in an awed voice. "I guessed you'd be big, but … Jesus Christ, Alex. I'm not very good at math and measurements, but *that* has to be at least twelve inches long."

"I've always had a thing for girls who don't have a head for math and measurements," I murmur.

"That's because we're better at giving head, aren't we?" she coos as she wraps her soft palm around my cock admiringly.

I suck in a breath of pure shock as my cock goes wild at her touch. Lust rages inside me and works me to a frenzy. No woman has ever got me like this. Not even when I was a teenager.

She moves her mouth closer, but I grab her shoulders and keep her at arm's length. "If you get your delicious mouth anywhere near my cock, I'm going to come right away."

Cindy takes her hand away from me.

Instantly, I miss the warmth of her touch and the intense pleasure she sent through my body, but I don't have to miss it for long. She puts her hands on my sides and pulls me back down on top of her.

Our lips meet again.

As I kiss her, she moves her hips, moving her wet pussy against my cock. I can feel the heat coming off it in waves. I have to be inside of her. I have to have her right now. I push off her, vaulting off the bed I reach for my suitcase. I grab the packet of condoms from it and as I walk towards her, I rip one open and roll it on to my dick.

I crawl over Cindy's body and capture her mouth again. Deepening the kiss, I push one hand into her hair. Her hands are on my back, roaming, caressing, bringing my skin to life. She arches her body up from the mattress and presses it against mine. I can feel her hard, little nipples against my chest.

I move my mouth from hers and reach down between us and grab my cock. I bring it to Cindy's opening, and marvel at how soaking wet she is, how ready for me she is. She gives me a smile drunk with lust. Her eyelids are half-closed as I tease her, moving my cock in a circle around the edge of her sweet pussy.

Her face changes when I ram into her in one brutal stroke. The look of surprise goes in a second, then her face twists with pleasure as I push all the way in and fill her up. Her pussy is warm and deliciously tight. I begin to move inside of her, stretching her out, making her mine. She moans and wraps her legs around my waist, grabbing at my ass and pushing me deeper inside her.

I angle my body so my cock rubs over her G-spot with each thrust. Each time my cock slams into her, she makes an 'ahh' sound. The sound is so full of primal need that it drives me all the way to the edge. I have to force myself to think of something else to keep from coming.

I stop moving, lean down and kiss her mouth. It's a deep, passionate kiss and it makes her melt under me. I kiss her neck and run my tongue up and down it.

Cindy's hips start thrusting desperately. She needs the friction. I start moving in time with her, making each thrust fill her right up. I can feel fire moving through my cock and up into my stomach. Cindy's hands move up my back and then she wraps her arms around my shoulders. Then her body starts to spasm.

She digs her nails into my back as her orgasm comes on. Her face contorts as she shouts my name and climaxes. Hard. So hard her body becomes stiff as a board and I feel her pussy clamping around my cock like a clenched fist.

I up the pace of my thrusts, short fast strokes that make her cry out incoherently. She sucks in a gasping breath as her eyes roll back in her head. The breathy noise of Cindy trying to recover from her orgasm pushes me over the edge.

My climax slams through me, tightening my muscles, making my stomach flutter. Pleasure radiates through me as I come inside Cindy. She clings to me, her face pressed against my neck. It feels as if we are hanging still in time, suspended in a world of pure pleasure.

As the pleasure fades, I roll off Cindy and lie beside her and get my breathing under control. It hits me then what I have done, but it doesn't feel like a mistake lying here beside her. It feels right.

I feel the mattress dip slightly as Cindy turns to face me. I turn onto my side and face her. She looks so beautiful with no make-up and her hair still mussed up from the sex.

She leans forward and kisses me. It's not the desperate kiss of earlier when we were both clawing at each other like unleashed demons. It's a tender, sensual kiss. A dangerous kiss. One that tells me it's not going to be so easy to let Cindy go.

She pulls back and smiles at me, a playful smile that makes her eyes twinkle.

"You can go back to the couch now," she says. "If you still want to."

I grin at her. "You know, I think I'll be ok here."

CINDY

I wake up and am immediately conscious of Alex lying beside me. I sit up, holding the sheet across my chest. The memories of last night flood in. The flirting over dinner and drinks, the awkwardness that fell between us, the terror of thinking there was a ghost in my room, and of course the way I practically threw myself at Alex.

I came to his room because I was genuinely scared, but then I started to want his touch, to want him. I'm telling myself it's because I was terrified and terrified people do weird, unreasonable things, but I know it's more than that.

When he told me if I moved the sheet again, he wouldn't be able to stop himself from fucking me, I should have left the sheet on. But I didn't. Of course, I didn't. How could I? I wanted him. I've wanted him from day one and I want things to change between us.

But now, in the cold hard light of day, I know it was probably a mistake. Things can't change between us. I'm his employee, nothing more. He told me so himself. Yesterday. If I hadn't thrown myself at him, he would never have taken me.

I debate trying to sneak away before Alex wakes up, but I remind myself I'm a grown ass woman who isn't in the habit of running away from her problems. No, I'm not going to sneak off. I'm going to wait for him to wake up and explain that I'm sorry about last night and ask him if we can just put it behind us. That's the grown-up thing to do. The right thing to do.

I let out a long sigh and jump with horror when Alex laughs beside me. I glance at him, instantly assaulted by how damned good he looks first thing in the morning. His face is softer than usual as sleep still stretches across it and his hair is all deliciously mussed. It takes a lot of will power for me to not reach down and brush his hair back from his face.

"I thought you were still sleeping," I say. My voice sounds throaty. As if I've been giving him blowjobs all night long, which, I suppose is what I have been doing.

"No. I'm awake," he says.

I nod, not really hearing him. I know I have to say this now and get it over with and just hope we can maintain some semblance of a professional relationship.

"Look, Alex, about last night. What happened, I agree with you that it shouldn't have."

"Good. We are in agreement." He pushes himself up into a sitting position.

I turn slightly so we're facing each other. "I honestly don't know what came over me. Believe it or not, I'm not in the habit of sneaking into people's rooms in the middle of the night, then having sex with them."

"Actually, I'm not in the habit of sleeping with my employees either," he says.

I smile, a shy smile full of the hope I feel. This isn't as awkward as I thought it was going to be and I'm starting to think we'll be ok, that we can just forget this ever happened and move past it. Forgetting it might be a stretch. I can barely look at Alex without remembering how amazing his cock felt inside of me, how his kiss awoke parts of me I didn't know were dormant. But I can move past it. I think.

"So we can both agree it shouldn't have happened," I go on.

Alex nods.

"And that it can't … no, not can't, but shouldn't, happen again."

Alex's eyes are twinkling, and I get the impression my discomfort is amusing him.

"We're both adults. We can move forward and put this one night down to drinking a bit too much and getting caught up in the moment," I finish.

"There's only one problem with that, Cindy," Alex says.

I feel dread in my stomach, even though he's smiling. He's going to tell me we can't work together after this or something. I'm going to lose The Macau because of one stupid, amazing mistake.

"What?" I ask quietly.

He looks me straight in the eye, his gaze so intense I want to look away, but I find that I can't. He holds me as surely as if he was holding me physically in place.

"I didn't drink too much," he says.

As he says it, he pushes a hand into my hair and pulls my face towards his. Our lips meet. I kiss Alex back as if my life depended on it. I am completely unable to stop myself because my body betrays me and responds to him. My clit starts throbbing with need, and my skin is tingling as if I've been walking in a storm. On their own accord my hands move out to touch Alex's chest, his arms, his back.

I don't know what exactly comes over me when I'm around Alex, but it's potent. It's like he casts some sort of spell over me, a spell that makes me lose all sense or self-preservation or responsibility. I don't care about the consequences of my actions at all. I just want him.

I feel myself moving, my body acting without my head's permission. I throw one leg over Alex and sit straddling him, kissing him, drinking him in. His hands move up and down my back and over my sides. I can feel his hard cock pressing against my pussy. My head screams that I have to stop this. Once (okay, more than once, but since it happened in one night, it can be classified as happening in one long continuous timeframe) can be classified as a mistake, but doing it in the harsh glare of sobriety ... I tear myself from his kiss.

"Alex, we can't do this," I gasp.

"We can't?" he replies with not an ounce of seriousness in his voice.

"It would be a big mistake."

"Mmmm."

"I work for you and we should remain professional. I hate the idea of women who sleep with their bosses." I frown down at Alex who is smiling.

"Uh ... huh."

"Is that all you can say?" I demand.

"No, but I'd find it much easier to believe you if you weren't straddling me and rubbing your hot wet pussy across my cock while you're saying it."

"I ... oh."

He's right, of course. I don't want to talk him out of this at all. I want him to talk me into it. To tell me it's ok for us to do this again. He seems to get the message and he obliges.

"Sure, you work for me, but we're also kind of on holiday. We're obviously hungry for each other, so why don't we get it out of our systems while we're here. Then when we go home, we can have that professional relationship you want without the chemistry."

I have to admit I like the sound of that. "So just a bit of no strings fun that ends when we go back to London?" I ask.

He shrugs. "If that's what you want."

"I can work with that," I say as I lean back down and kiss Alex again.

Can I though? Can I really let him go when my time here is over? Of course I can, I tell myself. It's not going to be any worse than letting him go now would be, and at least this way, I get some fun first. Who knows, maybe he'll be right and this will get it out of my system and I won't want him like this once we get home, the law of diminishing returns and all that. In my heart, I know it won't work like that, but I cling to the idea almost as tightly as I cling to him.

I reach down for Alex's cock, needing to feel him inside me, but he grabs my wrist and stops me. I pull my lips away from his. Has he changed his mind? His smile tells me no.

"I want to eat you out first," he says in a low husky voice that makes my pussy clench and a rush of liquid flood me.

He puts his hands on my shoulders and bucks his hips, rolling me off him and onto my back. I lay flat, looking up at him as he looks down hungrily at me. He kisses me, a quick kiss that leaves me wanting more.

"Ready?" he asks in that same husky, sex-filled voice.

I nod, and he brings his head down to my body and runs his tongue over my skin, between my breasts and down my stomach. He pushes my legs wide apart and I hold my breath, waiting to feel him suck my whole pussy greedily into his mouth the way he did last night, but instead, he skips past it. Ah, a different technique, a far more torturous one. He lifts one of my legs and runs his tongue up my inner thigh, sending shivers through my body. He licks back down to my knee and then moves to my other leg.

His touch is light, teasing, and it's driving me wild. He is waking up every cell in my body, filling me with a deep need that makes my clit throb, and my pussy craves his cock. I can't get any release as he teases me mercilessly, priming me for what's to come.

Finally, he releases my leg and he kneels between my legs, looking at my pussy. My legs are spread wide and I know all of me is on show, but I don't feel self-conscious, I feel utterly shameless. Empowered even. He looks up and meets my eye for a second.

The uncontrollable desire in his eyes sweeps a shiver up my spine.

He reaches out with one hand and he runs two fingers between my pussy lips. They graze lightly over my labia and then they finally reach my swollen clit. I am so turned on, so ready for his touch, that I'm trembling all over. Even his light touch sends a bolt of electricity through me and I gasp at the intensity of the feeling.

He grins at me and then he lowers himself and I can see only the top of his head and his hands. He lifts one of my legs and hooks it over his shoulder, his hand playing over my thigh. He holds my other hip in his hand, and finally, when I don't think I can take this anymore, he finds my clit with his tongue.

I'm so ready, so swollen, that the touch is almost painful. I gasp, forcing myself to stay in place, to take the sweet pain that flows through me. It only lasts for a few seconds and then my body adjusts to his touch and it is only pleasure, raw unadulterated pleasure that consumes me whole.

He swirls his tongue around on my clit, licking me back and forth and then side to side. I can already feel my climax building. Alex has primed me so completely I'm actually already on the verge of a climax before he even touches my clit.

Now, he sucks on my clit, pulling it into his mouth, his tongue circling it, working around it. His touch is rough and a little bit aggressive and I fucking love it. He gives a hard suck, one that makes me catch my breath, and I hear a pained 'ahh' sound leaving my mouth as I exhale.

My hands ball into fists beside me and my back arches as he continues his wonderful assault on my senses. My hips buck of their own accord, pressing my clit harder against his tongue as he releases it from his sucking grip and goes back to meticulously licking the sensitive petals of flesh around it.

When he presses down in the center of my clit with his tongue, the sensation is so intense, so unexpected, I feel my upper body being lifted clean off the bed. I moan his name as I flop back down, barely in control of myself now. My whole body is tingling, my stomach is rolling, and my clit is pulsing with the orgasm that's about to explode through me at any moment.

I pant for air, but no matter how much I get, it doesn't seem to be enough. My head spins as I feel myself coming undone. My moans turn into little animal-like whimpers as he works me into a frenzy. He never stops for even a second.

He just lets the pressure build and build.

Just when I think I can't take the relentless, sweet torture anymore, he pushes his fingers into my pussy, and I hear myself shouting his name over and over as my climax finally breaks, the release flooding through me as my body takes over from my mind, and carries me away on a carpet of ecstasy.

My eyes roll in my head, unfocused, unseeing. I can hear my own pulse as the blood rushes to my head. I scream Alex's name again as I hit the peak of my orgasm and then for a moment, everything is still and black and I can't see or hear anything. The blackness only lasts for a second, then I am thrown back onto the rollercoaster of pleasure that I am riding.

Then it's over. My senses come rushing back to me and my limbs feel heavy, sated. I pull in a deep breath and I hear myself panting, trying to get myself back under some sort of control. Alex doesn't wait around for me to get control of myself.

He pushes my leg away, rolls a rubber onto his ramrod stiff cock, then gets onto all fours and crawls up my body. It's an incredible turn on to see this powerful beast of a man claim me. He starts running his tongue over my skin once more. His lips find mine and I taste my orgasm on his tongue, on his lips. My juices glisten on his chin and throat.

He pulls back from my lips and without warning, takes hold of me, and flips me onto my stomach. He runs his fingers through my slit again and the squelching sounds reminds me of how incredibly wet I am, how much I still want him. I ignore the heavy feeling in my body and I push myself up onto all fours, inviting Alex in.

He moves his fingers away from me and he runs his nails down my spine. I curve my body, pressing myself into his touch. He moves his hands up and down my sides and then over my ass, and then I feel his cock, hard and huge on the edge of my pussy.

He takes hold of my hips and as he thrusts into me, he pulls on them, moving me onto him, impaling me on that huge cock of his. My breath catches in my throat as he fills me, stretching my pussy unbearably to accommodate his size.

He isn't holding back. He keeps his grip on my hips tight, pulling me all the way back towards him with each thrust, and pounds into me with such long hard strokes that they make me jerk forward like a toy without any control of its own movements I am consumed by him once more, by the carnal pleasure of having him rut inside of me.

He takes one hand off my hip, but it doesn't matter. I am moving with him, matching his rhythm without his guidance. I am in a frenzy, almost animalistic in my need for him to fill me.

I feel his hand moving over the front of my body, caressing my stomach and then it moves lower, and he presses his fingers against my clit. It feels like he's pressed something hot. It sparks against me as my already tender clit screams at his rough, insistent touch.

His name is wrenched from my lips in a cry that I don't recognize as my own voice as my orgasm explodes from nowhere, bursting forth through my full body. I can't suck in another breath and I hover, airless, weightless. I call his name again and again, as if that single word is my anchor to reality as I float up to the clouds.

I feel my arms give way and I fall onto my elbows, but I don't stop moving. My pussy clenches tightly around Alex's cock as another orgasm assaults my senses, bringing me even closer to undone. I call out Alex's name and then I let out a stream of unintelligible mutterings as my body screams with pleasure.

My orgasm begins to recede and I am me again. It feels as if it was only his name and his cock that kept me anchored, and stopped me from floating away and losing myself completely. He moves his fingers from my clit and I am both relieved and disappointed that the terrible, wonderful touch on it is over.

I feel his hand wrapping in my hair and he pulls me backwards. I come up easily, the stinging pain in my scalp only intensifies the pleasure I can feel in other parts of my body. He pulls me upright, against his chest and he wraps his arms around my waist, holding me in place against him.

I can feel his warm breath tickling my neck as he kisses it, and when he starts to whisper my name, I can hear the shaky quality of his voice. I reach an arm up and wrap it around his head, turning my head to the side and kissing him deeply as he thrusts hard into me.

He kisses me back, a rough kiss that tells me he's on the edge himself now. I clench my pussy, tightening my hold on him and he moans into my mouth. He pulls his lips away from mine and drags them along my shoulder, then I feel him pressing his face against my neck, breathing me in. He says my name in that lust filled voice that moves me so much and then he comes, his cock jerking and twitching, his cum pouring into the condom. And I mourn for that fact. I mourn that I cannot feel his hot seed inside me.

His whole body goes rigid and he doesn't breathe. His arms tighten around me, holding me to him so tightly it's like he wants us to be one. Then he relaxes, his muscles softening again, and sucks in a big breath. He holds me tightly against him.

Even when his cock slips out of me, spent, he still holds onto me. Then he pulls me to the side and we flop down on the mattress, my back still pressed against his chest. I can feel his chest heaving as I lay in his arms, enjoying the moment of closeness, enjoying knowing I can make him come just as undone as he can make me.

CINDY

The delicious afterglow of fabulous morning sex lays like a soft cloud around me, when Alex springs it upon me that Babushka told him last night that she was going to get up early today so that we could all enjoy a family breakfast together … which means, I have about fifteen minutes to get showered and ready.

I jump out of bed with a squeal. His laughter follows me as I run naked back through the connected door between our rooms.

Less than fifteen minutes later, I knock on his door. He grabs me and pulls me towards his body and I can immediately feel how hard he is for me.

"I don't think Babushka would mind if we are a little late," he whispers in my ear as his hand slips under my skirt.

I want to protest. I really do, but as soon as his fingers reach my slit, my legs part for him. A small moan escapes my lips as he picks me up like a damn caveman and carries me to his bed and throws me on it.

Everyone is at the table by the time we arrive, but the mood around the table seems somber. Both the ice sisters seem to be on their best behavior. At least they're not whispering about me in Russian today.

Babushka looks at Alex, then me. There is a twinkle in her eyes. "Neither of you look like you've had much sleep."

"As a matter of fact, none of us got any sleep last night thanks to all the screeching and wailing. Quite an achievement considering I'm in a whole other wing," Petra puts in sarcastically.

So much for her being on her best behavior. I feel my face turning red. We didn't make that much noise, I might have screamed once or twice, or maybe three times, but that was it. The other two times I bit down on the pillow.

Alex glares at Petra, and Babushka throws her a look that stops her from saying anything else, but she doesn't need to say anything else. She's already made me sound cheap and slutty. She looks down at her plate with a little smirk.

Babushka looks at me. "I can still remember when I made love all night long."

The ice sisters gasp in shock.

"What?" Babushka asks innocently. "You think I never had sex. How do you think your mother came into being?" She turns to me again. "Why don't you two have a nice relaxing day in your room? Just lock the door, get naked, curl up in bed, and watch movies together."

I feel myself blushing again and I take a long drink of my

orange juice to try to hide my face. The thought of being locked away in the bedroom with Alex naked. There'll be no movies watched. I know exactly what will happen if we're left alone together.

There's no denying that Alex knows his way around a woman. The sex last night was good, but this morning was something else. It's by far the best sex I've ever had, and even though I am still sore from it, I'd happily risk more soreness to have another go of that kind of pleasure.

Even just sitting so close to him at the table is enough to have me on edge, aware of his body so close to mine. A couple of times, our thighs brush against each other beneath the table and my clit throbs in response, a mixture of pain and desire. God, it's incredible how badly I want him.

"Cindy?" Alex says.

Every eye at the table is on me and I realize he has said something I've missed.

"Sorry," I mutter. "I was a million miles away." Thank God, people can't read thoughts. I take another sip of my orange juice and wish I could stop making such a fool of myself.

"I was just telling everyone how much you enjoy riding," Alex says innocently enough, but immediately I have a flashback of me bouncing on his hard cock.

I choke on a mouthful of juice and, thank God, I do not spray orange juice all over the table, but it throws me into a fit of coughing. Petra and Anastasia start laughing at my reaction. Babushka looks at me with concern, and Alex thumps my back.

He looks deep into my eyes. "Did I get that wrong, Cindy?"

You so know you didn't, I think to myself. Hell, we've already done a spot of riding this morning. It's clear he wanted to get a reaction. Well, two could play this game.

"No, you didn't get that wrong. I *love* riding. There's nothing to beat the sensation of being on top of a strong, powerful, beast, and feeling it move underneath you. It makes the blood in my veins sing," I say throatily, feigning the same innocence he did.

Now it's Alex's turn to almost choke on his breakfast and I smile into my glass. That'll teach him.

"You should take her riding one day while you're here Alex. Take her out to the creek. It's really romantic there," Babushka puts in, saving me from any comeback Alex was thinking up.

"I already have. We've even been on a ride to the lake," Alex says.

"Take her to the creek, but no galloping though. I don't want any accidents. Cindy needs to give you lots of big healthy babies," Babushka adds with a cheeky grin.

I swear that old lady says these things on purpose. I squirm in my seat with embarrassment as I try to smile nonchalantly, the way a real fiancée would.

"I'll remember that, Babushka," Alex says with a mocking smile. "Although, I think it'll be a long while before we start thinking about babies. I've got my hands full with just Cindy."

"Don't wait too long now," Babushka replies. She is no longer smiling. "I would love to see my great, great nephew or niece before I leave this body." She turns to me and leans forward. "Will you give me a great grandchild before I die?" she whispers.

Confused by the undercurrents I do not understand, I look to Alex for help. To my surprise, the blood has drained from his face.

The ice sisters are watching me with a mixture of dislike and glee, which isn't helping matters at all. But worse, I really, really, really hate lying to Babushka. More than I ever thought possible. She is a grand old lady with a heart of gold and Alex and I are cheating her. I wipe my mouth on my napkin and stand.

"If you'll all excuse me, I'm going to go up to my room for a while. Change of air from London, I suspect," I explain apologetically.

"Of course, dear. You relax." She smiles.

There is something lost and sad about her smile. As if I haven't passed a crucial test. I want to reach out and hug her, hold her thin body close to mine, and tell her, I would have a dozen of Alex's babies for her … but I can't. I'm only pretending. This is not my life. I have another life in London. In a week or two I will be gone, and never see her again.

"Oh, and I'm sorry about your heating," she adds. "Someone will come by today to fix it."

I smile my thanks and scuttle away before Petra can make any more jokes at my expense. I am halfway up the stairs when I hear footsteps behind me. I don't need to turn around to know it's Alex.

"You made a sharp exit there," he says, catching up with me

"Yeah. It's funny how everyone making jokes at my expense made me not want to stay at the table," I snap as I take the stairs two at a time.

As I reach the top of the stairs, Alex grabs my wrist, spinning me to face him.

"It was in the job description," he says, his eyes cold and hard. "Don't forget. This is a job."

The shock of seeing him so cold and distant is like being doused with freezing water. "I'm sorry." My voice sounds small and foreign, even to me. "I'm just tired. I guess I might take a nap after all."

He walks me to my door. "Get anything you need and come to my room in five minutes. You can nap there," he says.

He walks away before I can respond, which is probably a good thing, because he wouldn't have liked my response one little bit. Yes, I work for him, but if he thinks he can order me around like that, he has another think coming.

I go into my room and sit down on the edge of the bed. I don't doubt that Alex was serious about what he said, but I wonder what he will do when the five minutes pass and I don't go into his room. Will he come to get me?

The five minutes feel like an eternity, but they pass, and after ten minutes, I realize he's as stubborn as I am. He won't come to me, because he told me to go to him and I didn't. He's so frustrating.

I decide I am not going to just sit here thinking about Alex. The longer I sit on the end of the bed looking at the connecting door between my room and Alex's, the more likely I am to cave in and go to him. I stand up and grab my cell phone and then I move into the bathroom. I think it's time I had a long soak in the beautiful big bathtub. I start the taps running and then I call Raven.

"How's it going?" she asks.

I sigh loudly. "That *is* a very good question."

She giggles. "I knew you'd meet your match one of these days."

I throw a generous amount of vibrant blue bath salts into the water. "Well, he's not what I expected."

"You slept with him, didn't you?" she says.

"What the hell? How did you know?"

"I didn't," she says, and I can hear the smile in her voice. "But I do now. So? How was it?"

"It was freaking amazing," I admit. "You know how they say the earth beneath my feet moved. Yeah, there was an earthquake underneath my butt. I know it's a bad idea, and I know I'm living the cliché by sleeping with the boss. And I did remind myself of all of the reasons why sleeping with him is a bad idea, but everything I know and believe passionately becomes a puff of smoke that blows away when I'm with him."

"So what are you guys going to do? Make a go at it?"

I bite my lip. "No, he told me clearly he's not into long relationships. We've agreed that we'll have fun while we're here.

You know, get it out of our systems so that when we go home, we can go back to a professional relationship."

"So you're getting half of the Macau. You're having fun with someone you click with. And yet I get the impression you think it's a bad thing."

"I … I'm not sure it'll be out of my system by the time we come home. Or ever. I'm scared I'm letting myself fall for him," I admit slowly.

"Right," she says with a sigh.

"What should I do, Raven?"

"I learned a long time ago, that you must never help anyone make a decision on something like this. Only you know what is best for you, Cindy. I'll always be here for you."

"To pick up the pieces?"

"Or to celebrate because you took what you wanted with both hands and to hell with the consequences."

"Thanks, I feel so much better now," I say dryly.

She laughs. "You'll thank me properly at your wedding."

"Very funny."

"Stranger things have happened, Cindy. Look at what happened to me."

"You know what?"

"What?"

"I miss you, Raven. I really do. And I can't wait to see you again."

"Well, I'll be coming to London soon. Let's have a pizza night like the good ole days. Just you and me."

"Okay," I say happily.

We chat for another couple of minutes, then I end the call. I go back into the bedroom and strip off. Leaving my phone on the bed, I go into the bathroom again. Shutting the taps off I pour essential oil into the bath tub and climb into the gorgeously hot, sweet smelling water.

I sit down, enjoying the silky feel of the water on my swollen pussy. Laying back I close my eyes and relax. Raven is right. If I'm going to get hurt, I might as well have fun along the way. That way I'll have nothing to regret. I took the bull by the horns. So what if I lose a little blood along the way. There is majesty in dying on the horns of the bull.

I lay in the bath, and my mind goes to the way Alex's eyes are so intense when he looks at me. The way his kisses taste. The way he lights my body up in ways I never even knew were possible. I can't help but smile as I remember the way I felt wrapped up in his arms.

I'm in so much trouble here.

I am already in way too deep.

I force myself to think about something else, but it's hard. Eventually, I give up and get out of the bath. I wrap myself in a large white towel and go to the bedroom. I dry my hair and slip on a pair of leggings and a comfy top.

I think I am more than a little disappointed that Alex never came to me.

My intention is to go through to the lounge and watch a

movie, but when I look at the bed, it looks so comfortable, so inviting … and I really am exhausted.

I move to the big beautiful bed. There are no ghosts in the daytime. I tell myself I'm just going to lay down for five minutes. Who sleeps on such a beautiful day? The sun is shining in through the tall windows.

I have barely laid down when my eyes close and I fall into a deep, dreamless sleep.

CINDY

I wake up and stretch, relishing the feeling of my spine cracking. Then I sit up feeling refreshed and rested. The nap has done wonders for me. I glance out of the window and my jaw drops when I see the summer sun is already so low. No, that can't be right. It's still morning time surely. I look at my watch, sure I must have made some mistake, but no, I haven't. It is almost six p.m.

I have slept the entire day away!

My stomach rumbles reminding me that I haven't eaten since breakfast and I wonder if Alex came to see if I wanted to go for lunch, or if he's still mad because I didn't obey his command to go to his room. Dinner is usually around eight here from what I can gather so I get up and get changed into a yellow dress. I put on some make-up and I'm just running a comb through my hair when there's a quiet knock at my bedroom door.

My stomach flutters for a second, but then I realize if it was Alex, he would have used the connecting door. The excitement turns to curiosity. I go to the door and pull it open. I smile when I see Babushka standing there.

"I wondered if you would like to accompany me on a short walk before dinner," she says with a smile.

"Oh yes, I'd love to," I say. "I'll just be a moment."

Babushka nods and smiles. She has grown on me quickly and I very much like the idea of spending time with her. I also think the fresh air will do me good after a day cooped up in my room.

She has her cane, but she links her other hand through the crook of my elbow. She is slow on her feet, but she's sure footed and we walk slowly down the stairs, through the dining room, the conservatory, and into the grounds.

Babushka leads me in the opposite direction to the stables and I get a good look at the house itself from this direction. The place really is one of the most impressive buildings I've ever seen, and in such good repair too. Babushka sees me looking at the house and she smiles.

"It's in pretty good condition considering parts of it are almost five hundred years old, isn't it," she says.

"Wow. I knew it was old, but I had no idea it was that old. It's in excellent condition."

"The house has been passed down the family for generations. Along with the values needed to take care of a house like this. Or should I say a team of staff who know how to do that," she smiles, that irrepressible twinkle coming back into her eyes.

I laugh along with her and she goes on.

"I'm sure some of my older ancestors wouldn't approve of the changes I made to the place, but it had to be done. Growing up, the house was beautiful, but it was like something from the dark ages. It badly needed electricity, gas, and modern plumbing installed. It was a big job. Some would say a man's job, but my brother was a weak man, so I took it upon myself to oversee the transformation. It's a never-ending job, insanely expensive affair keeping old houses from falling into disrepair."

I stare at her curiously. The more I learn about Babushka, the more fascinating she becomes. She is most definitely the matriarch of the family. They all respect her and do what she wishes, but she is so much more than that. She's clever, and even now I imagine pulling the wool over her eyes would be damned hard. Unless of course it's something she wants to believe. Like how her favorite nephew has found love. I feel another surge of guilt run through me, but as always, I remind myself I'm here to make an old woman very happy, to maybe give her her final wish.

"You must love this house very much," I say softly.

"I do. There was only once when I wanted to leave it. When my husband died. Then I wanted to die too. For years I grieved, wearing only black and walking all those empty corridors. I thought he would come back. Even just once. I thought he couldn't leave me just like that. I waited for the sound of footsteps, his laughter, an apparition. Anything. But he never did. Then one day I cast aside my black garments and I moved on. I never remarried or anything, and the house became my, well my obsession. I think certain family members were a little disappointed when I rallied and they realized they'd have to wait for me to die to get their hands on the house and my money."

"Oh, I'm sure that's not true," I gasp.

Babushka gives a wry laugh. "Oh, I'm sure it is true, but it is what it is. It seems they've had a rather long wait." She winks at me and I can't help but laugh at her healthy attitude towards it. I'm almost certain she's talking about the ice sisters, although I don't come out and ask her. Good on her for getting one up on those two.

"I can't speak for the rest of the family, but Alex speaks very highly of you, and I know he doesn't feel that way."

I don't know why I feel the need to defend Alex. I tell myself I'm saying it to make Babushka feel better, so that she knows she has at least one family member who loves her, but I'm not sure that's the real reason I'm saying it. It's as though I feel guilty for our deception and I'm making sure the end justifies the means. So what if we are lying to her, we're not harming anyone and it is making her happy and that is the most important thing.

"Why? Do you think he's my favorite?" Babushka quips, then laughs uproariously.

I join her. Who can blame her for favoring the family member who isn't just waiting for her to die so they can take her home and its contents?

"I always worried Alex would not find a nice girl, you know. I mean he's handsome, but he's so closed off. It takes a special girl to see beneath that harsh exterior. He wasn't always like that you know. When he was younger, he was always smiling, always laughing. But then his parents died and he changed. He became a stranger overnight. He was so angry with the world. He chose a path I would not have wished upon my enemy. It was a very difficult period."

Her eyes cloud over with the memories of that time.

"I really thought he was lost to us. Every night before I went to bed, I would pray that no policeman would come to my door to tell me he was dead. I was so desperate I used to pay people to keep tabs on him. I was so frightened, but God was merciful. He kept him safe. And now he is the man of this family."

She smiles at me.

"Don't tell anyone I told you this, but when Anton decided he was ready to ask for Petra's hand in marriage, he didn't go to her father for permission. He went to Alex. And do you know what Alex said? He told Anton that Petra was a grown woman who could make her own decisions, and he didn't need his permission. He needed Petra's."

I smile to myself. I love that Alex realized that the outdated tradition of asking for a male relative's permission to marry a woman is as good as treating her like a possession and that he wanted no part in doing such a thing. Babushka is right. I knew it before and I'm certain of it now. Beneath the harsh front Alex puts on is a man with a heart of gold.

That doesn't help me though. In some ways, I almost wish he was an asshole underneath the mask. That would make it so much easier to not fall for him.

"You seem a bit off today dear," Babushka says, astute as ever. "You and Alex haven't fallen out, have you?"

If circumstances were different I would have liked to pour

my heart out to her and tell her I'm falling for Alex and I think I'm going to get hurt, but I can't do that. And the last thing I want is for her to start fretting over our relationship. My job is to make her feel good not the opposite.

"No, not at all," I smile. "As Petra said, we got up to no good all night long."

Babushka erupted in laughter. "You really must have Alex take you riding tomorrow. There's nothing quite like the freedom of riding through the countryside to make you feel like a million rubles," Babushka jokes.

"Yes, I think I'd like to feel like a million rubles tomorrow," I agree with a grin.

"I can tell you now from experience there are many parts of these grounds where you and Alex can get naked and get up to no good," Babushka adds, that twinkle back in her eyes.

I just laugh at Babushka's lack of tact and impropriety. I will really miss this kind soul when I'm gone from here.

"I think it's almost time for dinner," Babushka says as we arrive back at the conservatory door. "Are you hungry?"

"Starving."

ALEX

I hate to admit it, but I'm actually pleased and more than a little impressed that Cindy disobeyed my direct order. As perverse as it seems it only makes me even more hungry for her. I spent all day thinking up ways she could pay for her insubordination.

From my window, I watch her walking back with Babushka. It should have made me happy seeing the two of them getting to know each other. Knowing how accurately I had predicted what Babushka would appreciate in a woman. But it didn't feel good. It was hollow. I was cheating Babushka. And the stakes were high. If she ever found out it would destroy her.

I make my way downstairs to the music room and have a drink on my own. The time alone is necessary. Dinner tonight will be informal, more like a party. Babushka has invited some friends too, some of whom are old friends of mine. Usually Natalia gets to come to these events because Babushka was living in hope I would find a girl and she knew Natalia had a thing for me. If she comes tonight though there will be fireworks for sure.

I stroll into the ballroom where we all gather and have a drink first. Extra chairs have been brought in and arranged in small, intimate circles around the room, but the majority of the guests are standing, chatting and catching up with each other. I can't help but notice Natalia's absence. I smile to myself. Babushka might be getting on in years, but she's as sharp as a razor blade, and she knows Natalia has always had a thing for me.

Yakov, an old friend, comes up to me. As he talks my eyes keep returning to the door every time it opens. Eventually, it opens and Babushka and Cindy walk in. Cindy looks as beautiful as ever in a bright lemon sundress. The color brings out her tan and the way she's laughing at something Babushka says makes her eyes sparkle.

"Is that her?" Yakov asks in Russian. "Your fiancée?"

I nod.

Yakov pats me on the back. "Whoa! You've got a beauty there, my son. I wouldn't let such a rare bird fly out of my hand if I were you."

What did he know? That 'rare bird' didn't actually belong to me. It only came into my hands at night when the pipes in its room disturbed it. I watch as Cindy leads Babushka to a chair and helps her into it.

Cindy sits down next to Babushka and I smile to myself. I love how attentive she is to her, how she really seems to be making the effort with her. I just wish that was all I loved about her. I wish I didn't love the way her eyes sparkle when she laughs, or the way her hair shines. I wish I didn't love those killer legs of hers or how they feel wrapped around me.

I feel my temper starting to rise as Cindy sits laughing with my aunt. I've spent all day trying to get her body out of my head. To forget the way her tight little pussy clenched around my cock. To forget the way she made me feel things I didn't think I could ever feel. And I failed miserably. I got no work done, and I couldn't even sleep for thinking about her, and now I'm tired and grumpy, and seeing her there looking so fucking hot, and her not even coming over to acknowledge me, gets on my last nerve.

I realize Yakov is saying something and I force myself to look away from Cindy and listen to him. It lasts for all of about four seconds before my eyes go back to her. Yakov laughs beside me.

"You've got it bad, Alex," he comments. "You can't take your eyes off her for even a second."

I'm mad at myself, but I have to play the part. "Why would I want to look at anyone or anything else when such a thing of beauty exists in my line of vision?"

Yakov bursts out laughing. "I never thought I'd see the day you become a poet. Ah, the power of love."

Babushka nods towards me, then Cindy stands and starts moving in my direction. She smiles shyly at me and I feel myself returning her smile. The whole room drops away. I forget I'm supposed to punish her. I forget everything except how wonderful she looks in her lemon dress. Yakov claps me good-naturedly on the shoulder and moves away.

"Babushka seems to think you can't take your eyes off me," she says, her tone light and teasing.

"Hmm," I grunt. "Well, I have to keep up the ruse, don't I?"

"Of course," Cindy says.

Does she look a little disappointed or is it just my imagination? She touches my arm and I lose my train of thought as her touch wakes up the raw craving inside me.

"Are you still mad at me for not coming to your room, Alex?" she asks.

How can I tell her I'm not angry with her, I'm angry with myself for allowing myself to think with my dick?

"It wasn't a request. And you directly disobeyed me," I say, looking around and noting that our conversation is not being overheard.

She looks shocked. "You're not kidding, are you? You seriously think I'm going to be ordered around like that."

"You are an employee, and I am your boss, so quite frankly, yes I do," I say.

She glances around then, flashes a stunningly sexy smile at me. Anyone looking will think we are flirting with each other. Even my dick thinks that. "Let's get something straight here, just so there's absolutely no confusion. My boss or not, you do not get to order me to your room to have sex with you."

Where the fuck did that come from? I smile at her with the same glaring intensity she is employing. "I did not ask you to come to my room to have sex. I had something important I wanted to tell you."

213

Her mouth drops open. "You didn't?"

"Right then. I'm glad that's cleared up. Looks like we've got the chemistry thing out of our systems and discovered we are anything but compatible. So … let's get back to the business at hand, shall we?"

She nods her head slowly, her eyes blank. "Yes, I think that's for the best."

"Yes," I lash out, angry at the easy way she gave up. "And while we're laying down ground rules, here's one of mine. When you get scared tonight, don't come running to my room."

It sounds petty even to my own ears once I've said it aloud and I want to take it back. I am such a dick. No wonder I had to pay a girl to pretend to like me for my aunt's sake.

She smiles at me, the fake smile she uses when she's about to take Petra down. I hate that I have pushed her into a place where she feels she has to use it on me.

"Don't worry I won't be bothering you tonight or any other night for that matter. If I get scared, I'll go and see Babushka."

"Are you going to introduce me then or are you scared she'll fall for my charms?" Yakov's brother, Vladimir says, coming over to join us.

It's bad timing. The atmosphere between Cindy and I isn't exactly warm and fuzzy, but the chemistry is still sizzling between us. Even though she makes me so angry I see red, I still want to grab her, throw her against a wall, and fuck the living daylights out of her. The look in her eyes tells me she would still let me do it.

"There's no chance of that," I say, forcing a laugh. "Cindy, this is an old friend, Vladimir. Vladimir, this is Cindy, my fiancée."

I emphasize the word fiancée, to subtly remind Cindy why she's here. To be a professional and act the part of a loved-up fiancée even though I've made her hate me.

"Pleased to meet you, Cindy," Vladimir says formally.

Cindy smiles charmingly at him. "Likewise. So you're the one to go to for all of the stories about Alex as a teenager, huh? You will tell me everything, won't you?" she asks with a little laugh.

She's still playing her part, and I am at least grateful for that.

I put my arm around Vladimir's shoulders, laugh and shake my head. "There's no chance of that. It's the bro code. What happens between friends stays between friends," I say.

He laughs and nods his head, but then winks at Cindy. "I'm sure I can pass you a few juicy snippets though."

The rest of the dinner is hard. Cindy and I are very much acting our parts and sometimes it feels so real, I have to remind myself I won't be taking her up to my bed tonight.

I am glad when eleven o'clock rolls around and people start to leave. I excuse myself around half past eleven. We say our goodnights to everyone and go upstairs. We walk along the silent corridor without saying a word. At her door, she quickly says goodnight, and turns the handle. The door shuts before I can even respond.

I enter my room, close the door behind me and bite back the

roar of frustration. I move into the room and punch the mattress hard. It gets out some of the anger, but it does nothing to make me feel any better.

ALEX

Although I am determined not to go to Cindy, I can't sleep for thinking about her. Only a few steps separate us, but it might as well have been a deep chasm. It doesn't help that I can still smell her scent on my sheets.

I hear her moving around and then the sounds stop and I know she must have gotten into bed. I bet she's not losing any sleep over this. I mean I was a dick, there's no way around that, but I didn't really say anything we didn't already know. What we have is a business arrangement. She's probably done the sensible thing, shrugged it off and moved on, just like I should.

I roll angrily onto my side and close my eyes, but sleep won't come. I'm tired and I thought sleep would be easy, but it's the farthest thing from my mind.

Still, I must have finally fallen asleep after hours of tossing and turning, because I jump awake suddenly, awakened by a noise that I can no longer hear. I roll over and look at the clock. It's just gone half past two, which means I managed all of about thirty minutes of sleep. There are no more noises. It must be those damned pipes again. I close my eyes, determined to go back to sleep. I am just drifting back off when I hear it. A whimpering sound. And it's coming from Cindy's room.

I jump out of bed and stride towards the connecting door, but the noise has stopped. I hesitate at the door. There are no more noises. Just as I start to move away from the door, I hear it again. A high-pitched shriek. I fling open the door and burst into Cindy's bedroom.

Cindy's bedside lamp is on and I blink a few times against the bright light after the darkness of my own room. She's sitting up on the bed, her knees drawn to her chest and her arms wrapped around them. She's rocking back and forth gently and her face is as white as the sheets around her. Her eyes swing around towards me. They are wide with utter terror. If I had not seen it I could never have believed that such a strong and confident woman like her could look like that. A cold horror grips my belly. I never want to see her like this again.

"It's ok," I say quickly. "It's just me. I heard you …"

I don't get to finish the sentence before she bolts out of the bed and sprints towards me. She throws herself against me and I instinctively wrap my arms around her. As she clings to me I feel her body shaking. She's only wearing a thin night-dress and her skin feels cold. Her breath comes shallow and fast. I look around the room. There are no noises and nothing in the room. I won't tell her she is imagining it, but as far as I can see she is in no danger.

"Shh, it's ok," I whisper against her hair. It smells of coconut or strawberries. I can't help but suddenly become aware of all her curves pressed against me. I ignore the lust inside of me. I have to come to terms with the fact that I will always want this woman, no matter what the circumstances are. Even when she is this terrified!

"What happened?" I ask her gently.

She takes a shaking breath.

"I heard it again, Alex. My name. From the bathroom. I'm not imagining it, Alex. And it wasn't a dream."

I don't bother telling her it's just the pipes or the floorboards whispering. I know she doesn't believe that. And I'm starting to think it's not the pipes either, but I also don't think it was supernatural. This house has been standing here for a half-century with not a single report of a ghost before Cindy came to it.

"Why didn't you come to my room?"

She pulls away from me and I see a little of her fighting spirit come back to her. "You made it quite clear that wasn't an option."

"Yeah well, sometimes I say shit I don't mean."

"Yeah, well, I didn't know that."

"Now you do."

She bites her bottom lip and my cock stirs. I clear my throat. "I'll go take a look in the bathroom."

She nods gratefully and I can feel her eyes on me as I cross the room. I push the bathroom door open and turn on the light. There's nothing and no one there of course.

"It's all clear." I turn the light off and walk back towards her.

"Did you mean it?" she asks. "When you said I should have come to you?"

"Of course," I say.

"Good." She smiles tentatively, then turns away and quickly walks into my room. She really doesn't want to stay in her room for one second longer than necessary. Whatever noises she's hearing are terrifying her a lot more than I first thought. She's way too stubborn to change her mind and come to my room if she wasn't scared out of her mind.

I follow her into my room and shut the connecting door. Cindy has turned a lamp on and she's sitting on my bed. Her back is against the headboard and her legs are beneath the sheet. That's a good thing. I don't need those legs calling out to me.

I want to fuck her so bad, I can feel my skin tingling where her skin touched mine, but I don't want her to think she can't come to me unless she's willing to put out.

"I'll take the couch," I say.

"I think we're past that, Alex. Just get in the bed," she says. "We're adults. We can sleep in the same bed without making it weird."

Well, count me out of your adult games. It will be very weird to get in bed with Cindy and not have sex with her.

"It's okay. I'm happy with the couch." I turn away from her and start walking towards the lounge. The sense of déjà vu is crushing.

"I should have come to you this morning," she says.

I stop walking and smile. The last time this happened ... "Well you didn't," I reply, turning slowly towards her. She is smiling softly. The yellow light of the lamp has turned her hair to spun gold and her eyes gleam like blue sapphires.

"No. I didn't. But I'm here now," she says. She's flirting with me. She wants me with the same intensity I want her.

"Yes, you are. And it's late. Why don't you lay down and try to get some sleep?" I say. It's like we're both playing a game. After what she said this morning I'll be damned if she doesn't come right out and ask me to fuck her.

Never taking her eyes off me, she shuffles down the bed until she's laying down on her side facing me. "I don't think I'll be able to sleep though," she purrs. "Not with the thoughts that are running through my mind."

She runs her tongue over her lips, looking me straight in the eye as she does it. God she knows how to push my buttons. And I am under no illusion that she doesn't know exactly what she's doing.

She kicks her legs, kicking the sheet all the way down to her knees. I swallow hard as my cock responds to the sight of her bare legs. I know she can see my hard on through my boxers.

"You know what happens when that sheet comes off," I say.

"I know." Then she smiles and kicks the sheet completely off her legs.

And all reason leaves my mind as I walk like a mindless zombie towards the smell of fresh brains. I get on the bed and swoop down on her mouth. She kisses me back with passion. She pushes herself up and then she presses against my chest, pushing me back against the mattress. She keeps her lips on mine as I lay back and pull her on top of me. I push my hands beneath her nightdress, running them over her bare ass and up her back. She nibbles my lower lip and then she pulls back from me. She looks down at me, her eyes full of desire and I know that no matter what has happened between us, she isn't just acting this part because she feels obliged to. The desire I see in her eyes is real.

She moves her legs, nudging mine outwards. She kneels between my legs and pulls her nightdress over her head. She is quite a sight in the soft glow of the lamp, her body naked and perfect and mine for the taking. I start to sit up, but Cindy reaches out and pushes me back down.

"Hold your horses," she whispers. "It's your turn tonight to get the star treatment."

She shuffles backwards until she's out from between my legs and then she hooks her fingers into my boxer shorts. I lift my ass up and let her pull them free. She smiles when my rock-hard cock is freed.

"Someone is happy to see me," she whispers and I can't help but laugh.

She smiles down at me and then she pulls my boxer shorts the rest of the way down and off. She throws them to the ground and crawls back up the bed until she is between my knees. She takes my cock in her clenched fist and smiles again, and then she lowers her head and sucks me into her mouth.

Fire explodes through me and it's all I can do not to come on the spot. I swallow hard, forcing myself to stay in control. I don't want this to be over before it has even begun.

Her mouth is warm, her tongue velvet as she licks my length. She moves her head down, taking more of me into her mouth and her throat before bringing her head back up. My cock slips out from her mouth and I instantly miss the warmth. She rubs her tongue over the bottom of my cock, flicking it back and forth over the veins, teasing me. I let out an agonized groan which seems to spur her on.

She licks down my length and back up again, lapping at my cock like she's eating an ice cream. Her light teasing licks are almost too much for me to bear. I hate girls who lick my cock like a lollipop, but I let her do her thing. She's getting her own back for the teasing I did on her this morning before I gave her the orgasm of her life. After this I'm gonna grab her, sit her on my cock, have her ride me to oblivion.

The sheet is bunched in my fists and my need for her is almost an agony when she relents and sucks me into her mouth again. I watch her head bobbing as she sucks me hard. I see my cock, glistening with her saliva, disappearing into her stretched lips and I have to bite down on the inside of my mouth to stop myself from coming. Every cell in my body feels as if it is electrified.

I buck my hips, pushing my cock further into her mouth, and she takes it all. Swallows it like a good little girl. I grab her head and start to fuck her mouth. The way she deep throats is beautiful to watch. She caresses my balls, kneading them in time with her sucking and I can actually see fucking stars as she works me like a pro.

"I'm going to come in your mouth," I warn.

She doesn't stop. She sucks me harder, faster, and I realize it's her intention to make me come in her mouth. I stop trying to hold myself back and just relax and enjoy her mouth on me, her hand on me.

I feel my stomach tightening, my cock twitching and I know I've reached the point of no return. My climax hits home. I feel it in every part of my body; such intense pleasure that I can feel my heart slamming in my chest as the pleasure rips through me, and with a roar, I flood her, spurting into her mouth.

She drinks my cum down almost greedily, milking me, her throat working furiously, for the last drops. Her name plays in my brain. Cindy … Cindy … Cindy.

Finally, she pulls her blonde head away and wipes the back of her hand over her mouth.

"Fucking hell, Cindy," I whisper.

She smiles and lays down beside me, snuggling against me. I lift my arm and she moves closer. I wrap my arm around her as she snakes her arm across my waist. The weight of it on my body feels good. Surprisingly good.

I feel her cheek move against my chest as she smiles. "Fucking hell is right," she says and laughs softly.

I lay stroking my hand up and down her back. After sex, I'm usually ready to turn over and sleep. Not with her. She traces circles on my stomach with her nails. We no longer need words. Our bodies do all of our talking for us.

Without either of us saying a word Cindy finds my mouth between her legs. She sighs with contentment as I begin to lap up her sweetness. It's going to be hours before I get enough. Hours and hours.

CINDY

I wake up and I'm instantly aware of Alex's strong, solid body. That's because I'm wrapped up in his arms. Silly, but it makes me feel warm and safe and protected. As if I am a child again, without any responsibilities, financial worries or cares. Someone else will take care of my every need.

I close my eyes and luxuriate in the unfamiliar, but precious feeling. I've been independent and fighting my own battles for so long I finally understand how Raven, Rosa and Star feel. Why overnight their faces took a different character. My eyes snap open. But what they have and what I have is totally different. They have men who chased them like crazy and committed to them at the first opportunity, not men they had to literally seduce into bed with them.

Once again, I've let my guard down and let Alex back into my head. I need a moment to really think through what I'm actually doing. Very, very gently, I lift Alex's arm up and shuffle out of bed. He makes a sound and I freeze, but he only rolls over freeing me. I slide out of bed, pick up my nightdress, and move over to the door that leads outside onto a balcony. I have a similar door in my room. After pulling my nightdress over my head, I slide the door open and step outside.

The sun is just coming up and although there's still a slight chill in the air that brings goose bumps to my skin, it's nice enough that I choose to stay outside.

I move over to the balcony's railing and, resting my forearms on it, I look out over the gardens and grounds. It hits me again just how massive this place is, which although unconnected, that makes me wonder how big of a mistake I am making. I don't even know what I'm doing here anymore.

I can play the role of the doting girlfriend while Alex and I can maintain a working relationship or we could be more. But I don't think I can do both any longer. I can't have hot sex with Alex and not develop any feelings for him.

My body wants more. I want more.

I know what I agreed. Half of The Macau in exchange for acting as his fiancée, but suddenly I don't care all that much about having half the casino anymore. I don't want our relationship to be an act. I want it to be real. And if Alex doesn't feel the same as I do, which I don't think he does, then I'm just setting myself up to get hurt.

Alex is so hard to read. It's so hard to equate the man who held me so gently while I was out of my mind with fear with the man who I first met at the casino, who seemed to be a law unto himself. It's like he's two different people and I don't know which one is real. And until I can work that out, I might need to keep my distance from him.

I'm not one for playing games though. I'm not going to just silently withdraw from Alex. Once he awakes this morning, I'm going to talk to him and tell him what I've decided. In the best-case, long shot scenario, he will confess he feels the same, but quite honestly, I don't think I have a hope in hell that will happen. And in the worst case scenario …

A clatter sounds behind me and I jump and spin around, fear gripping me like an ice-cold glove. My hand is pressed against my chest when I see Alex standing behind me. He has put his boxer shorts back on. His abs look like slabs of dusky gold in the morning light.

"What the hell, Alex," I gasp. "Do you have to creep up on me like that? I thought it was … never mind. Just don't scare me like that again, ok?"

I see genuine concern on his face. "I'm sorry. I didn't mean to scare you. The sun is shining, and I thought you'd have heard me moving around."

He moves and sits on the padded settee and I turn so I'm properly facing him. He looks at me, raising a hand to shade his eyes from the rising sun.

"What are you so afraid of in this house, Cindy?"

It's not the conversation I thought we were going to have, but I did promise myself I was going to be honest with him and I decide to roll with that.

"I know you're used to it, but I'm not. And having the ghost of your crazy old great, great aunt, or whoever the hell she is, calling out my name in the middle of the night scares the living daylights out of me."

"Whoa there, back up. What crazy old aunt?"

"You know, the one they locked up."

"I don't know what you're talking about," Alex says, and to his credit, he sounds genuinely perplexed.

Was it possible that he did not know the story? "Petra and Anastasia told me the story of how one of your ancestors went crazy and had to be locked away in my room, and how she died in it … and now haunts it."

"You seriously believed those two?" Alex says, his face betraying his complete disbelief.

"Well no, not at first," I say, feeling suddenly naïve and stupid. "But then I heard it. Alex, you can say it's the pipes all you like, but it's my name she … it called."

Alex shakes his head.

"Well now that I know those two are involved, I can explain it easily enough. This house is full of secret passages and tunnels. I don't know where they all are, but they definitely do exist. They're messing with you, Cindy. They're in the tunnels banging around and whispering your name. They probably broke your heater too."

My jaw drops open. "Those little bitches!" I curse. Then I realize I've spoken out loud and instantly regret it. They are Alex's family, and I'm being paid to deal with them with class and grace. "I'm sorry. I shouldn't have said that."

"Oh, trust me, I've called them much worse than that," Alex says with a grin. "I'll tear a few strips off them later today. Rest assured you won't be tormented anymore."

"No, don't do that," I say quickly. "I don't want them to know it's bothered me enough to even tell you about it. Just let them think I haven't even noticed their little games. I think I want to give them a taste of their own medicine."

Alex grins at me. "I like your style."

We go quiet for a moment and then Alex speaks up again. "You know, when I was scoping out the casino and deciding whether or not to buy it, I watched you from afar. And I never would have taken you to be someone who bought into the paranormal. You seemed too … together."

"I'm a city girl. I have no experience of the paranormal so of course, I didn't believe in that sort of thing. And by the way, you sound as creepy as fuck when you admit you were watching me from afar."

Alex shrugs. "It was just good business. I had to know the casino would be in excellent hands once we concluded our deal."

I should be glad to hear that, surely. It means Alex thinks highly of my ability. I can't help think it's a bit creepy though. Like he's engineered this whole thing and I've played right into his hands.

"So this was all some elaborate plan to seduce me?" I ask.

Alex laughs, which is far from the reaction I expected. "Be honest, the idea of investing millions of pounds into a business just to bed you is a bit extreme even for me, don't you think?"

That was a rusty knife in an old wound, but I have to admit, when he puts it like that, it's crystal clear I'm over-reacting and letting my emotions cloud my rational judgment. It was me that made all the moves, and even now, all I want to do is reach out and touch the smooth skin of his stomach.

"I was honest with you," he adds. "I wanted a woman to present to my aunt who she would fall in love with. And that's really all it was about. Everything else that came with it, well that wasn't part of the plan."

I am inclined to believe him. Alex isn't the sort of man who makes grand gestures, but he is the sort who gets what he wants. If I'm really honest I'll have to admit that if he just wanted to have sex with me, he could have had me on day one. I bite my lip. Now is the perfect opportunity for me to make clear that we should go back to being employer and employee until I get my head straight. I've become too confused. I can't even think straight when he is around. I'm just about to tell him, when he says, "Look, now might be the time to tell you this. It's what I wanted to tell you when I … uh … ordered you to come to my room."

"Oh, okay."

"This is confidential information. No one knows except Valeriya and me. I'm telling you because it would seem strange to Babushka if I don't tell my own fiancée something so important."

I stare at him curiously.

"Babushka is dying. Eight years ago, she was told she had cancer of the saliva glands. At that time, she decided that she didn't want to go the chemo route. She had lived a long and fruitful life and she wanted to live her life here peacefully until it was time to go. The cancer has been spreading slowly. Her pain meds have been increasing steadily, but now her doctor has told her that she might have a year left, if she is lucky. Once it gets in her lungs she will suffer greatly and succumb to the disease."

My mouth drops open. "Oh, Alex. I'm so sorry," I whisper. Suddenly my shallow preoccupation with myself seems obnoxious and selfish. Now I understand why he was willing to give away half a casino for the right girl to play the part.

Alex doesn't say anything for a few seconds. His face is a mask, but his eyes give away the turmoil inside of him. Then he says, "Babushka doesn't want anyone else in her family to know so please don't tell anyone."

"Of course not. I know this is not much consolation, but I'll do everything in my power to make sure your aunt thinks we are the happiest couple in the world," I say.

Alex rests his elbows on his knees and looks down. I know he is in pain and he doesn't want me to see it. This is the way he deals with pain. He goes into himself.

I can feel tears burning in my eyes and almost feel the pain of the little boy he once was. How he let the pain of losing his parents fester away, how he shut himself off emotionally and then couldn't find his way back out of the prison he had created for himself.

For the first time, I feel like I am able to read Alex clearly, and I feel it deep inside me that every word he spoke was the truth.

I take a few steps forward and put my hand on his shoulder. He freezes.

I crouch down and press my lips against his. He resists me at first, but then he responds, kissing me passionately. His hands push into my hair and I wrap my arms around his waist, pulling myself closer to him, trying to kiss his pain away. Our kiss is salty, the taste of tears, and although I keep my eyes closed, and don't look, I don't think the tears are just mine.

ALEX

As I lead Cindy back to the stables, part of me is still in shock. I can't believe I opened up to her. She is the first human being I've allowed into my inner world since my parents died. She squeezes my hand and I squeeze back. I feel like the beast who is undone by the little child.

She looks up at me and beams. And I beam back.

We reach the stables and Boris waves. Earlier, I had one of the staff instruct him to have Nikita and Milan ready for a ride so they are both standing in the courtyard, saddled up and ready to go.

I stand back while Cindy climbs onto Nikita. Even after just one ride she is already so much more confident. I get onto Milan and turn to Cindy. "Are you ready to go or do you want to do a few laps of the courtyard to get a feel for Nikita again?"

"I'm ready to go," she replies excitedly.

Her cheeks are flushed with excitement and her smile is full of childlike innocence. It is clear she loves riding. I have definitely rekindled an old love within her. She needs a horse of her own. A gentle mare.

I tap my feet on Milan's sides and steer him out of the courtyard and onto the path leading to the creek. I can hear the clip-clop of Nikita following behind me. I dig my heels into Milan's sides again and he starts to canter, and I hear Nikita do the same. As soon as the path widens out, I maneuver my horse so that we are riding next to each other.

Cindy surprises me then. She shouts yah and digs her heels into Nikita's sides. She stands up in the stirrups and laughs as Nikita breaks into a gallop. For a second, I'm left behind, shaking my head in wonder at Cindy.

Then, I spur Milan on until we catch up to them. We gallop side by side through the fields. Cindy's hair billows out behind her and she laughs, a sound filled with pure delight. She looks free, like she's flying, and I love seeing her like this. She looks as if all of her worries have been lifted. There is almost no resemblance to the business-suited, utterly professional woman I saw at The Macau.

I recognize the lightness in her. It's the same lightness I always feel when I kick back and ride fast. We gallop into a small orchard and Cindy slows down. She looks around at the blooming apple trees, exclaiming at the beauty of the place.

To me, it's just part of our land, but I try to see it through her eyes and suddenly I see the beauty in it. Maybe she will change me. Maybe she will teach me the secret to seeing the beauty in the everyday stuff.

"Turn left as we leave the orchard," I shout over the rushing sound of the wind as we fly through it.

Cindy pulls on Nikita's reins, turning her to the left.

We ride for another few minutes before I start to pull up on Milan's reins when the creek comes into view. Cindy slows Nikita down too and we approach the creek at a canter.

"It's beautiful," Cindy says, her voice filled with awe.

She looks around her, taking in the scattered trees dripping with pale pink blossoms that coat the ground like a blanket. She looks out at the slowly trickling creek and the little Japanese wooden bridge across it.

Even though I have seen this place a hundred times, more maybe, I see it anew through her eyes.

"You look lost in thought," Cindy says as she dismounts from Nikita and waits for me to get off Milan.

"I was just thinking of Babushka. This is her most favorite place in the world. Until she was too ill to ride she used to come here all of the time. Sometimes she has Valeriya bring her out here on bright sunny days, but it's become a bittersweet journey for her now. It reminds her of the fact she can no longer ride."

I take the reins Cindy holds out to me and I lead the horses to the creek for a drink. I tie the horses to a post and Cindy and I walk away a little and sit down on the grass. "In the beginning I was a bit worried that Babushka would see through our act."

"She doesn't want to see through it," Cindy says. "Even if she had her suspicions, she would swallow them down, because she wants to believe you've found someone who makes you happy."

"Well that part isn't a lie," I say.

"I do?" she asks, her blue eyes huge and shining.

I grin. "You do."

"Er ... when you say happy ... what exactly do you mean?"

I cup her cheek with one hand and look deep into her eyes. "You make me happier than I've ever been," I admit.

"Do you want to know a secret?" she whispers.

I suppress my smile. I love this version of Cindy. So irrepressible.

"No one has made me feel the way you do," she confesses.

I lean forward and kiss her. A deep, sensual kiss, the melding of two people who are crazy about each other's bodies. She pulls back.

"Have you ever had sex outdoors, Alex?"

I shrug. "Of course."

She bites her bottom lip. "Well, I haven't."

I don't take my eyes off that bottom lip. "Then we'll have to remedy that right away."

"I totally agree."

She reaches down, grips her t-shirt, pulls it over her head, and carelessly flings it from her. Still grinning at me, she sends her bra the same way as her t-shirt. I moan low in my throat when I see her topless. Her breasts are white compared to her tanned stomach. Her nipples stand to attention as I push her onto her back and reach down and roll her nipples between my thumb and my fingers.

She closes her eyes, a smile playing across her lips.

I kiss that delicious mouth and she responds passionately, wrapping her arms around my neck and holding me in place, she kisses me deeply. Her tongue slips into my mouth, hooking my tongue and lightly sucking it back into her own mouth. I feel a jolt in my cock.

Releasing her mouth, I kiss her cheek, her jaw, her neck, then I trail kisses down her body. I run my tongue over every inch of exposed skin and feel the goose bumps erupting on her skin at my touch. As soon as I reach her leggings she kicks off her shoes and lifts her ass off the ground. I laugh at how eager she is, but it doesn't stop me from pulling down her leggings and her panties and yanking them off her feet. I lean down and kiss her belly.

Grabbing her hands, I pull her into a sitting position so she is taking her weight on the palms of her hands. Then I open her legs wide. She has never had the sun on her pussy and she sighs softly when the warm rays hit her most secret part. I kiss her again as I push my fingers inside her dripping wet lips. Her head falls back and her body arches with pleasure. I move my fingers around her clit slowly, bringing her near orgasm, but not close enough to actually climax.

Her thighs tremble and she makes a moaning sound when I start to move my fingers faster. She jerks her hips, pressing herself harder against my fingers and makes that now familiar 'ahh' sound as I move my other hand to her pussy and slip two fingers inside of her. I finger fuck her while simultaneously working her clit. In seconds she begins to gasp and the writhing of her hips speeds up. She is almost there, ready to climax and I don't hold back. I grip her body securely and work her like my life depends on it, moving my fingers faster and harder until I hear her suck in a breath and let it out in a scream. I watch with satisfaction as her orgasm blossoms through her. I feel her pussy clench around my fingers, her clit pulsing.

It's just beautiful. As long as I live I will remember this moment by the creek, the sun shining down, and my fingers buried inside this beautiful woman.

I wait for half a second, my fingers still and then I press down on her clit and her g-spot and she screams again. Her pussy clenches so tightly that for a minute, I can't move my fingers and I feel her juices coating them, coating my hand. I wait until she's really come undone and then I start to lap up the sweet juices pouring out of her.

She pants for a moment, her head still hanging back and then she lifts her head and smiles at me. I move upwards and kiss her and she kisses me back eagerly. She pulls away suddenly, and pushes me onto my back.

"Condom?" she asks, sitting astride my thighs.

"Left pocket," I say shortly, while my eyes take in the beauty of her bare body in the sunlight.

She jams her hand into my jeans pocket and pulls it out triumphantly. Tearing it open impatiently with her teeth she unzips my jeans. Then, lifting herself off the ground, she quickly pulls my jeans together with my boxer shorts down to my knees. Then she rolls the condom on to my hard cock and straddles me, sitting across me so I can feel her wet pussy pressing down on my cock.

She leans forward, her nipples on mine before she impales herself onto my cock. I groan as I feel her warm, wet pussy take me in. It's a huge turn on seeing Cindy take control. She begins to move. Slow, sensual movements that drive me wild. With each movement, she takes me all of the way inside of her and then she comes up so high that I almost slip out of her, but not quite.

She moves her hands sensuously over her body as she rides me and I am mesmerized by her movements. She rubs her stomach, her sides, and then she moves her hands to her breasts. She kneads them. Her eyes are closed and she's breathing slowly and heavily, her cheeks are flushed. She looks like a goddess, the goddess of ecstasy.

She takes her nipples between her fingers and works them, tugging on them, rolling them between her fingers. Her lips part slightly as her breathing speeds up, and still, she moves slowly on my cock, making me feel every nerve in it. I am on the verge of coming just watching her so I try not to focus too much on the sensation of her slippery pussy sucking me in. I don't want this show to end.

I know I'm fighting a losing battle when she releases her nipples and moves one hand slowly down her body to her clit. She rubs her clit slowly in time with her thrusts and I swallow hard, my breath catching in my throat.

Moaning she brings herself to orgasm and I feel her pussy clenching around me, a warm flood of liquid coating me. I catch her by the waist as she sways on top of me. Then she opens her eyes and looks at me. We are looking into each other's eyes as she comes again. That is the moment I can't hold back any longer.

I grab her hips in my hands and fuck her senseless, bucking my hips furiously. Within seconds, I am on the edge and I let myself go over, calling out her name as I come inside of her. I close my eyes for a moment, but then I remember the way I felt so connected to her when she looked me in the eye as she came, and I want to be able to do the same thing for her.

I open my eyes and look at her as I come hard, pleasure flooding me and making me call out to her even as I look her in the eye. She holds my gaze and when my cock slips out of her, she leans forward and grazes her lips over mine. She deepens the kiss, kissing me like she wants to consume me, like she wants to taste me.

I reach up and wrap my arms around her and she flattens her body as we explore each other's mouths with our tongues.

I know something has changed between us. It's something I can't put into words, but it feels amazing, like we're connecting on much more than just a physical level. The warmth of the sun on us, the weight of her body on top of me, the dull steady sound of her heartbeat, and the smell of the grass beneath me … feels almost unreal.

The sensation is so weird and so without precedent I am unable to speak. Then I realize she's fallen asleep. I should wake her so we can head back up to the house, but I don't have it in me to disturb her, to ruin this rare and precious moment. Instead, I close my eyes and let myself drift away too.

I wake up to Cindy gently shaking me and laughing. I open my eyes and instantly close them again as the sun blinds me.

I lift my hand to shield my eyes, then open one eye, and peer up at her. She's fully dressed again and she's smiling down at me.

"I just woke up. It's after eleven. I thought we'd better be getting back for lunch," she says.

I push myself up onto my elbows, fully awake now.

"Or we could just stay here and eat each other," I say. And I'm not joking.

She laughs and stands up before I can make a grab for her. "As tempting as that is, I'm kinda starving."

Reluctantly, I begin to button up my shirt. Standing, I pull my boxer shorts and my jeans up and fasten them. "Are you thirsty?"

She nods, and I beckon her closer to the creek. I crouch down and cup some water in my hands and drink it.

She raises an eyebrow. "Are you sure that's safe to drink?"

"If you mean have we had health inspectors out to test it, then no, probably not," I say. "But I've been drinking it all of my life out here and I'm still alive to tell the tale."

She laughs and copies me, cupping some water in her own hands and drinking it down. She smiles. "It's really good."

The water is always crisp and cool here, even in the middle of summer. "Come on. Let's head back."

I go and untie the horses and after another drink for them, we mount them and set off back towards home. I see Cindy shifting uncomfortably in her saddle.

"Bit sore?" I laugh, teasing her.

"I'm pretty sure you know the answer to that one," she laughs back.

"What will happen to all these apples?" Cindy asks as we get to the orchard.

"The staff make apple cider. You can try some later."

"I'd love to," she says with a laugh. "I was thinking of asking Babushka if she would like to come out for a short walk with me after lunch."

I smile broadly, pleased that she's making such a big effort with Babushka.

CINDY

Lunch is remarkably pleasant considering Petra joined Babushka, Alex, and I. We ate finger sandwiches and scones in the conservatory and we drank some homemade elderflower juice that Petra had picked up at the farmer's market she'd been to that morning. If it wasn't for the fact she was drinking it too, I would have been a tiny bit afraid she would have poisoned it. She was on her best behavior, speaking in English, and asking me questions that didn't feel like disguised insults, but I was on to her now. After lunch, Alex excused himself as he had some calls to make.

I turn to Babushka once he is out of the door. "I was wondering if you would like to take a walk with me," I say to her.

She smiles at me but she shakes her head. "I'd like nothing more, dear, but my arthritis is playing up something terrible today and I was actually planning on having a lie down after lunch."

"Oh, I'm so sorry," I say, trying to not show my alarm and hoping it is nothing serious. "Is there anything I can do?"

She smiles sweetly. "That is so kind of you, but no, dear. Valeriya will give me one of my pills and I'll be out like a light until dinner."

"I'll take a walk with you," Petra offers with a bright smile.

Oh shit. A half hour over lunch is one thing, but can I really stomach more time with her? I shake my head and smile politely. "Oh no, it's fine. I can go by myself. I'm sure you have plans and I really don't want to spoil your day."

"Nonsense," she replies. "I don't have anything planned and a walk sounds like a great idea with the sun shining like that. I'd only end up in the drawing room reading, and I think some fresh air sounds much nicer."

I can't think of any other way to get out of it without being rude and so I find myself nodding. "Then that would be lovely."

There can only be two reasons Petra is offering. Either she's realized she was acting like an obnoxious brat and she's now making an effort to get to know me a little better, or, the more likely scenario, this is another way of torturing me. If that's the case I'm ready for her.

Valeriya appears and helps Babushka from the conservatory and I wonder for a second if Petra's claws will come out now. It doesn't happen though. Instead, she smiles pleasantly at me.

"Are you ready now or did you want a cup of tea or something first?" she asks.

"I'm ready whenever you are."

"Great. Please wait here a minute," she says and is gone before I can ask why. A few seconds later I start to wonder if this is her plan. To leave me sitting here like an idiot waiting for her when she has no intention of coming back. If that's her plan, then the joke is on her because it's really quite nice sitting here. I take my phone out and send a text to Star, Raven, and Rosa.

I look up when Petra returns. She pulls a bottle of wine and two glasses from behind her back. "I thought it would be nice to have a glass or two of wine at the fountain down by the stables."

I agree that it would be and we leave the conservatory. Petra asks me lots of questions about my life in London and I carefully divulge select pieces of sanitized information about my life. She hangs on my every word, smiling and nodding.

"I actually love London," she gushes.

"You should come and visit Alex and me sometime," I say just to get a reaction.

"I might just do that," she agrees.

We both know she won't, but she does a damn good job of pretending she will.

We reach the fountain and sit down on the bench in front of it. Petra opens the wine and pours two glasses. She hands me one and I wait for her to pour herself a glass. Only when she sips herself do I sip from my glass. It's refreshing and fruity.

"Good choice," I say lightly.

"It's one of my favorites. I love the honey and blackberry

accents," she says. She puts her glass down on the bench and turns towards me. "I wanted to apologize to you, Cindy. I was such a bitch to you."

"It's okay," I say quietly. She seems sincere, but I can't let my guard down.

"It's really not who I am," she adds. "But I had already told myself before I met you that I would make sure I didn't like you. Because if I didn't like you then I wouldn't care about what Alex is doing to you. But the thing is, I do like you, and I think you deserve to know the truth. I'm only sorry you have to hear it from me instead of him."

Oh, here we go. I look at her innocently. "What do you mean?"

"I'm sorry to tell you this, because I can see that you are deeply in love with him." She takes a deep breath. "He's using you, Cindy. You're just a pawn in a game you don't understand. Once he's duped Babushka, he'll dump you."

Petra can't possibly know about our fake romance? So what the hell is she talking about? "Stop talking in riddles and just tell me what you want me to know," I say, my voice harsh.

She looks down into her glass for a moment and then she looks up directly at me, her gaze unwavering and full of intensity. "There's a clause in Babushka's will. Alex gets everything if he is married by the time she dies. If not, then Babushka's whole inheritance, everything you see here and quite a lot you don't, will go into a trust fund to maintain the estate and the rest of the family. So you see: no white wedding, no money, no house for Alex."

I stare at her blankly. To say she pulled the rug out from

under my feet doesn't describe. It's more like she pushed me into an abyss. I feel as if I'm falling, screaming silently, arms flailing, grasping for something to hold on to and catching only air. I never saw this coming and I don't know what or who to believe right now. Is this another lie like the ghosts?"

I never take my eyes off her. "Are there ghosts in my room, Petra?"

She shifts uncomfortably. "I'm sorry about that, okay. We just couldn't resist. We didn't mean any real harm. But this is not a lie. If you don't believe me go and ask Alex. He might lie to you, but you'll see from his expression if he is. A woman in love will always know when the man she loves is lying to her."

Could this be true? Is what Alex and I have all a lie? Maybe his plan was to offer me the other half of the casino if I went ahead and married him. Or did he expect me to fall in love with him. He is a powerhouse of raw sexual magnetism and pure male beauty so I can't imagine many girls who wouldn't eventually fall for him. The truth is if he had asked me to marry him today I would have said yes. For him, for Babushka, for me ...

But it can't be true. Alex doesn't need Babushka's money. That's self-evident. Then I think of all the eighty and ninety-year old billionaires who still go to work every day rain or shine to earn even more money they will never spend in the little time they have left on earth.

But he loves Babushka. I know that's real. I have to believe in Alex over Petra. I mean this woman has done a complete one eighty on me today. I don't like her and I never have.

"You're not mad at me for telling you, are you?" Petra says, cutting through my thoughts.

"No," I lie. I need to let her think I'm at least considering her story, or this whole thing could blow up.

"But you do believe me, don't you?" she insists.

I try to think how I would react if I had always just been Alex's fiancée and had never known there was more to it. I'm not entirely sure how I would react, but I can't just tell Petra I believe her story blindly, or she's going to smell a rat. "Actually, Petra, I don't believe a word you've told me. And I'm telling Alex what you told me."

To my surprise she looks relieved, which means I must have given her the right answer. She wants me to ask Alex, which would also mean she is telling me the truth or that she just wants me to believe she would be happy.

"I'm so sorry to do this to you. I know you love him and it must hurt a lot, but if you take some time to think about it, perhaps the circumstance of how the two of you met, the quickness of your relationship, there will be clues, and you'll soon see the truth."

Little does she know ... I take a deep breath. "Now that you've administered your poison, you can be on your merry way, and take your wine with you so you can celebrate properly."

"I know you are angry now, but one day you will thank me," she says, standing up and taking a step away from me. She doesn't reach for the wine bottle. "I'll be in my room if you need to talk to someone."

I watch her walk away and there is only one thought in my

head. You scheming little bitch. She really does hate me with a passion and I can see now why Alex wanted a fake girlfriend here, someone who Petra couldn't emotionally blackmail. I don't need to think about this. I believe Alex.

I do need to warn him that Petra really has it out for him though. I stand and start walking towards the house, but I remember he had some important calls to make. I can talk to him after dinner tonight. She can't do much damage today. She has to give me a bit of time to digest what she's told me.

I decide to go down to the stables and go out for another ride on Nikita. Anything to keep me away from the evil sister. I'm sure she'll be using all those tunnels in the house even more now to watch my reaction to her news. Well if she's watching me now she'll see me taking Nikita out and looking like I don't believe a word she has told me.

CINDY

I smile my thanks at Boris, who, despite the language
barrier, seemed to understand perfectly that I wanted
Nikita saddled up just from my hand gestures. He holds the
reins for me while I mount her. I'm getting better and better
at getting onto her every time I do it, and if I keep riding
twice a day for the rest of the break, I might even get to be
reasonably graceful at it.

Boris hands me the reins once I'm seated. I thank him and
tap my heels into Nikita's sides and she starts to move. I
stroke her neck as we leave the courtyard and head out into
the fields. I will not spoil my ride by thinking of the lies Petra
told me. I will trust Alex. I take Nikita in the direction Alex
and I went this morning. I'd quite like to take a closer look at
the orchard.

I'm not confident enough riding yet to gallop when I'm out
on my own, but I want to feel like I'm moving, to feel the
breeze in my hair. I want to feel free like I did earlier, to
feel like I am flying. I settle on the middle ground; a fast
canter. It's not quite as much of an adrenaline rush as a

full-on gallop is, but it feels nice and I feel like I'm in control.

We dash across the greenery and I look to each side, taking it all in. Even though I've seen it already just this morning, I'm still taken by the beauty of this place. If I stayed here for ten years, I don't think I would ever reach a point where the natural beauty didn't awe me. If I saw it every single day, I would still want to take it all in each time I passed through it.

I'm on the outskirts of the orchard, ready to slow Nikita down so we can take a slow, lazy walk through the orchard and I can really appreciate it all when I hear a loud noise. In the still, silent orchard, it sounds like a gun shot. A small squeak of surprise leaves my lips, but my reaction is nothing compared to Nikita's.

The sound spooks her completely and she rears up, a terrified whine escaping her lips. I cling to the reins for dear life, as I try to soothe Nikita, telling her it's ok, but there's no soothing her. She snorts in fear as she comes back down on all fours, but it is only for a split second.

Then she rears up again.

This time, I can't hold on. I feel the reins jerk through my fingers, and before I know what's happening, I'm rushing through the air. Not flying, but falling backwards, toppling. I slam to the ground and pain explodes through my body. My shoulder hits something hard, a rock maybe, and my ankle twists beneath me. I feel my head bang against the ground. For a second, I actually see stars, and I think I will pass out, but the moment passes. I take deep breaths. I'm alive. I'm fine. I'm probably just winded.

Nikita bolts over the open fields and I'm left out here alone.

Except … I am not alone. Seconds before the noise sounded, I saw a flash of pink through the trees and I was about to head in that direction to check it out, but the noise that sounded like a car backfiring or a gun going off filled the air and I was thrown off Nikita's back.

It dawns on me that Petra was wearing a pink dress at lunch today.

This only convinces me further that the friendly routine was all an act. She was trying to come between Alex and I. Maybe she saw I didn't look as shaken by her revelation as she expected me to be. She must have worked out that I didn't believe her and decided to get her revenge on me in this way. Revenge for what though? I still don't have any idea what the hell I've done to her to make her hate me so much that she'd pull this kind of stunt. If my head had hit the rock my shoulder hit, I could have been killed. Hell, I could have broken my neck.

This has to be more than just some petty jealousy over Alex's fiancée.

I sit up gingerly, half afraid Petra will burst out of the trees with a knife or something, ready to finish the job. I hold my breath listening, but the only sounds are the leaves rustling in the breeze and birds chirping. All I can see in every direction is shades of green.

There is no pink anywhere. Petra has gone. She must have made her escape while I was falling to the ground. She didn't even bother sticking around to see her handy work in action. Well, more fool her because she didn't get anywhere near the amount of damage I suspect she wanted to. Alex said there were tunnels all over the house and grounds so there could be some kind of tunnel from which she appeared and disappeared. In fact, it would make sense for there to be a tunnel directly to the orchard. In times of trouble you could pop out here and be hidden amongst the trees.

I reach up with my good arm and feel the back of my head. A stinging pain where I touch makes me gasp. I can feel a pretty big bump there but when I bring my hand around in front of my face and check it, there's no blood. I steel myself to look down at my ankle, hardly daring to see if there's bone poking out of it.

There is no bone sticking out. I tell myself not to be so dramatic. Sure, it's a bit painful but it's not so painful that I couldn't walk on it. I lean forward, ignoring the pain in my shoulder and I reach down and roll the bottom of my leggings up. There's a blue bruise forming on the inside of my ankle already. I poke and prod at it, gritting my teeth as pain shoots up my leg. I'm no doctor, but I don't think anything is broken.

Wow! Looks like I've just had one hell of a lucky escape.

I push myself slowly to my feet. By the time I am standing, my weight on my one good leg, I am covered in a film of cold sweat and I feel quite sick. I blink away the tears of shock and self-pity that fill my eyes.

I take a tiny step, testing out my ankle. It hurts like all hell, but it holds. I limp forward a step and then another. The tears run freely down my face now as each limping step jerks my shoulder. It's going to be a hell of a long walk back to the house, but fucking hell, Petra, you evil bitch, you won't get rid of me that easy.

ALEX

I look up from my laptop at the knock on the library door. "Come in," I call with a frown.

To my surprise, Boris slides awkwardly into the room. He looks nervous, twisting his hands together, and refusing to look me in the eye.

"What is it, Boris?" I ask immediately.

"Cindy went out on Nikita alone," he mutters.

I nod, impatient. Has he come here just to let me keep tabs on Cindy or is he worried he shouldn't have allowed her to.

"Nikita came back a few minutes ago. Alone," he adds, his eyes sliding away from me again.

He's still talking, but I'm no longer listening. If Nikita came back alone, it has to mean something has happened to Cindy. She must be hurt. If she'd gotten off Nikita and forgotten to tie her up, Nikita might have wandered a little, but she wouldn't have come right back to the stables. And certainly not in a manner that made Boris feel the need to come and tell me about it.

Panic rises inside me. Cindy could be unconscious somewhere. She could have broken an arm, a leg … her neck. Jesus! I shove my laptop away, the report I was reading forgotten, and jump to my feet. I streak past Boris. I can hear his feet behind me as he follows at my heels.

We tear through the house and across the gardens to the stables. One look at Nikita confirms that she was spooked. Her eyes are wide, the whites showing around the edges. She's covered in sweat and panting.

"Take care of Nikita. I'll go and find Cindy," I shout over my shoulder to Boris.

He nods his head but he still doesn't move. Just stands there shifting from foot to foot.

"What is it?" I demand. If he knows something, he needs to tell me what it is.

"I … I'm sorry," he says. "I should never have allowed Cindy to take Nikita out alone. But she's usually so gentle and I just thought—"

"It's not your fault," I say, cutting him off. "Just keep your phone on you. As soon as I find her I'll call to bring the truck around."

He nods and goes towards Nikita.

Without taking the time to saddle Milan, I jump onto his back. Pushing him to his maximum speed, I leave the courtyard and follow the grass that is a little churned up from Nikita's dash home.

Looks like I'm heading in the same direction we went this morning and I think I know where she was going to. The orchard. She seemed pretty taken with it this morning so it makes sense she would go back there. I really have no idea how far she might have gotten, but she can't have gone beyond the boundaries of this land. I'll stay out here all day and all night if I have to, but I will find her.

I picture Cindy clinging to a panicked Nikita, holding on for dear life and then being thrown to the ground. I stop the thought before it can go any further. I don't need the picture in my mind right now. Cindy will be fine. Nothing could have happened to her now. Not when I just found her.

I feel cold sweat run down my back as I gallop as fast as Milan will take me.

I can see the orchard in the distance and hope that's as far as Cindy went. She could have gone to the creek again, or she could have gone in any of the other directions. I have no fucking idea which path she might have chosen.

Again, I can feel the panic rising, threatening to take over. I never fall apart when things go wrong. I'm cool and level-headed even in the most dire, life and death circumstances so I can't understand why I am teetering on the edge of paranoia like this. I swallow the nausea and fear down, telling myself I need to be rational. My mind needs to be razor sharp. The last thing Cindy needs is for me to turn into a useless basket case.

As I close the gap between me and the orchard, I see Cindy. She's coming towards me, and relief like I have never known floods me. She's ok. She's ok. God, she's ok. I can already see that she's limping heavily, barely daring to put any weight on her right ankle. One of her sleeves has torn away, and it's hanging down her arm by a single thread or two.

Fuck.

I grip Milan and spur him to go even faster. I can see the relief on her face when I pull up next to her and jump down.

I don't give her a chance to say anything before I look her up and down and run my hands all over her body. She doesn't seem to have any serious injuries. I can't see any blood which I take to be a good sign, and although her ankle is clearly painful, it's not broken, or she wouldn't have been able to walk at all. I scoop her up in my arms and bury my face in her neck. "You gave me a such a fucking scare, Cindy." My voice sounds hoarse with fear.

"I'm fine, Alex," she says. "I could have walked to the house myself, you know."

I pull back and look into her white face. She stares back at me. She's in shock. I lay her down on the grass. "You'll be fine," I tell her pulling my phone out. I give Boris my exact location and cut the call.

"It's mostly just my ankle," she says calmly. "I banged my head, but it's fine. My shoulder hurts too, but it's nothing major, just a bruise or two, I reckon."

"Yes well, Doctor Ivanov will be the judge of that," I say.

"I don't need a doctor. I just need some ice for my ankle," she says in that same calm voice.

I let it go. She's getting the doctor whether she likes it or not, but I can't achieve anything by arguing with her about it out here.

"Oh, shit! Nikita," Cindy says suddenly. "There was a noise and it spooked her and she bolted. We have to find her, Alex."

I can't help but smile. Even after the accident and when she's clearly in pain, even if she is trying to hide that fact from me, Cindy appears to be more worried about Nikita's fate than she is about her own.

"What's so funny?" she asks, frowning.

"Nothing. I just thought it was sweet that you were worried about Nikita. She's fine. She made it back to the stables. It's how I knew to come and look for you."

"Oh, of course," Cindy says. "I didn't even consider how you knew to come and look for me. How did you know where to find me?"

"I followed Nikita's hoof marks, but I had a good idea where you might be heading to as well."

She nods and looks at me. "Thank you for coming to get me."

I can't stand to see her like this. Meek and quiet. It's not her. It's not her at all. I have to try and make her feel better somehow.

At that moment I see the truck thundering across the plains. Boris is going so fast it looks like it could turn turtle any moment. "Here comes help. If he doesn't run us over first," I say.

She gives a snort of laughter which, to my great relief, sounds a bit more like her.

ALEX

Boris takes Milan and I carefully put her into the passenger seat then get into the driver's seat. We don't talk on the way back. She leans back with her eyes closed and I concentrate on driving as smoothly as possible as not to jar her ankle. When we get back to the house, I drive the truck right through the courtyard and through the grounds to the door. As soon as I stop, Cindy immediately moves to get out of the truck and winces as she turns.

"Just stay there," I instruct.

I don't care if she thinks it sounds like an order and gets offended. It is an order and she's goddamned going to follow it. She could be doing even more damage to her ankle by walking on it. She makes a humph sound, but she stays seated and when I come around to her side, she doesn't object to taking my hands and letting me help her out of it.

She does object when I pick her up again, but I ignore her protests and carry her in through the conservatory and through the dining room.

"Alex, I'm fine to walk," she says again.

"And I'm fine to carry you," I reply.

She gets it finally that arguing this matter would be pointless so she sighs and rests her head against my chest. I hold her a little tighter as it suddenly hits me how much worse this could have been. I can't stand the thought of even the smallest hurt for Cindy.

I go up the stairs and take her into my room. Tenderly, I lay her on the bed. She pushes herself up into a sitting position and although I would prefer her to stay on her back until she's been checked over by Doctor Ivanov, I let her win this one.

"I'm going to call the doctor," I say. "I know you think you're fine, but it won't hurt to get checked out."

She shakes her head quickly. "Alex, seriously, it would be a complete waste of the doctor's time. I am fine. I've twisted my ankle and bruised my shoulder and that's it. I'm working class. You don't call a doctor for that. You put an ice pack on the ankle, maybe a bandage. And that's literally it."

I really don't like the idea of her not getting checked over just to be on the safe side, but deep down, I know she's right. It doesn't seem like she's seriously hurt, and what's Doctor Ivanov really going to do for her ankle that I can't do myself? It's like she said. He'll put some ice on it for a time, and then he'll bandage it. He might prescribe her some painkillers.

I decide to relent. I really don't want us to fight right now. But I'll be keeping a very close eye on Cindy and if her ankle isn't any better by tomorrow, I'll call the doctor whether she likes it or not. And at the first sign of a concussion, I'll do the same.

I stand up and move to the telephone in the corner of my room.

"Alex, no," Cindy says.

"Just relax. I'm not calling the doctor. You won this one. I'm just calling downstairs to get some ice and some bandages sent up."

I speak to one of the staff and ask for what I need. Then I start pacing impatiently as I wait for the things to be brought to me.

"Will you stop that! You're making me nervous," Cindy says.

"Sorry. I can't help it. I hate not being able to do anything. You don't—" I stop and turn at the sound of a discreet knock on the door. One of the maids holds out the items I requested when I open the door. I thank her and go back to sit down beside Cindy.

I gently roll her leggings up and look at her ankle. It's swollen and bruised, the skin shiny and a deep purple color. I wince when I see it. Cindy grins, peering down at it.

"It's a corker of a bruise, isn't it?" she comments happily.

"You're not meant to sound happy about it," I say with a frown.

I pick up the ice pack and lay it on her ankle.

She hisses, but before I can tell her, that's it, I'm calling the doctor, she explains, "It didn't hurt. It's just cold. I got a shock, that's all."

I think she's underplaying how much her ankle is hurting. Looking at the bruise, it must be hurting like hell, but I'm convinced now it's not broken. Even if she was running on adrenaline earlier and walking though the break rather than be left outside, alone and injured, that adrenaline would have been long gone now and she wouldn't be able to bear anything or anyone even touching her ankle.

I leave the ice pack in place for a few minutes while I unravel the bandage and get it sorted and ready to use. I gently lift the ice pack away and begin to bandage her foot.

She watches me for a moment. "You're good at this."

"I've patched up a lot of men with worse injuries when I was younger. I guess it's something you don't forget," I say.

I finish up and Cindy smiles at me. "It feels so much better now it's supported."

"Good." I smile at her. "I'm sorry this happened to you, Cindy. I should have been around."

"It wasn't your fault."

"Even the most experienced rider gets thrown sometimes. It's just one of those things. I hope it hasn't put you off riding."

"No, of course not. I love riding."

"Nikita is usually so calm and it generally takes helluva of a lot more than outside noises to spook her," I say, thinking about the incident rationally for the first time.

"Yeah. Like someone making a noise that sounded like a gunshot, for example?" Cindy says.

I frown. "What do you mean?"

She shakes her head. "I'm probably just being paranoid."

I realize in my panic I didn't ask what happened leading up to Cindy being thrown from Nikita. "Paranoid is not a word I would have associated with you. Tell me everything."

"There was a noise, a damned loud one. It sounded like a car backfiring, or a gun shot. That's when Nikita reared and I fell. I realized I'd seen a flash of pink through the trees right before hearing the noise. It appeared to be the same pink as the dress Petra wore at lunch. It sounds crazy, but I can't help feeling that she was the one who spooked Nikita. That she wanted me to fall and hurt myself. But even as I'm saying it out loud now, I know it sounds ridiculous."

I feel anger coming over me in waves. Fucking Petra. I don't know what game she's playing exactly, but this is a damned sight more serious than spooking Cindy in her room. Letting her think the ghost of some crazy old relative was in her room was child's play compared to this. This could have caused a serious injury. Hell, it could have paralyzed, or even killed her.

"It doesn't sound ridiculous at all. It sounds exactly like something Petra would do," I say in a low voice so filled with anger that Cindy recoils slightly.

I stand.

"Where are you going?" Cindy asks.

"To have a little chat with my bitch of a cousin," I reply.

"Don't do that, Alex. What if I'm wrong?" she says.

"Petra is sly, vindictive, and one hell of a liar, but I have always been able to see through her lies. I'll know whether she is behind this or not, don't you worry about that."

"I'll come with you," she says immediately.

"Cindy, please, just stay here and don't move your ankle. I won't be long, I promise. I'm not going to hurt Petra, even though I would love to give her the hiding she never got as a child. I'm just going to let her know I'm onto her dangerous games and make it clear she stops right now or she'll have a very different me to deal with. I promised you nothing would happen to you while you were here with me, and now something has. But I'll make damned sure nothing else does."

She nods but she doesn't look overly happy about it. The fact she gives in so easily tells me she's scared of what Petra is capable of and what she might do next. She won't be doing anything else, I'll make damned sure of that.

I stalk out of the room before Cindy can say anything else. I have to. I can't let her see how mad I really am, or she'll be hobbling along behind me trying to calm me down. I wasn't lying to Cindy. I'm not going to hurt Petra. This time.

I need to get a handle on my temper before I look for Petra. If I go in ranting and raving at her, she's not going to take my threats seriously. Everyone knows I have a temper and my immediate family learned quickly to just ignore my outbursts. I need to dig down inside of myself and find that cold anger I know still lurks there. The kind of anger that terrified people back in the days before I sorted my life out and began making my money through legit businesses.

I push all thoughts of Cindy away, because when I think of her, hurt and in pain, my emotions take over and all I can see is red. I know deep down this isn't about Cindy. Petra couldn't care less about Cindy one way or the other. This is about me. This is between me and her. Cindy is collateral damage in this, and that's how I need to think of her for the moment. I will protect my assets, just like I always have in my business.

It works.

The rage inside of me shifts, becoming a cold, deadly focus. By the time I reach the bottom of the stairs, I am different. Gone is the emotion, the ranting and raving. In its place is a ruthless determination that I have never allowed myself to show in front of my family before today.

I move through the house. A maid who is carrying a tray of coffee informs me Petra is in her bedroom. The coffee is for her. I tell her to take the coffee back to the kitchen. Then I go back upstairs and tap on Petra's suite of rooms. She shouts for me to come in.

I push the door open. "Leave it by the table," she says carelessly, not even looking up from the magazine she is reading.

I say nothing and Petra looks up with irritation. I see her register my ice-cold eyes, the set of my mouth and the way I stalk towards her. I see fear, real fear, flickering in her eyes.

"Alex? What … what's wrong?" she asks.

"I think we both know the answer to that one, Petra," I say.

My voice doesn't sound like my own. It sounds cold, robotic almost. It's totally devoid of any emotion. Petra flinches at the sound of it. She scrambles off the bed, putting it between us, and for a second, I remember the child she used to be. How the hell did we come to this?

Cindy's white face flashes into my mind, and although I push the image straight back out, seeing her for that fraction of a second is enough to remind me that this Petra isn't the same girl who grew up with me all of those years ago. Just like I'm not the same boy. Life has taken its toll on us both.

"Cindy was out on Nikita earlier and a noise spooked her. Cindy was thrown to the ground," I say.

"Is she ok?" Petra asks, her eyes widening convincingly.

"She's fine," I say.

Petra's mask slips for half a second. The bitch looks disappointed and it's all I can do not to fly across the bed and strangle her, but I keep my cool. That flash of giveaway expression was enough to confirm Cindy is right about her being behind this.

"Petra, I have something to say to you, and I'm only going to say it once, so I want you to listen closely because it's very important."

She nods. Her eyes flit between me and the door. She's sizing up if she has any chance of escape if I go for her. It's further confirmation of what she's done. She'd be up in arms if she had been wrongly accused. She would be shouting and cursing about how she gets the blame for everything around here, which is not actually true, but a little thing like the truth wouldn't get in the way of an outburst for Petra.

"If anything untoward at all happens to Cindy while she's here; any accident whatsoever, even something as small as a paper cut on her finger, I am going to find you and I am going to hurt you so bad you will wish you were dead. I mean that literally. Do we understand each other?"

Fear flashes in her eyes. It's not like she doesn't know what I have been capable of. The stories of my *Bratva* days are not secret. She swallows hard and nods once.

"Good." I turn to leave.

I close the door behind me and take a moment to compose myself, pushing away the cold, ruthless man I swore I had left behind for good. Once that was me all the time, but I gave up settling my problems with violence.

I think I scared Petra enough that he won't need to come out again.

I hope I have, because I really don't like this side of myself, but if Petra doesn't get the message, my nasty side will come out again, because I'm not messing about here. If she so much as looks at Cindy wrong, I will go through with my threat. No one is going to hurt Cindy ever again.

Not on my watch.

CINDY

By the time Alex returns to his room, I'm starting to feel much better. My shoulder is barely aching and my head has stopped spinning. I didn't dare tell Alex I felt a little bit light-headed, because if he had known that, I never would have been able to talk him out of calling for the doctor. The ice and the bandage have worked wonders on my ankle, and I've even been up and tested it while Alex was gone. It still hurts a bit and I have a slight limp to my step, but it's nothing I can't handle. I'm not sure what Petra hoped to achieve with what she did, whether she wanted to kill me, or just hurt me, but either way, she failed. I'm fine. I've done worse to myself falling down the stairs at home after a glass of wine too many.

I look at Alex as he comes into the room.

"How did it go with Petra?" I ask.

I wonder how far he has gone. I mean she needed telling, but I don't imagine Alex is the nicest guy towards anyone who gets on the wrong side of him.

"It was her, but she won't be trying anything like that again, I promise."

"I think she must want me out of the way so she can get all of the money for herself," I say with a laugh.

Alex frowns, looking confused, and I decide to tell him what Petra told me now. I think it's kind of funny how far Petra will go to try and split Alex and I up, and while I don't think Alex will find it funny, I still think he deserves to know the truth. If Petra is willing to tell a virtual stranger stories like that about him, who else is she telling these lies to?

I pat the bed beside me and Alex sits down.

"After lunch today, Petra invited me to have a glass of wine with her. Turns out she was only pretending to be nice to me so she could try and get into my head. I think she thought I would believe her story. I didn't because I know you better than that, but I have to hand it to her, the girl is damned good at manipulating people. If I didn't know you as well as I do, I might have believed her, she was that convincing."

Alex's frown deepens. "What did she tell you, Cindy?"

I take a deep breath. "She told me that you're using me. Our relationship is a lie to fool Babushka."

He narrows his eyes.

"That was my initial reaction too. I thought she had somehow worked out what we were doing, well how we started … our deal. Then I realized she couldn't have and I only thought that because she was being so vague, so I asked her to spit it out. That was when she tried to convince me that there's a clause in your aunt's will that says that you will only inherit her money and her estate if you are married. If

269

you're not, then everything will go into a fund that will provide for Petra and the others. I mean talk about scraping the bottom of the barrel for a story. I don't know what she's trying to achieve with these stories. Maybe she just wants to make you miserable."

I keep on babbling because as the words are pouring out of my mouth I'm beginning to realize that she was not scraping the bottom of the barrel. The story actually made perfect sense, especially since the reaction I'd been expecting from Alex, either anger at Petra, or maybe even laughing at how pathetic she is, doesn't come.

He doesn't say anything. He's just silent. In fact, his face has gone white and he's staring straight ahead of himself and in that moment, I know it's true. Petra clearly has an agenda here. One that involves getting me out of the way at any cost. She must have thought after our little conversation that I would stick by Alex no matter what so she tried to get rid of me another way.

Because she too wants that money at any cost.

"Alex?" I say when it's clear that he's not going to be the first one of us to break the silence that's fallen over the room. "Please tell me this isn't true."

He looks at me and I can see sorrow and pain in his eyes, but it's clear that everything Petra said is true. He's just been using me to get his hands on Babushka's money. Everything has been a lie. I'm not here fooling that sweet old lady for her sake, I'm here so Alex can walk away with the whole lot. For a brief second, the horror of knowing how thoroughly I was fooled by him made me almost wish I hadn't told him what Petra said.

But no. I'm glad I told him. I would rather know now what kind of a man Alex is than learn about it down the line in a divorce court once he has access to all the money. No doubt, he would have made me sign a pre-nup. What a joke! He sure knew how to pick the right girl for the job, because I would have insisted on signing a pre-nup to show him I had no interest in his money.

I finally see the true man beneath the mask. His face might be handsome, but inside, he is ugly. Ugly to the core.

"I don't want to lie to you, Cindy," he says softly.

Not only is he not trying to say it's not true, but he's not even defending himself or trying to explain to me why he's done any of this if it wasn't about the money.

I can't help but think of Babushka. Of how much she loves Alex and how this news would break her heart into a thousand pieces. I know then that I will take the coward's way out. I won't tell Babushka what I've learned. I can't be the one who breaks her heart like that. But I also can't be a part of duping her. It was one thing when I thought I was part of something that would make an old woman very happy, but not this. I have grown fond of Babushka over the last few days, and I don't care if Alex doesn't pay me a red cent. In fact, he can take his stupid casino and shove it up his ass. I am not being a part of duping an old lady out of her money.

"Fine," I say simply.

What else is there to say? He's not giving me any sort of an explanation and he's not denying it. I could get angry and yell at him, tell him what I think of someone who would do something so terrible. But what good would it do? Alex must know himself that what he's doing here is the lowest of the low. He doesn't need me to tell him that. And it's not like any of what I thought was between us is even real. He's not going to give a rat's ass what I think.

"I'm kind of tired now. Would you mind leaving me alone for a while?" I add when he says nothing.

I don't wait for him to say anything else. There's nothing he can say that can fix this. I lay down and turn my back to him. Please just go I think to myself. Don't make this harder than it has to be.

Alex stays sitting beside me on the bed, but he makes no move to touch me or to try to get me to talk to him. I close my eyes, willing him to go, and after a few minutes, I feel the mattress move as he stands. I hear him walking across the room and I open one eye a slit so I can see him. He picks his laptop up, then walks towards the door. I hear it open.

"I'm sorry, Cindy," he says.

The door closes behind him and I clench my jaw tightly. I can feel the tears of fury burning the backs of my eyes. Sorry? That's not enough. It's not even close to enough. I thought we could get through anything together, but I didn't bank on something like this coming up. And there is no us to get through anything because it was all a pack of lies. I was being duped every bit as much as Babushka was, and it took Petra of all people to bring the truth to light.

CINDY

I lay stiffly on Alex's bed for about ten minutes. I know I need to get back to my own room, to my phone so I can make arrangements to get out of here. But first, I want to make sure Alex is really gone. I don't want a slanging match with him. I just want to be able to slip away quietly and have this whole fucking mess over and done with.

I wait for as long as I can bear to, and then I sit up. I put my good foot down first and then I stand up, putting my hand on the headboard for balance. I test my weight slowly on my twisted ankle. A stab of pain goes up my leg, but it's nothing I can't handle and my ankle doesn't give way or anything. Alex might be a scheming bastard who wants to get richer than he already is off the back of his aunt, but he sure can apply a bandage with precision.

I limp towards the connecting door between our rooms and I find myself laughing like a mad person when a crazy thought pops into my head. I feel as if I'm suddenly in the starring role in Misery. Here I am, a prisoner in a strange house, unable to walk properly, needing to escape, and feeling like there's no way out.

Of course, there's a way out I tell myself as I move into my own room and push the connecting door closed. It's called a cab and then a plane. It's that simple.

No one is holding you here against your will, I remind myself. It's not a movie and this isn't going to turn into some action sequence where I have to try and escape my captors.

Even if Alex catches me packing and tries to stop me from leaving, I know Babushka won't allow him to keep me here if I tell her I want to leave. I don't want it to come to that though. I have done enough damage to Babushka. I won't do anymore.

I pick up my phone and the light catches on my beautiful, fake-engagement ring. With my heart feeling as if it had turned to stone, I take it off and carefully place it on the bedside table. Then I go to sit on the edge of my bed. I open up Google and begin looking for flights. Panic seizes me and tears threaten when I see all the flights leaving tonight start jumbling up before my eyes.

I feel trapped. Panicky. There is only one way out and it involves doing something I never imagined I'd ever do. I never imagined a situation like this. I can't help but think my life is in danger here. Not from Alex. Even though his feelings for me were lies, it's a stretch to think he'd try to kill me. But Petra just might. She's already tried it once. And I keep thinking about Alex mentioning secret passages in the house. She could get into my room and slit my throat in my sleep without anyone even knowing she'd left her room. And I refuse to sleep with Alex again. I think I'd rather be murdered.

I call Star. She answers on the second ring.

"Oi you! I'm surprised you have time for me with all the hot sex going on over there."

At the sound of her voice, I burst into tears. I didn't even know they were coming, but once they start, I fear they won't stop.

"What the fuck?" Star never swears and hearing her do it makes me cry harder. Star makes soothing noises down the line, letting me cry it out. I finally get myself under control when my sobs turn into a series of broken hiccups.

"Tell me what happened?" she orders, her voice brisk and businesslike.

I tell her everything. About Alex and I and how I thought we had something special. Then about Petra's revelation, and my 'accident'. And finally, the worst part, how I confronted Alex with what Petra said and he didn't even try to deny it.

"I have to leave here, Star. I can't stay another night. It was one thing lying to make Alex's great aunt happy, but I won't be a part of someone trying to deceive her so that he can take her money. And then there's Petra. Alex warned her to leave me alone, but I don't know whether or not she'll listen to him. She might slit my throat while I'm sleeping."

"I totally get it. I'd be out of there too," Star says.

I sniff. I really do have good friends if nothing else. Star hasn't even said I told you so. And she would have been well within her rights to do so.

"The thing is, Star ... I hate to ask you this, but I'm desperate. Is there anyway Nikolai can get someone to pick me up from here? I remember you saying that he keeps a plane in Russia ..."

"What time do you want to fly?" she interrupts me.

"As soon as possible?"

"Right. Let me make some arrangements and call you back."

"Thank you," I say. Knowing that Star is on my case causes such relief to flood through me that I almost start crying again, but I hold the tears back. I have to stay strong and get away from here. I can cry all I want to, all I need to when I get home.

ALEX

I don't recognize the number of the caller, but since it is my private line that no one other than family and a few close friends know, I take the call.

"Alex, this is Star. I am a friend of Cindy," a woman says coldly.

A cold claw grips my insides. I know what this call is about. She doesn't wait for me to answer her, but goes on.

"I'll be sending a plane for her to your estate in two hours. I don't think you deserve to be told, but my husband says you are capable of shooting the pilot of any plane landing on your land if I don't ask for your permission first. So consider this call as my notification that I want my friend back and I'm sending someone to get her. She may not be precious to you, but she is extremely precious to me. So please do not stop her from leaving, or I will come there myself to collect her."

A bitter smile curves my lips. How well her husband knows me. That is exactly what I would have done if anybody had tried to come between me and my woman, but as it happens this offer is exactly what I need. I need Cindy gone. And there is no better way than in one of Nikolai's planes. I trust him.

"All right. Send your plane. A driver will take her out to the airstrip to wait for you," I tell her.

She gasps. I know what she is thinking. She's thinking I'm a monster for cheating my own flesh and blood and for using her friend. I guess I am, if she had seen the things I've done, this would be nothing in comparison.

"Thank you for that." Then the line goes dead.

How very, very stupid I've been. I exhale and look out of the window. Oh Cindy, Cindy, Cindy.

CINDY

I end the call with Star, relieved that there will be a plane in two hours to pick me up. Quickly, I grab my suitcase and start throwing my things into it. In my haste, I throw everything in so haphazardly I can't then fasten my suitcase. I feel my hands clenching with a strange panic. I don't want to leave this paradise, and yet I want to run away from this place as soon as I can. My heart feels like it is breaking.

He betrayed me. Used me. Lied to me.

I should have listened to my instincts that night at the casino. He was too slick, too smooth, to James Bondish. But foolishly I bought his bullshit because I was taken in by his beauty.

I sit down and tell myself I have to calm down. Two hours is a long time. I don't have to hurry, I will be ready by then. I take everything back out of the suitcase and put it back in neatly. I check the time when I'm done. Twenty minutes have passed. I will wait an extra ten minutes in my room before venturing down and asking someone to drive me to the tarmac.

I wish I could go and say goodbye to Babushka, but I know I can't. Not without somehow breaking down and making her suspect what Alex has been up to, and I know I can't do that. But she's going to be hurt that I left without saying goodbye, but I know Alex, the consummate liar will make up something about me having to go urgently to take care of a sick relative or something. She will never see me again and I hope she will find it in her heart to forgive me.

I have five more minutes to wait when the connecting door in my room opens and Alex walks in. He looks at my suitcase and then at me and I see his jaw tighten as if he is controlling himself. It makes me want to go to him and throw my arms around him and tell him I won't leave him if he wants me to stay.

But I don't.

I hate liars. Even gorgeous liars like him.

So I look away from him, refusing to meet his eyes.

ALEX

I stop dead when I see her suitcases on the bed. I was wrong earlier when she turned her back on me and I thought I was breaking inside. Seeing her standing over her packed cases is a hundred times worse. I know she has to leave this place. After what happened earlier, and after she found out about the clause, I don't blame her for wanting to leave. She has her dignity and her pride. I would want to leave too if I was in her shoes.

"Let me help you carry your suitcases down," I hear myself saying. My voice sounds strange to my ears.

I walk towards her and she doesn't back away, but she makes no effort to come to me and when I reach her, I have to physically stop myself from reaching for her.

She looks me in the eye and I can see her heart is breaking. I don't want her to be hurting, but in some ways, the hurt I can see in her eyes gives me hope. I can still reach her. She hasn't turned herself off from me completely. Not yet.

"No need. I'm sure one of the staff will help me."

I expected that answer. I stare at her blankly. I feel so lost.

I see a flash of anger cross her face. "What will you tell Babushka?"

"What do you want me to tell her?" My voice almost falters. What a mess this has turned out to be. I underestimated Petra. I didn't think it through. I was careless. I should have known better. There was too much money at stake.

"Please," she whispers, "tell her I'm sorry I had to go, but that it was lovely to meet her."

Then she goes to step around me, struggling to pull her suitcase behind her. The weight of it makes her stumble and I reach out then. I grab her wrist and even as she breaks my heart I feel the sparks when we touch. I know she feels them too, because she gasps before she pulls her arm away from me.

"Don't you dare touch me," she hurls at me.

"I'll fix it all, I promise," I whisper.

She snorts out a laugh. "Fix it? How the fuck do you expect to do that?" she yells. Then she stops and takes a deep breath before continuing in a calmer voice. "I don't need you to swoop in and fix things for me. Nah. You've got your hands full here. Anyway, I'm a grown woman and I don't need you or anyone else to take care of me. Now if you don't mind, I'd like to go downstairs and ask for some help with my suitcases."

She leaves me then, limping pitifully, and I let her go. I watch her back as she slowly and painfully walks away from me. She never looks back, and I feel as though my whole future has been ripped away. As though the only light left in my life has been extinguished. I dared to let myself believe I could still have a happy ending.

I go to the top of the stairs and watch her grasp the banister as she hops down the stairs. As soon as she gets down safely I call the driver to bring the car around. Then I go back into her room and pick up her two suitcases.

I take them downstairs and arrive next to her as she stands in the middle of the foyer. She is obviously waiting to ask someone for help with her suitcases. Her lips tighten when she sees me carrying them.

"The driver is waiting outside for you."

She presses her lips together and her chin trembles and I think she might start crying, but she doesn't. Wordlessly, she crosses the wide space and goes outside. The driver rushes to relieve me of her luggage. He puts it in the boot of his car and she is in such a hurry to get in she almost falls. I can't help it, I catch her in my arms.

"I said don't touch me," she says between gritted teeth.

Ignoring her I help her into the back and close the door. She doesn't look at me. Just stares straight ahead, her face red with the emotion she is trying not to show.

I watch as the car pulls away. Then I turn around and something catches my eye. I look in the direction of my aunt's quarters and I see her standing at her window. She looks at me sadly. She shakes her head and I shake mine too. At that moment, I can't stop my eyes from filling with tears.

Then I go back to my room and I sit down on the bed. Petra played this game like a master. I look around me. The room feels empty, like Cindy's presence filled it up and now it's gone and nothing in the world makes sense anymore. I pick up the corner of the sheet and press it to my face, sniffing it and taking in Cindy's scent.

"I'll win you back, Cindy Forrester if it's the last thing I do," I whisper into her sweet scent.

CINDY

It's been a week since I left Russia. Since I left Alex. My flight home was unbearably sad and lonely, but it all went smoothly. Everything went without a hitch. I spoke to Star as soon as I got on board and she was at the airport as she promised she would be. She took one look at my tear-stained face and took me to the nearest off-license. She bought three bottles of wine and we went to my place. We talked and drank into the early hours of the next morning. I sobbed my heart out to her. She made all the right noises and she still didn't say I told you so.

Then Rosa arrived and Star left and I sobbed all over again.

I finally collapsed into bed around seven a.m. the next morning, telling myself I would feel better when I woke up now I had it all out of my system. I didn't. Not only did I have the worst hangover I'd ever had in my life, but I was still just as sad, just as empty feeling. And I missed Alex so fucking much.

Rosa made me a whopping breakfast and gave me a glass of wine to drink. Hair of the dog, she said. I felt slightly better.

I knew he would still be trying to keep up the ruse for his aunt's sake, and I didn't expect to see him for the first two days at work. He would still be in Russia. But once he was due home, I expected him to show up at the casino. I was half looking forward to it, because I missed him so much, and I was half dreading it, because no matter what I felt when I looked at him again, on his side of it all had been a big fat fucking lie.

I didn't even know if I still wanted to work at The Macau. All the excitement I felt about my career was gone. Everything felt empty and pointless.

I waited and waited, but I never had to face him because he didn't show up. I went about my nights in the casino as usual, doing my job, and jumping every time a big guy in a suit walked in, but it was never him. What a coward. He wasn't even going to show his face. I told myself I didn't care, but I did. The least he owed me was an apology.

Actually, he didn't though. Not really. He paid me what he promised me at the start of our arrangement. His lawyer sent me the deeds to half the casino. When I looked at it, I didn't feel happy. I felt dirty and stupid because of what I'd unwittingly done to get it.

And yet despite feeling so lost, angry and stupid, and despite knowing Alex didn't want me, that he never had, I still found myself wanting to see him more and more with each day that passed.

There was no out. I *wanted* him to show up at the casino. I needed him to. We need closure. I need closure.

Tonight has been another night he didn't show up. He never once called to see how the business was running.

I sigh as I let myself into my home. It's been a long night at work, made longer by my constant checking of the CCTV screens for Alex. I feel exhausted. I know I look like shit too. My brain tells me I have to let this crap go. I have to stop thinking about Alex. Stop hoping I'll see him and just move on with my life. But my heart won't let go. Damn him. He really did a fucking number on me.

I lock my front door and shrug out of my coat. Then I kick my shoes off tiredly and head into the lounge. I am instantly on high alert when I see that one of my lamps is on. I didn't put that on. The high alert turns to spine tingling fear when a man stands up from my couch.

"Hello, Cindy."

The fear turns to uncontrollable fury. The man is Alex.

"Did you miss me?" he asks softly.

"Did I miss you? Are you fucking kidding me?" I shout hysterically. "How the fuck did you get into my house?"

I take a step towards him and the hurt and the longing and the pain all turns into an all-encompassing, inexplicable rage when I see that Alex's smile has its usual effect on my body. My body wants him to fuck me. I scream then, a sound of total frustration, incomprehension, and pain as I launch myself at him, my fists flying. Alex sees my attack coming and he catches hold of my wrists easily. He holds me out at arm's length so my kicking feet can't connect with him. Then he just watches me calmly as I scream and shout and try to twist my way free.

Eventually, I use up all of my anger and I just stand there, my chest heaving with the exertion of it all.

"Are you done?" he asks softly.

I nod miserably and he releases my wrists. I debate going for him again, but the anger is gone and I'm just bone-tired. The truth is I'm tired of feeling this way and I just want him out of my life. I'll hear him out, get the closure I need, and then I'll resign and start over. Somewhere else. He can have his damn fifty percent back. I don't want it.

I sink down heavily on the couch and Alex sits beside me. One thing is really bothering me more than anything and I repeat my earlier question, although without the fiery anger this time.

"How did you get in here?" I say again.

"You keep a spare key in your locker at work," he says, as though it's perfectly acceptable for him to help himself to that key and use it to come into my house without permission.

This should anger me further, but it doesn't. I just accept it. I'm done raging.

"I'm sorry. I would never have used it, but the conversation we're about to have isn't one I was willing to have at the casino and I didn't think you'd let me in if I just knocked on your door like a sane person."

A ghost of a smile curves my lips. I really have missed him, although there's no way in hell I'm going to tell him that.

"Yeah, you bet I wouldn't have," I agree.

"I caused you pain, Cindy, and I'm truly sorry for that. I

won't blame you if you tell me to get out and never come back. But I won't leave until after I've explained everything to you. I owe you that and I need you to hear it. And then if you still want me to leave, I'll go."

"Whatever," I shrug tiredly. "Let's hear the next batch of lies you've cooked up."

"I've never lied to you. The only time I was less than transparent, the only thing I am guilty of is when I let you believe what Petra said was true and, I think you'll at least understand why I had to do what I did when I explain."

"What?" I whisper in shock.

"It's true. Everything I said about wanting to make Babushka happy was true. She really does want me to find someone and be happy with her and I wanted to give her that before she left this earth. And until Petra interfered you made her really happy, you saw for yourself how happy she was to think I'd found the one. It was never about anything else. Here's something else interesting for you to know. I am the rightful and the only heir to the Obolensky fortune. The titles only passed to Babushka because my father died and she was the next in line. After her death, I am the next in line, but I am not interested in her house or her money. I have my own money, more than I need, and until I saw how truly beautiful Winter House was through your eyes I never wanted it, or had any intention of going to live there."

"What about the clause Petra was talking about?" I ask in shock.

"That clause is indeed in my aunt's will. I told Babushka to add it years ago."

I have to admit I didn't see that one coming. I want to reject the explanation as lies, but Alex seems so genuine and I know in my heart he's telling me the truth. "Why?"

"Basically, my relatives are freeloaders and parasites. They have no issues with doing nothing and living off Babushka. She allows it because she likes to be surrounded by them. After all, they're family and blood is thicker than water, but deep down, she knows what they're after. Her money. And that's why she made a little joke about them being so eager to get their hands on some of her money that they could arrange for her to have a fall, or even slowly poison her."

My mouth drops open at the idea of them trying to kill her. Killing me, a complete stranger is one thing, but a sweet little old lady like Babushka?

"To be honest, at that time, I thought she was being a bit paranoid, but there's nothing I won't do to keep her happy so even though I didn't believe it, I came up with the idea of the clause. The clause would mean it would be in their interest to make sure Babushka lived as long as possible so they could continue to live in the style they had become accustomed to. In the event she died, a trust would take over and they would all get a pittance compared to what they enjoy now. Since I didn't want anybody to suspect why we were changing the will, we let everyone think it was because Babushka wanted me to get married and produce heirs. It worked. Everybody believed it and everyone was happy because nobody could see me settling down with anyone. In fact, it was more likely they would be attending my funeral than my wedding. That is until now when I wanted to make Babushka happy with the thought that she was going to get what she wanted all along and ..."

"You brought me into the picture," I finish for him.

He nods. "Anyway, what none of the family knows, is that the will they've seen with the clause isn't Babushka's real will. Her real will is with her lawyer. It gives Marina and Viktor a good payout as she's already bought them a house. It gives Petra and Anastasia enough to live in a fairly grand style. I will inherit Winter House, regardless of my marital status and Valeriya will live in the house for as long as she wants. The rest of Babushka's money will be used to start a charity in Russia for homeless children. If you don't believe me, I can show you a copy of the real will."

CINDY

As Alex explains his side of the situation, I had a hundred questions, but they've all mostly faded away. His explanation makes sense. Much more sense than thinking that he needs his aunt's money, or that he'd purposely con the one family member he has who loves him completely.

"I … oh my God, Alex, I'm so sorry. I can't believe I believed that of you," I say.

He shrugs.

"Petra got into your head. She's good like that. How else could you react?"

"But why didn't you tell me all this that day?"

"I wanted more than anything to tell you the truth that day, but Winter House wasn't the place to do it. As you learned, there are tunnels and passageways everywhere and I was pretty certain either Petra or Anastasia would be around your room hoping to hear us talking. I knew I could not keep both you and Babushka safe. Even though it devastated me to send you away in the way I did, I knew my best bet was to get you off the property and back to safety while Petra and Anastasia thought we had fallen out. Once you were gone I knew they couldn't harm you and I could more effectively sort out Babushka's situation to my satisfaction."

"Everything I said to you from the moment we met is true, Cindy. I am in love with you. Completely, hopelessly in love with you. And that means total honesty. Even if it hurts."

I stare in his familiar stormy eyes and feel my heart skip a beat. He loves me! It wasn't all a lie. What we had was real. I open my mouth to speak but nothing comes out. I close it again and just sit in silence, trying to process everything he's told me, but mostly just hearing him say he's in love with me. It vibrates inside my head. And it sounds beautiful.

"Cindy? You do believe me, don't you?" he says, a tinge of worry in his voice.

I nod, still mute for the moment. I shake my head slightly, hoping to clear it.

"I … yes. I believe you about your aunt's will. It makes sense. And I desperately want to believe you about the rest …"

"But?" Alex prompts me.

"But it's been a week since I left you in Russia. You've been home for what? Days? And you're just coming here now. That doesn't feel like the actions of someone who is completely and hopelessly in love."

"Actually, I've just got back. I came here straight from the airport. Well after I waited for you to go down to the casino floor so I could sneak like a damn thief into your locker and get your key," he says with a sheepish smile. "I know I could have called you from somewhere outside of the house, but this wasn't a conversation to be had over the phone. I needed you to be able to look me in the eye as I spoke so you could see the truth of my words."

"You've just got back? Why?"

"After I saw for myself that my aunt wasn't just being paranoid I started to fear for her safety too. I stayed on a bit longer to convince her to come to London and then to arrange to have her and Valeriya's things sent here."

"You got her to agree to it?" I ask, surprised.

He nods. "Yes. It seems you made quite an impression on my aunt as well as me. She wants to be around us. But don't worry. No pressure. Now that she is away from danger there is no longer any need to pretend. You can tell her we ended things between us, if that's what you want."

"Or I could not do that," I say with a smile.

He stares at me. He looks like he hardly dares to breathe. "What do you mean?" he whispers hoarsely.

"You said that nothing you told me at the house was a lie. Well it wasn't for me either. Everything I said and felt was real. Alex, I love you so much I thought I was going to die this week without you."

"You would take me back after everything that happened?" he asks.

I nod. "If you can forgive me for doubting you," I say, nervous suddenly.

"There's nothing to forgive," Alex says, sweeping me into his arms

His mouth is suddenly on mine. As we kiss, it's like no time has passed at all, like none of the bad stuff between us ever happened. I can feel it in his kiss that he feels exactly the same. He pulls me closer to him, and it's like we're made to fit together.

We had a whirlwind insta-lust attraction and a rocky road that lead us here, but now that we're here, I know for sure I never want to walk away from Alex again. A week without him was more than I could bear. I was ready to give up everything for him. I can't even begin to imagine living the rest of my life without him. I don't want to imagine it. Not even for a second. I'm never letting him go again.

Alex takes his mouth from mine and already I miss his lips, his tongue. He has woken my body back up and I want him so badly. He pulls me close and holds me against him for a moment.

"I love you more than words, more than money, more than anything else in this world, Cindy. I want you to never forget that," he whispers into my ear.

I cling to him for a moment and then I pull back so I can look at his face again.

"Should we take this to my bedroom? Or do you need to get back to your aunt?" I ask.

He stands up and offers me his hand. I slip my hand into his with no hesitation and he pulls me gently to my feet.

"First things first," he says as he slips the beautiful ring I thought I'd never see again on my finger.

I look down at the ring with a mixture of amazement and delight. Wow! This time it's for real.

"And now, bed for you, I think," he says. "My aunt will be just fine without me. Why do you think I brought Valeriya home with her?"

My laughter dies in my throat when he throws me over his shoulder like a sack of potatoes and starts heading for my bedroom. I missed Alex with all my heart, but Alex missed me with his body. He falls on me with the intensity and hunger of a man who has been locked away in prison for years and years and this is his last day on earth.

All the pain and darkness magically disappeared. Soon the morning sun will come out and flood my home, but it is already flooding my heart.

CINDY

SIX MONTHS LATER

I stand in the bathroom, needing a moment of alone time. The old cathedral where we're getting married is filled with gorgeously dressed people. All of our friends are here, along with my family and Babushka, who I guess is my family now too. The rest of Alex's family didn't get an invite to the wedding, although a fair few of his old friends have flown out to be here today.

Everywhere I turn there is noise and movement. It's all happy noise – laughter, tears of joy and chattering, but I just needed a moment of silence.

The bathroom adjoins the room I claimed for myself and my bridesmaids, Star, Rosa, and Raven, to get ready in. They're still in there, sipping champagne and chatting. I know they were worried when I announced I needed a moment alone to center myself, but they'll get over it when they find out why and hopefully, they'll understand why I didn't talk to them about it.

I clutch the edge of the sink and look at myself in the mirror and smile at my reflection. I look radiant, even if I do say so myself.

My dress is silvery white with a tight bodice and a big white flowing skirt. A beautiful diamond and silver sparkly tiara holds my veil in place, my curls peeking out from around the sides of it. My make-up is flawless. My skin looks like porcelain with my cheeks tinged with just the right amount of blusher to make me look excited.

I didn't need the extra color, I am excited. I can't wait to marry Alex.

As I look into my own eyes in the mirror, I see the truth shining in the unshed tears there, and I know I have to tell him now. I should have told him sooner, but I told myself no, I could wait. But I can't. I feel like it's now or never and I choose now.

I nod to myself, telling myself I've made the right choice. I turn away from the mirror and leave the bathroom before I can talk myself back out of this.

"I won't be long," I say to the girls as I pass through the room.

I head for the door to the room, ignoring the questions being called out behind me from Rosa and Star. I walk along the corridor blindly, vaguely aware that people are greeting me as I pass by them, and I'm rudely ignoring them.

Halfway down the corridor, I pick up the many voluminous, whispering layers that make up the skirt of my gown in both hands and start to run. I am aware of passing Babushka as she joins the other guests who are beginning to make their way downstairs to the banquet hall where Alex and I will be married. I hear her asking me where I'm going, but I don't stop, only give her a big smile. If I stop, there won't be enough time to catch Alex before he leaves his room.

I keep running and finally, I arrive at his room. It's at the opposite end of the corridor to mine. Mine is beside one staircase, his another. We agreed to the idea so that we wouldn't see each other on the day, at least not before the ceremony.

I go into the room without knocking. I am greeted by a room full of groomsmen, all of whom look at me in shock as I burst into the room.

"Where is he?" I ask, scanning the room and instantly seeing Alex isn't among the men gathered there.

"He's in the bathroom," one of the men says.

"Cindy, what are you doing here?" Alex's best man asks. There is a note of urgency in his voice.

"I need to talk to him. Now," I say.

"Is everything ok?" someone else asks.

"Yeah, I just need to talk to him," I repeat.

I sense the mood in the room changing. The groomsmen are starting to shift about uncomfortably, pulling at their suits and ties. Maybe they think I've changed my mind and either I'm about to call off the wedding, or stand Alex up.

Before I can tell them to relax, all is well, a door opens and Alex steps into the room. He looks gorgeous in his gray suit and white shirt, a perfect contrast to the groomsmen who wear traditional black suits. For a second, our eyes meet and we just drink each other in.

"Isn't this meant to be unlucky?" Alex teases me with a wink.

He said the tradition of not seeing each other on the day of the wedding was stupid, an old wives' tale, but I insisted and he agreed to it, and now here I am being the one to bring bad luck to us.

I don't reply. If I do, I know I will cry and I don't want to cry. I also don't want to have this conversation in a room full of Alex's friends and I try to tell him that with my eyes. I don't know if he gets the message, but without looking away from me, he addresses the whole room.

"Gentlemen, can you give us a minute, please?" he asks.

He speaks in English and I know some of his groomsmen speak little to no English, but they all seem to get the message as the others start to file out of the room. Soon, it's just Alex and I left in the room.

"What is it?" he asks.

I want to speak, to reassure him, but I have a huge lump in my throat, and all I can do is shake my head. To tell him that it's not bad news.

"Cindy, you're really worrying me now," he says, a suddenly deep sadness filling his eyes.

I take a deep breath and I swallow hard, pushing away the lump, and when I finally get my words to come out, my voice sounds shaky.

"Alex, I'm sorry to do this now," I say. "I should have told you sooner, but I didn't and then I told myself I'd tell you later, but I have to tell you before we get married. I don't know why, but I just know I have to."

"So, we're still getting married," he says, looking relieved.

"Yes," I say quickly. "God, yes. Of course, yes. I just … Alex, I'm pregnant."

For a second he just looks at me like I haven't spoken and then his face opens out into a wide smile. It is the widest smile I have ever seen on his face. Then he starts to laugh with pure joy. In a flash, he closes the gap between us and, wrapping his arms around me, he picks me and whirls me around. I laugh too. My veil flies behind me and swirls around us, until it is wrapped around us.

"Alex," I whisper in his ear.

"What?" he whispers back.

"You're pleased?"

"Pleased? I'm deliriously, fantastically, and ecstatically pleased," he says.

I feel sheer relief flood me and it hits me why I wanted to wait until after the wedding to tell him about this and why I suddenly knew that I couldn't do that. I wasn't sure whether he would be happy about this. We've never really talked about when or even if we'd have kids.

"Have I spoilt it by coming here, though? Now you won't get to turn around and see me coming to you in my white dress."

"Oh, Cindy. You haven't spoilt anything for me. You coming here to tell me I'm going to be a dad is something I'll remember to the day I die. It's … well … different. A real Cindy Forrester thing to have done," he says, not able to keep the grin off his face for even a second. "Plus it's the best wedding gift anyone could have ever given me."

He sets me back down on my feet and untangles us from my long veil, then he leans in to kiss me and I jerk back.

"Lipstick," I caution with a laugh. "My eyes are probably enough of a mess with all the tears."

"Mess? You look absolutely beautiful," he says seriously.

He kisses my cheek tenderly. I hug him to me again, then release him quickly before I can start to feel the way my body responds to being in his arms.

"I have to go," I say. "I'm due to get married in less than five minutes and I need to get my make-up fixed first."

"Yes, go. You don't want to keep your poor groom waiting at the altar."

"Oh, Alex, I can't wait to become Mrs. Obolensky."

"Get in the queue. I was here first," he teases.

"Stop bickering. We're not married yet," I throw over my shoulder as I hurry towards the door.

"I love you," Alex calls.

I'm in the hallway when I shout the sentiment back to him and smile to myself as I hear the collective sigh of relief from the groomsmen who were lining the hallway and are now filing back into the room.

I debate skipping getting my make-up fixed, but I decide against it. I'm the bride. It's tradition for me to be late. And besides, I plan on only ever doing this once and I don't want to look a mess for it.

I hurry back to my room, but rather than feeling like I'm running, this time, it feels like I am floating on air. As I get to the room where Rosa, Star, and Raven are waiting, I can hear that someone inside there has put on one of my favorite songs. I smile to myself.

Yes, it is a nice day for a white wedding.

A very nice day.

EPILOGUE

ALEX

Eight Months Later

Babushka stands as Cindy and I walk into the room. Usually, I would gesture for her to sit back down, but today nothing will keep her in her seat. She comes towards us eagerly, her face filled with joy and anticipation. Completely ignoring me, she goes towards Cindy and peers at the bundle Cindy is carrying.

"Babushka, meet your great, great nephew, Leonid Joseph Obolensky," I say.

"Hi there, Leonid." Tears run down Babushka's withered cheeks as she smiles down at him. Then she looks up at me. "Your father would have been so proud of you, Alex. So proud."

The image of my father flashes into my head. Yes, I suppose

he would have been. But I wouldn't be here today, if not for Cindy.

I help Babushka gently back to her seat and Cindy puts our son into her frail arms.

"Leonid Joseph. That's a good, almost biblical name for a strong boy," she says, smiling with approval. "Now tell me, Alex. How did such a good biblical baby come into the world only eight months after your wedding?"

I grin at Babushka's nosy, mocking question and Cindy starts fussing with Leonid's blanket so she doesn't have to look her in the eye.

"Well, if you really want to know …" I say trailing away when Cindy gives me a horrified look.

Babushka laughs and I can see the twinkle in her eye.

"Ahhhhhh … look at that gorgeous little face," she says, not looking up. She only has eyes for baby Leonid. "He's going to be a little stunner, just like his mum and dad."

She finally manages to tear her eyes away from the baby's face long enough to glance up at Cindy. "I'm sorry I couldn't come to the hospital. I really wanted to, but Alex wouldn't let me."

"Quite right. A hospital is no place for you. You are safest here, at home."

"Yes, I suppose all those antibiotic-resistant bacteria are a worry when you're old and decrepit," she says mildly. "Enough about me, how are you feeling, my dear?"

"Absolutely fine." Cindy smiles. "Having Leonid here is worth the pain. Anyway, I found out giving birth is an apparently really good time to swear continuously at your husband. It's totally acceptable, even encouraged. The air was blue while I was giving birth."

Babushka laughs uproariously. That is the one thing that has not dimmed even with the sickness eating her up from the inside. Her beautiful laugh.

"It was different in my time," she tells Cindy. "All I could think of was I didn't want to push out a roll of crap while I was trying to get my Marina out."

Cindy grins at Babushka's frankness.

Unfazed Babushka continues. "Still, I remember that feeling of holding my baby for the first time well." Her eyes fill with nostalgia. "There is no feeling purer or greater than the love you feel for your newborn baby."

Cindy smiles softly and sighs. "No, there isn't."

"You are a lucky girl, Cindy. He is an absolutely beautiful baby."

"I know. I'm so glad you got to meet your great, great nephew, Babushka."

Babushka beams at her words and looks down at Leonid again. "Just to give you both fair warning, you do know I'm going to spoil him rotten, right?"

I know she means it as well. "I wouldn't expect anything else," I say with a laugh.

"I'm so pleased you two got together. You're a lovely couple. Or you were. Now you're a lovely family," she says.

Cindy smiles at her and my aunt winks at her.

"Tell me the truth, Cindy. It was when you went out riding together to the creek, wasn't it? The moment you fell in love with him. It was the magic of that place."

I feel a little pang of fear. Is Babushka starting to get confused? "We went to the creek only when we came to your house remember, Babushka."

"I know," she says, her tone suggesting that I'm the one who is confused.

"We were already engaged then," Cindy reminds gently.

Babushka throws her head back and laughs. "I think we can drop that one now, don't you think?"

"What do you mean?" Cindy asks, her tone cautious.

"Did you two really think I didn't know your whole so-called relationship was made up? Honestly. That proposal story was sweet and all, but it was so far from your style Alex."

"But if you knew, why did you go along with it?" I ask.

Babushka smiles at me. A wide smile that is so full of love it is almost heartbreaking. "I knew you were trying to make me happy. I didn't want to throw it back in your face, but I also knew the spark was already there ... and if I played along so both of you could spend some time acting like a couple that somewhere along the way, you would become one. And it worked, didn't it? Look where we are now. I've lived many more years than you have and I could see what the two of you couldn't. That you were made for each other."

I look at Cindy at the same time she looks at me and the

same expression is in her eyes that I know is in mine. Love, pure love and immense gratitude that we found each other, that we have Leonid, and we still have Babushka with us.

The End

COMING NEXT - SAMPLE CHAPTER

WITH THIS RING

WITH THIS RING

FREYA

(Unedited)

"Freya!"

I looked up from the dirty vodka martini I was mixing.

"Monsieur Garlic-Cock wants you, darling," George said in his totally inimitable way, as he paused by the service station, a tray of ten cocktail glasses expertly balanced on the palm of his hand.

I could have asked him how he knew Monsieur Bisset's cock smelled of garlic, but I just laughed at his sass, and said, "Tell him he knows where to find me."

"There goes my tip," George said sourly and sashayed away, a gorgeous smile on his lips.

I looked in the direction of the middle-aged French businessman. He raised his glass and nodded at me. Monsieur Bisset flew into town once a month and he usually ended up in our bar to celebrate his victories in the boardroom. His goal seemed to be female attention, usually mine, but he was not too fussy. After a certain point in the night an orifice to wet his cock was more than enough. Of course, being filthy rich he couldn't understand why I kept rejecting his advances. I told him I didn't need money once, and he took that to mean I was holding out for more. In his eyes, I was a lowly waitress who should be grateful that such a fine gentleman as him had looked my way.

I pushed the dirty martini over to Dan, the curly-haired American guy, sitting at the bar. He was a regular, a funny guy. He gave me a wink which I returned before I moved onto mixing the next drink on my order list.

"I see I'm not the only one after you," he commented.

"Would I be as desirable if you were?" I quipped.

"Fair enough," he agreed, taking a long sip of his drink. He put his glass on the bar and grinned at me. "Fuck, this tastes as good as I can only imagine you will."

I took the flirt in good stride. It was part of the job. You want to be a barmaid in an underground cocktail bar beneath the Chelsea Market, then you can't be a paid-up member of the #metoo movement as well.

"Come on. Give me a chance, babe," he cajoled. "It's been months."

I reached up to the top shelves for a new bottle of rum. I needed it to make a Long Island Iced Teas. As I unscrewed the top I responded to Dan's unwise remark. "If I ever do Dan, beware. It might end with me sucking you dry—"

He tapped the counter excitedly. "But that is exactly what I want!"

"With a sexual harassment lawsuit," I completed dryly.

"I'll take that too," he said, after a brief contemplation.

I burst into laughter that rang across the bar.

"It'll be worth it," he joked. "Just for one taste."

I blew him a kiss and delivered the Long Island to the amused, bearded man sitting next to him. He tipped his fedora to me, and I gave him what I'd been told was my most electrifying smile. Julia came by then with a tray in hand, and passed on another message from Bisset. "He says there's a five-hundred-dollar tip waiting for you if you bring the drink to him yourself." She looked a bit jealous as she said it.

I shook my head to cover my irritation. "Tell him my place is behind the bar."

The message was relayed and a few minutes later Monsieur Antoine Bisset himself, made his way over. "You have me wrapped around your little finger, haven't you," he said, his accent thick with French charm or alcohol.

"No one has you wrapped around their little finger, Monsieur," I say firmly.

He took his seat and watched me as I worked, until his ogling started to irritate me.

"What else will you have today, Monsieur?" I asked, with a big plastic smile.

"You are a wild girl, Freya," He sucked in his breath. I waited patiently while he ran his gaze from the top of my fiery red hair, down on my chest, linger there deliberately, then back up to my eyes.

"The usual." he said.

I nodded and went to the locked cabinet to retrieve the £4,700 bottle of Louis XIII cognac that was kept specially for him.

I picked up one of the large glass goblets I'd been keeping warm on top of the coffee machine and poured a healthy amount of the ridiculously expensive drink into it. I swirled it to further warm the drink then, with the proper reverence for the price of the drink, placed the goblet on a coaster in front of him. "Should I send the rest over to your table?"

"Fuck no!" he cursed. "I'll take it with me on my way out. Perhaps it'll be enough reason for you to stop by my hotel room and share a glass with me." Without breaking eye contact, he slipped his usual hundred towards me.

I took the cash and tucked it into my back jeans pocket. "There will never be a reason in the world big enough, Monsieur." I smiled to take the sting away.

"That pussy of yours is not going to lick itself. Someday you're going to come to your senses, Princess."

Dan roared triumphantly. "Join the line Mon-fucking-sieur."

He ignored Dan and shifted his attention to his drink. He took an elaborate sniff of the potent fumes, then a sip of the sinfully smooth luxury.

"Ahhh…" he moaned at the pleasure.

I turned away to take care of the other patrons waiting to be served when my eyes suddenly met *his*.

I froze

Right there in the midst of the crowd… he was watching me. His gaze was icy blue… and cold, and unmistakable and just as always, my stomach turned.

I blinked, and briefly lowered my head in disbelief.

He was here?

Why?

When I had myself under control I lifted my gaze to him, but he was gone.

A frown furrowed into my forehead as my eyes roved across the bar. Every sound and sight beyond that of his haunting gaze faded into the background as I searched around the dimly lit space for him, but he had disappeared like a puff of smoke. After a few seconds I started to wonder if I'd just imagined him.

But why the hell would I?

I hate him. He was an arrogant, insufferable, rude, sanctimonious, annoying, ignorant, uncivilized, brutal thug. Immediately, I abandoned the search for such a low-life, and turned around to settle my breathing. It was uneven, and it aggravated me to no end that even imagining seeing him never failed to stir the most unpleasant storms inside me.

"Bastard," I swore under my breath as I turned to a customer waiting to get my attention. But it was now a feat to focus on his order. He had to repeat it twice. I nodded and set to work, but my mood had turned sour. The rest of the night became an ordeal. I kept expecting him to turn up even though I had told myself a thousand times that he was just a figment of my imagination.

I usually headed out of the bar with a little skip in my step at the end of my shift at 3am, but thanks to the memory of that devil, I felt taut and irritable.

I'd just turned the block when I found Bisset waiting on the deserted side street, his foot against the wall. I wasn't surprised, but I was disappointed. Despite his clumsy advances and smutty jokes I'd considered Garlic Cock fairly decent and able to respect set boundaries. Meeting outside the bar meant there was no going back.

"You're waiting to harass me, Monsieur?" I asked coldly.

He smiled charmingly. "Never, mon chéri. I thought, maybe, the bar is too crowded for you to … express your interest. Perhaps, you are shy in front of your employers and colleagues. I thought maybe—"

I cut him off. "You figured wrong. I'm not interested in you."

"That's unfair, baby girl. Just look at you… I'm about to lose my mind just staring at you."

I sighed. "Look, don't make this ugly. Maybe you have drunk too much, but if you stop now we can laugh about this the next time you come to the bar."

"I'm not drunk."

"Well, I'm going home. Alone."

He stepped in my path, his hands spread out and I could smell the alcohol I had fed him, pungent and overindulgent.

"My car and driver are right around the corner," he slurred. "It's running, waiting for you. Let's go for a drive. I'll show you some very beautiful places. Secret places. Where rich people go to feed their needs. You'll never get the chance to see on your own."

My stomach turned at the thought of the ugly things he had in mind. "I've lived in this city for five years. I've seen all that I need or want to see of it."

"No, you don't understand," he rasped urgently, his eyes shining. "This city has an underbelly. An exciting place that only those in the know can hope to experience. I promise you, you will love it."

"Thanks, but no thanks." I attempted to walk past him again.

Suddenly his face changed. The affable Frenchman was gone. Here was the real thing. The thing I would have seen if I had said yes at any time. "What will it take?" he asked. "because I'm not going home without you tonight."

I lost my patience. "Out of my way," I said and tried to push him aside, but he grabbed my hand and turned me violently around. It twisted my wrist and the pain made me wince.

He drew me to him and brought his nose close to my neck. Sniffing me he pressed his unimpressive cock against me.

"Do you feel what you do to me? Just give me one night," he pleaded. "I'll fuck you so good you'll never forget me."

I was as still as a tree. "Let me go."

Of course, he didn't listen.

I gave him one more chance. "Monsieur, let me go."

Instead the fool pressed his lips to my skin for a kiss.

I pushed myself back and smacked a blow so hard across his face I knew he saw stars.

Shocked, he staggered away from me and hit the wall. His mouth was agape with disbelief. "You fucking bitch," he said in wonder as he pulled away the hand he had held to his bruised face. "You hit me!"

I shrugged. "I did warn you."

He came for me then.

I wanted to roll my eyes into my skull.

He grabbed my shirt and pulled me up to his face. "How dare you? You fucking cheap whore!"

I struck his wrist hard with the edge of my hand, and he howled in pain. You can't blame a man for making that racket when his limb has shifted out of joint. To his credit, he lunged again for me, but his legs crumbled under him from sheer pain. It sent him crashing to the cold ground. Some people standing out the kebab shop in the distance turned at the sight of his drunken howl.

It was not the end of the matter though. That ridiculous cognac had put fire into his veins.

"I'm going to kill you," he screamed and came for me. I waited and at the right moment swung my frame around just in time to land a swift kick across the unprotected side of his face.

He flew backwards, and collapsed on the ground, a battered, pathetic mess. I glanced at the square heel of my boots and wondered just how much damage it had done to him. I felt a bit guilty: I did take all the hundreds of dollars he pushed across the bar to me. The money would go towards the orders for fashion samples that Bethany and I would need in the next few days. Anyway, someone had to teach him some manners. He would think twice about using this technique to approach another woman.

"Sorry Monsieur," I said.

I was just about to walk away when I felt a commanding presence behind me. All the hairs on my body instantly stood and I swiveled around in response to the danger I could sense. There was indeed danger. A man detached himself from the shadows. It was the last man I wanted to see. The owner of the pair of icy blue eyes that had disrupted me in the bar and put me in my bitter mood.

Maxim Ivankov.

So he really had been present at the bar. I couldn't wait to find out why. He walked up to me and stood with the street-light directly overhead. It made him appear even more forbidding and brutal. I could feel my heart start to thump.

"Why the fuck are you on my tail?" I snarled.

He smiled darkly, and it startled me, just like it always had.

"It's nice to see you too," he drawled. His voice was like waves crashing upon rocks. It could take centuries but in the end, it would pulverize the rocks into sand. "What's it been, seven years?"

"Well, thanks for helping."

He gazed down at Antoine, and shook his head. "You didn't need the help. The idiot didn't know what he had coming."

"Neither do you apparently," I said and instantly felt a frisson of fear strike me at the threat I had just issued to the one man I knew who could hurt me with just his gaze.

"What did you say?" he asked, his voice sending chills down my body and I knew that I had overstepped my boundaries. We were mortal enemies and the less involvement I had with him the better for me.

"Fuck off," I mutter under my breath, and began to walk away.

At first there was nothing but the sound of my footsteps. I prayed he wouldn't come after me. He didn't.

"Call your father," his voice rang after me.

My heart slammed into my chest. For a second I couldn't move. What did that imply? Was my dad alright?

His father and mine had been bloody rivals for as long as anyone could remember. Between them, death was usually almost always on the table.

I whirled around to confront him, but he was gone, as silently as he had arrived.

Pre-order the book here:
With This Ring

ABOUT THE AUTHOR

Thank you so much for reading my book. Might you be
thinking of leaving a review? :-)
Please do it here:

Highest Bidder

Please click on this link to receive news of my latest releases
and great giveaways.
http://bit.ly/10e9WdE

and remember
I **LOVE** hearing from readers so by all means come and say
hello here:

The Man In The Mirror

A Kiss Stolen

Can't Let Her Go

Highest Bidder

Saving Della Ray

Made in the USA
Columbia, SC
20 April 2020